Suddenly the world seemed to explode

Tower hurled himself down the remaining steps and out onto the stone floor of the hall. Smoke was drifting in the hall, and the acrid smell of burning high explosives filled the air. He pulled the trigger of the SAW and sprayed the room ahead of him with a series of short bursts. Men were yelling and running as he fired again, and he heard Blake shout, "Down!"

Tower threw himself to the floor. From above and behind came the crackling roar of M-16 rifles and SAWs opening up. Omega Force's men were moving down the stairs now, raking the hall with bursts of fire.

The fight went out of the enemy. Some threw down their weapons while others ran desperately for the door. The assault party swept past Tower, firing as they went.

Blake appeared from nowhere. "All secure, Captain. This place belongs to us."

"Damn good work," Tower said. "Find the radio operator and send a message to the general. 'Assault successful. Send in the main body.' And tell them to be careful . The opposition is still in the lower part of the castle. They may be in a bad mood."

PATRICK F. ROGERS

OMEGA
ZERO HOUR

A GOLD EAGLE BOOK FROM
WORLDWIDE.

TORONTO • NEW YORK • LONDON
AMSTERDAM • PARIS • SYDNEY • HAMBURG
STOCKHOLM • ATHENS • TOKYO • MILAN
MADRID • WARSAW • BUDAPEST • AUCKLAND

First edition June 1993

ISBN 0-373-63208-8

Special thanks and acknowledgment to
Patrick F. Rogers for his contribution to this work.

ZERO HOUR

"War is merely politics carried on by other means."
—Carl von Clausewitz

1

Captain Yitzhak Meir stared intently at his surface-search radar scope. There was no shortage of targets. The radar display showed more than a dozen ships or boats within thirty miles of the *Gaash* as she moved steadily toward Cyprus. He would have to depend on his radar. The night was dark and a warm light rain was falling. His lookouts were good, but they weren't likely to spot the target until it was very close. That was the problem. If he were free to sink the damned freighter when he found it, his mission would be simple.

Meir sighed. He was glad, not for the first time, that he had no close family to worry about him. Somehow his missions were never simple. Still, he was fortunate to serve with well-trained and dedicated officers and men, and the *Gaash* had the best equipment the Israeli navy could buy.

The *Gaash* didn't look like a powerful warship. She displaced only two hundred sixty tons, and neither her single 76 mm gun nor her small 40 mm automatic cannon was suitable for blasting enemy ships out of the water. But appearances were deceiving. In what looked like six harmless cylinders aft, she carried six Gabriel II antiship missiles. They could destroy ships twenty times her size if Meir was allowed to use them.

Meir had used Gabriels in combat and he had the utmost faith in them, but his orders were to use them only as a last resort. He was to intercept, board and search the Jordanian freighter, *Ba'ir*. Israeli Intelligence believed the freighter was transporting a new and deadly weapon intended for use against Israel. They wanted the weapon intact for analysis. Meir could sink the *Ba'ir* only if she refused to stop and be searched.

Meir didn't like the mission. He was a straightforward man, and his appearance reflected his attitude. At the moment his stocky body seemed energized, and there was a frown on his square face. Not for the first time, he wished the bright boys in Tel Aviv had some experience aboard a ship before they were allowed to plan naval operations. It had doubtless seemed simple when some Intelligence officer had planned it, sitting at a desk in Mossad headquarters in Tel Aviv. It didn't seem so easy at sea, operating in the dark two hundred miles from home. He looked at the radar scope again. One target appeared promising. It had to be a ship of some size, steaming steadily toward the south coast of Cyprus. Its radar return was strong and steady. Nothing else was on the right course. If the Mossad's information was right, this had to be the target.

Very well, time to earn his pay. Meir snapped an order, and the rumble of the *Gaash*'s four diesel engines deepened as she increased speed to thirty-two knots. Her crew was already at battle stations. The weapons officer reported that the missiles were checked out and locked on. Meir watched the radar display as the symbol of the *Gaash*'s position closed steadily on the target. He could see no change in its course and speed. If the freighter's captain was aware of the *Gaash*'s presence, he was taking no action. Even if he had detected them, he wasn't expecting to encounter the Israeli navy off the coast of Cyprus.

The rain was slackening. Meir made a quick calculation and determined that he would intercept the freighter in about six minutes. It would be in sight now if the weather was clear. He looked through his night-vision binoculars. Yes, there she was, a small freighter headed for the coast of Cyprus. The *Gaash*'s 76 mm cannon turret swiveled and ointed at the freighter. Meir smiled grimly. Time for some iendly conversation! He picked up his microphone. The adio was set on an international emergency frequency. The eighter should be monitoring that. He pushed the transit button.

"Freighter *Ba'ir*. Freighter *Ba'ir*. This is the Israeli deense force ship *Gaash*. Stop your engines, and prepare to e boarded."

There was no reply. Meir repeated his message. Still no nswer. Time to communicate a little more directly! He urned to his weapons officer.

"Put one across his bow, Aaron!"

The *Gaash*'s 76 mm Oto Melara spit a tongue of orange lame. A high-explosive shell shrieked toward the freighter. Meir watched through his binoculars. A fountain of water uddenly shot forward fifty feet in front of the freighter's ow. It was impressive shooting, and it carried a message nderstood in any language. Almost instantly, Meir heard n agitated voice on his radio.

"This is the captain of the Jordanian freighter *Ba'ir*. We re in international waters. Why in the name of God are ou firing on us?"

"To attract your attention, Captain. You didn't reond to my message. I repeat, stop your engines and preare to be boarded. If you do not do so at once, I will sink ou."

"There is some mistake. I am a merchant ship in interational waters. I am carrying commercial cargo to Cyrus. My ship is of no interest to the Israeli navy. You have o authority to stop me!"

Meir smiled grimly. "Perhaps all that is true, but our inormation is different. We believe you are carrying terror veapons for use against the state of Israel. You will stop our ship and be searched." He turned to his weapons oficer. "As for my authority, Aaron, put another round cross his bow!"

The 76 mm cannon fired again. A second high-explosive shell shrieked toward the *Ba'ir*. Meir watched through his binoculars. This time the fountain of water splashed the freighter's bow.

"I trust you find my authority convincing, Captain. I don't believe in wasting ammunition. The next round goes into your bridge. Stop your engines!"

For a moment there was silence. Then the freighter's captain replied, his voice hoarse with rage. "Do not fire again. This is piracy, but I cannot fight a warship which has guns and missiles. I have stopped my engines, but I warn you, I will protest! My government will protest! By God's name, you will pay for this!"

Meir looked through his binoculars. The *Ba'ir* was stopping. He slowed his engines and began the delicate process of coming alongside the twelve-thousand-ton freighter. He must not give the *Ba'ir*'s captain any chance to ram. Despite her powerful weapons, the *Gaash* could easily be smashed to pieces by the larger ship. It was up to Meir to be sure that the freighter's captain didn't get that chance.

"A wise decision, Captain. Don't start your engines again until I say you may. Now, throw a cargo net over your starboard side and stand by to be boarded. And one other thing, Captain. It may occur to you to kill my boarding party or seize them and hold them hostage. I warn you, if I lose communication with them for a second, I will assume the worst and I will destroy you. I have six missiles locked on your ship. Sixty seconds after I give the firing order, your ship will be a burning, sinking wreck, and there will be no survivors. I will see to that personally. Do you understand, Captain?"

"I understand. I will do as you say, but you will regret this. See if you do not!" The *Ba'ir*'s captain added a few sizzling remarks in Arabic, most of which Meir understood.

He shrugged. He didn't believe that he was the son of Satan, and he certainly hadn't done any of those things with his female relatives. However, he had no time for exchanging pleasantries. He concentrated on bringing the *Gaash* alongside the *Ba'ir*. This was a risky maneuver. Despite what he had said, he was too close to the freighter to use his missiles. The weapons officer had the 76 mm gun and the 40 mm automatic cannon ready to sweep the freighter's side. That would have to do.

He looked aft. His boarding party was ready. The ten elite Israeli naval commandos were heavily armed and protected by body armor and gas masks. It was risky, boarding the freighter in the open sea. She could be carrying a lot of men, and they could be heavily armed, but Israeli naval commandos were some of the best-trained fighters in the world. They could look after themselves. And if they were overwhelmed by sheer weight of numbers, Meir hadn't been bluffing. He would back off, use his missiles, and send the *Ba'ir* down.

MAJOR JAMAL TAWFIQ LEANED over the rail of the *Ba'ir* and watched as the Israeli patrol boat slowly pulled alongside the freighter. There was nothing unusual in Tawfiq's appearance so long as you didn't look too closely at his face, especially his eyes, which indicated a man of great confidence. He was dressed in the shabby working clothes of a poorly paid seaman, but he wasn't a sailor. Born in Iraq, Tawfiq had once commanded a special forces battalion of the elite Republican Guard. If he ever returned to Iraq, the secret police would shoot him on sight. A man without a country, he believed devoutly in the idea of the Arab nation, a state that would unite all Arabs in a single, rich, and powerful nation. A nation free from foreign domination, where all true believers would live as God intended. That was all Tawfiq had left to believe in. For that, he would fight and kill and die.

He seemed to be merely gawking at the *Gaash* as she came alongside. His AK-47 was lying on the deck, impossible to see from the low-lying Israeli boat. He glanced casually to the left and right. His men were ready, keeping low and out of sight. They were heavily armed with AK-47 automatic rifles and RPG-7 rocket-propelled grenade launchers. They were good men, combat veterans to a man. They were quivering with eagerness to strike, but no one had his finger on the trigger. Good, no one would fire until Tawfiq gave the order.

That was just as well. They would have just one chance to kill the Israelis. If they erred, Tawfiq had no doubt that the Israeli captain would carry out his threat and sink the *Ba'ir*. That wasn't a pleasant thought. Like most Iraqis, Tawfiq was a poor swimmer. Very well, he would not fail.

Now, where in God's name was Captain Kawash with the weapons? He looked carefully, casually, behind him. If the Israelis were watching him, he must do nothing that would alert them. He saw Kawash approaching, carrying a three-foot-long, silver-gray cylinder in his arms. A sergeant followed with a second cylinder. They were moving slowly and carefully. Tawfiq didn't blame them for being cautious. If half of what he had heard about this weapon was true, it was incredibly dangerous.

Captain Kawash set his cylinder carefully down by Tawfiq's feet. Kawash looked pale but ready for action.

"Is it armed?" Tawfiq asked.

"Yes. It is like a grenade. Pull the safety ring, and throw it. It will go off on impact."

"God is great! I will take this one. You go aft with the other. Try to put it close to that automatic cannon aft on the Israeli's deck. Be sure to wait for my signal. Go with God, my brother!"

Tawfiq glanced over the side. The Israeli patrol boat had stopped alongside so that the sides of the two ships were almost touching. The Israeli commandos grasped the net that hung over the freighter's side and began to climb the thirty feet to the deck. Now or never!

Tawfiq wasn't given to making speeches in combat. He shouted "Fire!" as loudly as he could. Instantly, his men sprang to their feet. Tawfiq heard the reassuring rattle of AK-47s and the hiss of rocket grenades as his men poured fire on the Israelis. The Israelis were helpless, easy targets for the AK-47s. Bursts of automatic-rifle fire killed them all. Tawfiq heard the crackle of machine-gun fire as the startled Israeli boat's gunners fired back.

Tawfiq bent down, pulled the safety ring, and lifted the cylinder. A large and powerful man, he easily swung the cylinder over his head and hurled it over the side, straight down at the Israeli boat's deck. It struck just forward of the *Gaash*'s bridge. For a moment nothing seemed to happen. Tawfiq's heart froze. A dud? No, God is great! A gray-white, nearly transparent vapor was hissing out of a dozen vents in the cylinder's side. He looked toward the aft of the Israeli boat. Good! Kawash had thrown his cylinder as instructed, and it, too, was emitting vapor.

CAPTAIN MEIR WATCHED as the naval commandos began to climb the cargo net. Another minute, and they would be on the *Ba'ir*'s deck, and things would be under control. He turned to his radioman.

"Send a message to headquarters. *Ba'ir* intercepted approximately fifteen miles off Cyprus. Boarding her now. We will—"

Suddenly, the *Ba'ir*'s rail was alive with yellow flashes as a dozen light automatic weapons were firing. The commandos were being slaughtered. Although his machine gunners were firing back, they couldn't use the *Gaash*'s cannons while any of the commandos were on the net.

Meir snapped an order when he saw the last commando fall. The muffled throb of the *Gaash*'s engines began to increase as all four propellers began to turn. The radioman yelled something. Meir looked up. A cylinder that looked like a diver's air tank slammed down on the *Gaash*'s deck. A second cylinder dropped near the cannon aft. Bombs? No, the cylinders merely lay there. Then he saw the vapor pouring from their sides, spreading rapidly over the deck. Gas attack!

Instantly he shouted into the intercom. His voice rang throughout the *Gaash*. "Gas! Gas! Gas attack!"

Meir ran a tight ship. His men were well trained, and orders were orders. Every one of his officers and men was carrying a gas mask in a pouch strapped to his left side, exactly as prescribed when at battle stations. Meir unsnapped his pouch and pulled his gas mask out. With the skill that comes from long practice, he slipped it over his head and felt the reassuring pressure of the mask against his face. He took a deep breath, put his hand over the filter canister, and blew out hard to vent the mask and check the seal. Everything was working perfectly. He glanced quickly to the left and right. The helmsman and the weapons officer already had donned their masks. The radioman was almost ready. The damned cylinders were still spewing out vapor, but now every man in his crew should be masked and safe.

The *Gaash* was moving away from the freighter now. Meir could see bodies floating in the water. The damned terrorists had killed every one of the commandos. Meir swore bitterly. He would avenge them. He wasn't a man who made idle threats. He would sink the *Ba'ir* as soon as the *Gaash* was far enough away from the freighter to use her missiles. As he had said, there would be no survivors.

"Weapons officer. Stand by. Fire a salvo as soon as we are beyond minimum range. Launch four missiles. I want that ship sunk!"

"Missiles locked on, Captain. Ready to launch in... in—"

Meir looked at the weapons officer. Something was wrong. He was slumped motionless over his control console. The radioman was lying unconscious on the floor. The helmsman was clutching the wheel as if he were about to fall. Meir smelled a faint, sweet, flowery scent. That was wrong! He shouldn't be able to smell anything with his gas mask on. Suddenly he was on fire! Every nerve in his body was burning! He couldn't breathe! His vision blurred, he fell heavily to the deck. He tried desperately to move, but his body would not obey his brain. Mercifully he was dead in thirty seconds.

The *Gaash*'s dead helmsman's hands were still on the wheel. All of her forty-man crew were dead at their posts. Manned only by dead men, the *Gaash* moved steadily on through the night toward the coast of Cyprus.

DONALD PRESTON SAT waiting tensely in the consulate briefing room. He nervously adjusted his tie and checked the way his trousers broke just at the tops of his shoes. His clothes looked very expensive in a quiet, understated way. On paper Preston was the assistant cultural attaché at the U.S. embassy in Athens. Actually he was the assistant CIA officer at the Athens station. He was worried, and with good reason. The next two hours were going to be extremely critical to his career.

Dr. Peter Kaye, the man he was going to brief, had a fearsome reputation in the Agency. Nothing and no one stood in Kaye's way! On his own initiative, Preston had asked him to come to Cyprus. That was taking a chance. The CIA encouraged initiative, but it didn't encourage failure. He had better be right! If he was not, neither his tall, blond good looks nor his family influence was likely to save him.

There was a knock on the door. A Marine guard ushered in a tall, thin man in an expensive but wrinkled suit. He did not appear happy. He had the coldest black eyes that Preston had ever seen, eyes that dominated his whole face. The Marine left and closed the door behind him.

"Preston?" the tall man inquired. "I'm Kaye." He didn't move to shake hands.

"Pleased to meet you, Dr. Kaye," Preston said brightly. "Would you like some refreshments, or shall I proceed with the briefing?"

Kaye glared at Preston. It was obvious that he considered that to be a foolish question, and Kaye wasn't a man who suffered fools gladly.

"I've spent the last twelve hours traveling from Washington to this godforsaken place, Preston, because you saw fit to send me a priority message. Cut out the nonsense and tell me just what you think is so damned important."

Preston snapped on the viewfoil projector. A map of the eastern Mediterranean appeared on the screen. Preston was an excellent briefer and he knew the facts. He began to speak formally, keeping a wary eye on Dr. Kaye.

"Yes, sir. I sent that message in response to your request of six weeks ago to all Middle Eastern stations for any information on the activities of a new Arab terrorist organization, the Arab Nation Movement, and its leader, Colonel Nizar Sadiq. I believe we have hard information that Colonel Sadiq is conducting a major operation in the Cyprus area. All evidence is that this operation is directed against Israel. Our informants have picked up references to a mysterious weapon which is to be used in the attack. We do not know the precise nature of this weapon, but it is rumored to be extremely powerful, a weapon of mass destruction."

Preston paused to let his words sink in.

Kaye's expression had changed. He looked intensely interested and leaned forward in his chair. "Go on, Preston," he said quietly.

Preston continued smoothly. "In addition to Colonel Sadiq, your message mentioned his right-hand man, Major Jamal Tawfiq. You also requested information on the freighter, *Ba'ir*. Six days ago the *Ba'ir* left Malta for Cyprus. Major Tawfiq and thirty of Colonel Sadiq's men went aboard the ship at Malta. It is probable that the *Ba'ir* reached Turkish-controlled Cyprus within the last twenty-four hours and landed her cargo."

"That's interesting, Preston. It's good work, but why do you think it's a major crisis?"

"Because something occurred while you were flying here from Washington that confirms absolutely our previous information. The Israelis have the same information. They sent a missile armed patrol boat, the *Gaash*, to intercept the *Ba'ir*. We were able to monitor radio transmissions between the patrol boat and Israel. The *Gaash* stopped the *Ba'ir* and was sending a boarding party to search her. While the *Gaash* was reporting this, the message suddenly broke off, literally while the radio operator was in midsentence. Israeli navy headquarters has made repeated attempts to contact the *Gaash*. They haven't received any reply. It seems certain that the entire crew was killed instantly by some kind of weapon employed from the *Ba'ir.*"

Kaye stared at him. "You used the word 'killed,' Preston. Was the Israeli patrol boat sunk, and the entire crew lost, or are you implying something else?"

"A few hours ago, the *Gaash* came ashore on a beach in southern Cyprus. It suffered only superficial damage, but the entire crew was killed. I have aerial photographs taken by a Navy reconnaissance plane and photographs taken by one of our agents in the area."

Preston flashed a series of pictures on the projection screen. Kaye stared intently. "You're sure this is the Israeli boat?" he asked softly.

"Yes, sir. The *Gaash* is a Saar 3 class fast attack craft, built in France for the Israelis. Other countries operate similar craft, but this is an Israeli vessel. Only the Israelis arm them with the combination of Gabriel antiship missiles and a 40 mm automatic cannon aft. Look at this picture. The hull number painted on the bow is 333. That is the *Gaash's* hull number. I don't think there can be any doubt. This is the *Gaash*."

Kaye seemed convinced. "Has anyone gone on board to investigate?"

Preston shook his head. " No, for several reasons. I don't know what killed the Israelis, but I suspect some sort of advanced chemical-warfare agent. It may still be active. Anyone we send on board that boat had better be wearing full protective equipment. That's not available here on Cyprus. All we have are gas masks issued to the Marine guards. That may not be enough."

A new picture flashed on the screen.

"This is a blowup of a picture taken by our agent, Grivas. It shows the 40 mm gun mounted aft. You can clearly see the bodies of the gunner and one of the loaders. They are both wearing Israeli military Type 15A1 gas masks with Type 90 filters. Those masks are as good as any of ours, perhaps better, but they seem to have been completely ineffective."

Dr. Kaye nodded. The picture of the dead Israeli crewmen was extremely convincing.

"You said for several reasons, Preston. What are the others?"

"Grivas has continued to observe the boat from a distance. A few hours ago, he reported that a heavily armed team of ten or twelve men arrived and established a perimeter around the boat. Grivas was an officer in the Greek army. He knows weapons. He said they were carrying AK-47 automatic rifles. Grivas worked his way close enough to hear them talking. He said they were speaking Arabic. They haven't tried to go on board the *Gaash*, but they seem to be guarding it. I think anyone we send to investigate will have to be ready to shoot their way in."

"Do we have any paramilitary capability here on Cyprus?"

Preston shook his head. "No. You can buy just about anything in the world on Cyprus, but there is no paramilitary team available here that we could trust with a highly classified mission."

"What about the Marine guards?"

"They are part of the Marine's embassy protective force. To use them, we would have to get the approval of the Marine Corps commandant and the State Department. That could take weeks, and you know what State Department security is like. We would be reading about it in the *Washington Post!*"

Kaye sneered. Like most CIA men, he had little use for the State Department. He smiled at Preston. It was undoubtedly intended to be friendly, but it reminded Preston of a shark about to bite.

"All right, I accept that. What alternatives do we have?"

Preston considered this. So far, he seemed to be doing well with Dr. Kaye. It wouldn't do to blow it with a stupid suggestion. "I don't believe that the problem can be solved with the resources available to the Athens station," he said finally. "Perhaps we could contact the U.S. Army headquarters in Germany. They could send a chemical-warfare team and some Green Berets from the Tenth Special Forces Group. It would require approval from Washington."

"That's good thinking, Preston. You've done a good job. You were right to contact me. This is obviously very important. We must take action immediately."

Preston didn't fail to notice the "we." He allowed himself to relax a little. "Shall I contact Army headquarters in Germany?" he asked.

"No. I think we need the first team for this. I'm going to contact Washington via satellite communications and ask for a team from the Army's chemical and biological research center. If anyone can handle this, they can."

That sounded reasonable to Preston, but there was still one problem. "What about a paramilitary team?" he asked.

"I am going to ask for Omega Force. Have you heard of them?"

Preston was startled. "Omega Force? Yes, I've heard of them. Some sort of Army hush-hush special-operations force, but they're a bunch of cowboys! Shoot anything that moves and blow up everything that doesn't. Do we want those kind of people involved in a sensitive operation?"

"Certainly. There is likely to be a lot of shooting and blowing things up before we're through. I've worked with them before. I don't like them, but they're good. And one other thing." He smiled sardonically. "If the operation is a failure, they can take the blame."

2

Captain Amanda Stuart crouched behind the Volkswagen van. She held a silenced MP-5K 9 mm Heckler & Koch submachine gun ready for action. She asked herself for the hundredth time how she had gotten herself into this. Amanda was an Army brat. Her father was a highly experienced soldier. If he had told her once, he had told her a thousand times never to volunteer for anything.

The German captain crouched beside her and spoke in flat, precise English. His green beret showed that he was an officer in one of the German army's elite commando companies. His icy blue eyes in his narrow face radiated arrogance.

"All the terrorists are inside the building, Captain Stuart. We aren't sure exactly how many, but there must be five or six, and they are armed. They've taken a number of hostages, including women and children, and have threatened to torture and kill them if we don't immediately comply with their demands. But we cannot comply and we cannot wait for reinforcements. You must assault the building and neutralize the terrorists. I will wait here to prevent any terrorists from escaping."

Amanda snarled to herself. Thanks a lot for the help, Hans!

The German captain continued methodically. "I will cover you until you enter the door. From there on the tactics to be employed are up to you. Be careful not to hurt any of the hostages. Remember, these terrorists are cold-blooded murderers. They will kill you in an instant if they have the chance. Do not hesitate. Shoot to kill! Is this clear?''

Amanda nodded.

"Very well. I will give the signal to attack sometime in the next two minutes. Good luck, Captain Stuart.''

Amanda smiled bleakly. She was going to need all the luck she could get. The seven-pound weight of the Heckler & Koch in her hands was reassuring, but she would rather have had an M-16A2 rifle. That was what she was used to, but the German army wasn't passing them out. Her green eyes narrowed as she concentrated on remembering her training. The problem was that Amanda wasn't a Green Beret or a Ranger. She was a U.S. Army Special Operations helicopter pilot, and a good one. Unfortunately that wasn't terribly useful in close-quarter combat.

She had to make a decision. The Heckler & Koch had three firing modes. Each time she pulled the trigger, she could select one shot, bursts limited to three shots, or full-automatic fire like a machine gun. That was tempting, but if she froze on the trigger, the H&K would empty its magazine in two seconds. Oh, well, in for a nickle, in for a dime. She pushed the selector switch to full automatic. Her .45 Colt automatic was ready in its holster. Should she—

"Go!" the German captain shouted.

Amanda shot forward, her long legs driving her toward the door. If the Olympics had a record for twenty-yard sprints while carrying a submachine gun, Amanda might have broken it. No one fired at her. She flattened herself against the wall next to the door. A woman began to scream inside the building, desperate, agonized screams that went on and on.

She raised a booted foot and kicked in the door. Dashing inside, she angled to the right so as not to be silhouetted against the opening. She was in a dimly lit room, but she could make out the figure of a man ten feet in front of her, turning toward her. Amanda saw a submachine gun in his hands, its muzzle swinging straight toward her.

Amanda didn't hesitate. She squeezed the trigger. The Heckler & Koch vibrated in her hands and sent a 6-round burst tearing through her target. The man went down. Sensing movement, she turned to her left. A dim figure loomed in a doorway. She dived to the floor and rolled to one side. She saw a series of quick orange flashes and heard the deafening roar of a high-powered weapon firing indoors.

She fired back, sweeping the wall with a long burst. It wasn't pretty shooting but it was good enough. The figure in the doorway fell to the floor. There was a large, battered couch to Amanda's left. She rolled behind it. It wouldn't stop high-powered bullets, but any cover was better than none. Suddenly the room was flooded with light. Amanda heard a woman swearing angrily in German. Amanda stayed prone and chanced a quick look around the side of the couch. She saw a tall, blond woman in a lovely blue dress with a small but deadly-looking automatic in her hand. Amanda pulled her trigger. A burst of 9 mm bullets struck the woman in blue. She went down instantly, dropping the pistol.

Another figure appeared in the doorway—a large man with a double-barreled shotgun. Amanda pulled the trigger without thinking. A red dot flew from the Heckler & Koch and struck the big man in the chest, but he didn't go down. Amanda had used the old soldier's trick of loading a tracer round as the last shot in her magazine. She had fired her last round. Her submachine gun was empty. No time to reload. She dropped the H&K and reached for her .45. Suddenly there was an explosion of orange fire as the shotgun fired, and Amanda knew that if she had been standing, she would have been dead.

Time seemed to slow down. It seemed to take forever to draw the big Colt and point its front sight at her target. She fired twice, as fast as she could. Two heavy .45 caliber bullets smashed into the big man's chest, and he went down. There was a sudden, deafening silence. The fight had taken less than twenty seconds, but was it over? Amanda counted quickly. She had, to use the quaint German phrase, "neutralized" four terrorists. But the German captain had said there would be five or six. She snatched up the Heckler & Koch, snapped in a fresh 30-round magazine, and worked the cocking lever. She was ready.

Listening intently, she heard a woman sobbing softly. She sensed movement to her right. A door had opened, and a dim figure was moving slowly from a dark room into the light. She snapped her submachine gun to her shoulder but didn't pull the trigger. It was bad form to shoot to kill before you identified your target.

A woman in a torn, red dress slowly entered, pushing a large black baby carriage. A man was crouched behind her, one arm locked under her chin. The other arm held a flat black Glock automatic against the side of her head. "Throw out your weapons and surrender!" he yelled in a hoarse voice. "Do it now, or I will kill her and the child!"

Amanda knew it would be suicide to give up her weapons, but she couldn't just lie there while the hostages were killed. She could see the man's face over the woman's shoulder. She aimed carefully at the man's head, pushed the selector switch to semi-automatic and slowly began to squeeze the trigger, knowing that a Heckler & Koch MP-5K was as accurate as a rifle out to one hundred yards.

"Surrender or I'll kill them!" the man yelled again.

As Amanda looked at him through her sights, the expression on his face was one of murderous rage. Slowly, steadily, she increased the pressure on the trigger.

"I will count to five. If you do not throw out your weapons and come out with your hands up, I will kill them both. First the woman and then the child! One! Two! Three!—"

The Heckler & Koch vibrated in Amanda's hands and sent a full-metal-jacketed 9 mm bullet through the terrorist's head. He staggered away from the woman, the Glock still in his hand. Amanda shot him again, just to make sure. He fell to the floor and lay still.

Amanda scanned the room, looking through the sights of her submachine gun. No one moved. There was silence except for the soft sobbing of the woman by the baby carriage. Amanda waited tensely while the seconds ticked by, then finally she allowed herself the luxury of a deep breath. Thank God, it was over. She got carefully to her feet and swept the room again. She turned toward the entrance. The rest of the Omega Force group should be arriving any second. Amanda felt a glow of pride. She had certainly not done badly for her first time out. She—

A submachine gun snarled behind her. Desperately, she pivoted, trying to swing her Heckler & Koch on target. But too late! The woman in the red dress had snatched an Uzi from the baby carriage and was firing burst after burst straight at her. Amanda fired back. She knew it was too late, but at least it made her feel better. A dozen 9 mm bullets smashed into the woman in red, but she didn't fall. She stood there with the Uzi in her hands, frozen, immobile as a statue.

A siren sounded and red lights flashed. Amanda heard the amplified voice of the German captain.

"Cease fire! Clear all weapons! Cease fire!"

Swearing softly, Amanda removed the remaining rounds from her weapons. She heard the sound of applause. Major Jack Cray, the commander of Omega Force, was standing in the door, clapping politely. It was like him to do the right thing and clap. But only Cray would do it so politely, with that sardonic look on his rugged face! Still, Amanda felt a lot better with Cray nearby. The German captain standing beside Cray, glanced at his clipboard.

"We are running a bit late for the next event, but we have time for a short critique," he said quickly. "Captain Stuart did very well for her first time through a shooting house. Her use of cover and concealment was excellent. She shot well and hit all the targets. Her emergency use of her pistol showed excellent reactions under stress. Unfortunately—" Amanda winced "—she failed to think that the woman in red might be a terrorist rather than a hostage, and she was killed. Learn from this that a terrorist can look like anyone."

The German captain paused for a moment and forced a smile. "Do not feel too badly, Captain Stuart. The lady in red gets everyone the first time. I had my weapon slung over my shoulder when she got me."

Amanda smiled politely. She was still nervous and tense. The shooting house was undoubtedly marvelous training, but the computer-controlled, simulated human targets were almost too real. The only thing they didn't do was fire back with real bullets.

"All your people did very well, Major," the German captain continued. "Your Sergeant Hall shoots remarkably well. I have never seen such shooting."

He consulted his clipboard again. "Very well. The next event is an exercise in recapturing a hijacked airliner. I think you will find it very interesting."

He stopped and frowned as a jeep roared around the corner and came to a screeching halt outside the shooting house. The driver, a tall, blond man wearing an American Army camouflaged battle dress uniform, leaped from the jeep and ran toward Major Cray. He was Captain Dave Tower, Omega Force's second-in-command. Amanda was instantly alert. She knew Tower well. He was normally cool and calm, no matter what was happening. If he was excited, something important was going on.

Tower handed Cray an envelope. "Message for you from General Sykes, Major. It has every priority there is!"

Amanda Stuart and Dave Tower looked to Cray. General Sykes was the operations officer of the United States Special Operations Command. He wasn't given to idle conversation, so his message wouldn't ask how the weather was or how they liked Germany. Amanda would have bet her last dollar that it was an operations order. She wouldn't have lost her money.

"It's from General Sykes at SOCOM headquarters. Omega Force is on alert to deploy to the island of Cyprus. General Sykes is flying there now. He wants us to meet him there. We are to requisition weapons and equipment from the Tenth Special Forces Group here in Germany and be prepared for combat operations on arrival. All Omega Force personnel here will go, including Sergeant Blake and Sergeant Hall. He doesn't say anything about the operation. We will be briefed when we arrive. That's it, let's go!"

Amanda felt left out. It was irrational, perhaps, but she was a professional officer, proud of her capabilities. She had been with Omega Force during its raid into Libya, and she hated to see them going into action now without her. Still, she was a captain in the Army. She had understood since she was sworn in as a lieutenant that orders were orders.

She put a smile on her face. "It looks like you're going on an operation, Major," she said softly. "Well, good luck to all of you. You can tell me about it when you get back."

Cray smiled. "Thanks, Captain, we'll probably need all the luck we can get. But there's one other thing. The general wants us to come in a Special Operations Blackhawk helicopter. We need a pilot who is familiar with special operations and the Blackhawk. Rumor has it that you're the best Blackhawk pilot in the 160th Special Operations Aviation Regiment. Want the job?"

Amanda seemed to hear her father saying, "Never volunteer for anything, damn it! Never volunteer!" It didn't matter. She was a Special Operations helicopter pilot, and a damned good one! She wanted to fly with the first team.

She smiled back at Cray. "You've got yourself a pilot, Major. Let's go!"

GENERAL JIM SYKES WAITED patiently in the lobby of the consulate while the Marine guard checked his identity. Sykes felt out of place in civilian clothes. He would have felt much more comfortable wearing his battle dress uniform and his web equipment. Twenty-five years in the Rangers made him feel uneasy when he was separated from his combat gear and weapons.

The Marine guard studied Sykes's identity card, carefully comparing the picture on the card with Sykes's face. He saw a stern, no-nonsense face that seemed to exude command presence. The eyes measured, the nose demanded, and the chin jutted. Sykes could sense a change in the Marine's attitude as he completed his check and nodded.

Sykes had definitely gone up in the world! He was no longer some lousy tourist who had wandered into the consulate. He was a brigadier general in the United States Army, and Marines were impressed by generals. The Marine made a quick phone call, and a Marine corporal appeared and led Sykes down toward the basement of the building. They stopped in front of a door marked, Warning! Do Not Enter Without Authorization! The Marine knocked, and a young man appeared.

"General Sykes is here, Mr. Preston," the Marine said, then left.

The tall, blond young man behind the desk smiled, showing his perfect, white teeth. "Welcome to Cyprus, General. I'm Donald Preston from the CIA's Athens station. Come in, we've been expecting you."

CIA! The alarm bells began to ring. Sykes had been afraid of that. Like most Special Operations officers, he didn't trust the CIA. A number of his friends were buried in out-of-the-way parts of the world because they had gone on missions for the CIA. Sykes had had more than one close call himself. With friends like the CIA, he didn't need enemies.

Sykes was an impressive figure, over six feet tall, with close-cropped iron gray hair and penetrating gray eyes. Diplomacy wasn't his strong suit. He wasn't a paper soldier. He had earned his rank in high-risk combat operations, not commanding a desk in the Pentagon. He stared at Preston intently.

Preston sensed the chill in the air. Inwardly he shrugged. He didn't care whether Sykes liked him or not. Outwardly he smiled brightly and extended his hand. They shook hands. Preston counted his fingers carefully. Yes, all five were there! Years of unarmed-combat training had given Sykes an extremely strong grip.

Preston led Sykes to a conference table. A man and a woman sat at the table looking at a map on the wall. The woman looked up and smiled. She was a tall, attractive woman in her late thirties, with hazel eyes and prematurely gray hair.

"General Sykes, this is Dr. Cora Hill of the Army's chemical and biological research center. Dr. Hill is an expert in advanced chemical and biological warfare."

Dr. Hill extended her hand. General Sykes hesitated: was it safe to touch her? He took her hand. She undoubtedly washed her hands after playing with her pet viruses.

"And," Preston continued smoothly, "I believe you already know Dr. Kaye."

Kaye looked at Sykes with his cold black eyes and smiled thinly.

"Oh, yes, we know each other quite well," said Kaye. "We were on the mission into Libya together a few months ago. How are you, General?" Kaye didn't offer to shake hands.

Sykes felt a cold knot in his stomach. Peter Kaye! Of all the people Sykes knew in the Intelligence game, he trusted Kaye the least. Kaye would have cold-bloodedly abandoned Omega Force in Libya. Sykes was not about to forgive him for that. If Kaye was involved in this operation, there was real trouble. He would bet on that.

Kaye continued to smile. "Sit down, General, and have some coffee. Preston was about to brief Dr. Hill. He will fill you in on the situation."

Sykes figured that Kaye would probably hesitate to poison him in front of witnesses. He took some coffee and sat back as Preston turned on the viewfoil projector and began his briefing. Sykes listened attentively as Preston repeated what he had told Kaye earlier. Sykes had to admit that Preston did a good job. He covered the *Gaash*'s interception of the *Ba'ir* and the subsequent events quite well.

Preston finished. Kaye smiled again. That made Sykes nervous. He wished he had his back to the wall!

"Thank you Preston," Kaye said smoothly. "Very well, Doctor, General Sykes, you see that the situation is critical. Do either of you have any questions or comments?"

"Just one comment," Cora Hill said quietly. "You were very wise not to send anyone on board the patrol boat. Israeli chemical protective gear is as good as ours, perhaps better. If whatever killed the crew of the *Gaash* is still active, sending anyone on board without advanced protective equipment would be fatal. Ordinary military protective gear will not be adequate."

Sykes suppressed a shudder. He was a soldier, and not particularly squeamish, but something about chemical warfare turned his stomach. If anything, biological warfare sounded worse.

"What do you mean by 'still active,' Dr. Hill?" Kaye asked.

"There are basically two types of lethal chemical and biological agents—persistent, and nonpersistent. A nonpersistent agent can be extremely lethal, but it disperses rapidly. A persistent agent will contaminate an area and remain lethal for days or weeks. We have no way of knowing which type of agent was used against the Israeli patrol boat. We must assume that a persistent agent was used and that it is still active. There is no way I can tell from a distance. I must board the patrol boat and collect samples. There is simply no other way."

Whatever else Cora Hill was, she was brave. Sykes could think of nothing in the world that would make him volunteer to go aboard the Israeli patrol boat, even with Dr. Hill's "advanced protective equipment."

"Yes, Doctor," Kaye said. "You are the expert. That's why you're here. Of course, the problem is how to get you access to the *Gaash*." He paused and smiled at Sykes. "We do have the problem of this group of armed men guarding the area, but that is why General Sykes is here. In that field, he is the expert. We all defer to his superior knowledge when special operations are involved."

Sykes kept his best poker face on and showed no emotion. Inwardly he was seething. Kaye's plan was obvious, but it was clever. If Sykes and Omega Force were successful, Kaye could take the credit for calling them in. If they failed, military operations weren't Kaye's responsibility. Sykes and Omega Force would take the blame.

"Why is the situation immediately critical?" asked Sykes. The Israeli boat is aground. Its crew is dead. It's not going anywhere. What's the rush?"

"Two reasons, General. At the moment the terrorists control the boat. They may move it or destroy it at any moment. Also, the Israelis are conducting a massive search for the *Gaash*. If they locate it, they will launch a military operation to recover or destroy it. In either case, we will not have access to the boat, and we will not learn the characteristics of the weapon that was used. That information is vital to the security of the United States."

Dr. Hill nodded. "Dr. Kaye is right. We cannot tolerate a situation where foreign powers have a weapon which can defeat American chemical-warfare protective equipment. We must find out what it is and develop defenses against it. Surely, General, as a military man, you understand that."

She was right. Sykes could imagine thousands of American troops destroyed by a lethal agent that easily penetrated their protective equipment. He could visualize the panic that would follow, the kind of panic that destroyed armies and lost wars.

"I understand," Sykes said reluctantly. "We've got to get you on that damned patrol boat as soon as possible."

"Excellent, General. I was sure you'd understand," Kaye said smoothly. "Now we need to plan. What resources are available?"

Sykes frowned. Was that a subtle put-down? Every other time Kaye spoke, he seemed to have a double meaning. Sykes decided to let it pass. Much as he disliked Kaye, this was no time for exchanging insults. He smiled grimly.

"You're looking at them. Unless we can use the Marine guards, and you tell me we can't, I'm the U.S. military presence on Cyprus."

It was Kaye's turn to frown. "For the moment, that's true, General, but how long will it be before Omega Force arrives?"

"When I left Washington, the CIA's request to deploy Omega Force had gone to the National Command Authorities. I assume they will authorize SOCOM to deploy Omega Force. I put them on full alert before I took off. The Air Force has a Lockheed C-5B standing by. Omega Force can start loading on the C-5B two hours after they get the order. Since it's about an eleven- or twelve-hour flight, they could be here fourteen hours after the NCA authorizes deployment."

Kaye looked perturbed. "Fourteen hours or more? That's completely unacceptable! We can't wait! Can't any of your forces get here sooner?"

"That depends on what you mean by forces, Doctor. The Tenth Special Forces Group in Germany is the closest unit under SOCOM control, but if we use them, we are launching a combat operation from Germany. The Germans are extremely sensitive about that. God only knows how long it would take us to get their permission. It would certainly be a matter of days, not hours. There is—"

"That's utterly useless, General. We have to do something now!" Kaye said abruptly.

Sykes frowned. Like most generals, he wasn't used to being interrupted. He suppressed the desire to strangle Kaye and continued firmly. "As I was about to say, there is an alternative. I don't like it, but it may be the only chance we've got. The Omega Force command group was in Germany a few hours ago. I ordered them to come to Cyprus before I left Washington. Major Cray and four of his key officers and men should be here in an hour or two. They are bringing special-operations weapons and equipment. As soon as they get here, I think we can get that patrol boat back for you and Dr. Hill."

Kaye looked skeptical. "You and five men from Omega Force are going to defeat a terrorist force?"

Sykes smiled grimly. "Why not, Doctor? You've only got twelve terrorists, haven't you?"

FOUR HOURS LATER, Sykes and Major Cray lay concealed in a cluster of scrubby trees, studying the beach below through their binoculars. It was definitely the right place. They could see the Israeli patrol boat aground at the water's edge. It looked exactly as it had in Preston's pictures. Nothing had changed. At the moment, there was nothing to do but wait. Captain Tower and Sergeant Blake were scouting the area very carefully.

So far, there was nothing to indicate that the CIA report had been inaccurate, but rushing into a raid on the assumption that your Intelligence must be accurate was an excellent way to get your head blown off. Cray was too old a hand to make that mistake. Besides, he did not know Grivas, the agent who prepared the report. The stocky, balding Cypriot looked competent, but could he be trusted? Preston said he had served in the elite Greek army commandos. A man who took money to work for one foreign group might well take more money to work for another.

Cray scanned the area again, slowly and carefully, trying to pick up every detail. It was up to him to plan the attack. Their lives depended on doing it right. He could see six men. Two were guarding the dirt road that ran along the beach leading west. Two more were watching the road that led from Nicosia. The two pairs of sentries were positioned to intercept and stop anyone who approached the Israeli patrol boat from either direction. They stayed about three hundred yards to the east and west of the *Gaash*. They didn't appear to want to get any closer. Cray did not blame them.

Two more men were sitting by a small fire near a clump of trees close to the road. They, too, didn't seemed to be armed, but as Cray watched, one of them reached under a blanket and drew out a long slender tube and checked it carefully. Cray was good at weapons identification. He recognized a Russian RPG-7 rocket-propelled grenade launcher. The RPG-7 was a deadly weapon, firing 85 mm rockets with five-pound, high-explosive warheads. It was effective against almost anything but a main battle tank and was a favorite weapon with Arab soldiers who had access to Russian weapons. Seeing it did not make Cray happy. It told him he was up against professionals.

Someone spoke softly. Cray recognized Dave Tower's voice to his right. It was not a whisper, but a low speaking tone. Cray smiled. Tower was careful. He knew that the hissing sound of a whisper will carry much farther than normal speech in a low tone of voice. Even near a beach, with waves breaking softly on the sand, Tower was taking no chances.

"It's Tower, Major. I'm coming in."

The tall, blond captain approached carefully, keeping low to the ground, out of sight of the men on the road below. Like his colleagues, he was dressed in the rough work clothes of Cypriot fishermen. Preston had insisted on this. He was adamant that no military uniforms could be worn. Cray didn't mind the clothes. The dark blue-and-black shirts and pants were almost as good as camouflage as long as they stayed in the shadows. But the whole idea seemed ridiculous to him. No matter how they dressed, they did not look like happy fishermen, unless Cypriot fishermen carried automatic rifles, knives and pistols. If they encountered a Cypriot military or police patrol, their hardware would be a little hard to explain.

Tower dropped to the ground and lay prone by Cray's side.

"It's them, all right," Tower said softly. "I got close enough to hear them talking. They weren't saying anything important, but they were speaking Arabic. There's an eastern Arabic accent and a western. They have eastern accents. They sound like Iraqis to me. And one of them said that Colonel Sadiq knows what he's doing. I don't think there's much doubt. They are some of the same people we ran into in Libya."

Cray didn't ask any questions. He had faith in Tower's judgment. One of the reasons Tower was Omega Force's second-in-command was that he could speak perfect Arabic and knew more about the Middle East and its factions than any other Special Operations officer. Another reason was that he was an outstanding combat leader.

"How do you size up the situation?" Cray asked.

"They are reasonably alert, but they don't expect to be attacked. We can probably surprise them, if we're lucky. They're here only to ensure nobody messes with the Israeli patrol boat. They've been told to stay away from it, and from what I can see, they have. There would be tracks in the sand around the boat if anyone had gone on board. I counted six men, all with AK-47Ms and at least one RPG-7. I didn't see any heavy weapons or special equipment."

"You saw six? Grivas thought there were twelve. Where do you think the rest are?"

Tower shrugged. "Probably in that clump of trees near the fire, but I couldn't get close enough to find out. There are a lot of tracks around that fire, so there could be more of them than Grivas saw."

Cray frowned. He did not like it. Modern infantry weapons were incredibly lethal in the hands of men who knew how to use them well. Most of Colonel Sadiq's men were ex-Iraqi army soldiers, veterans of Iraq's eight-year war with Iran and the fighting in Kuwait. If there were men on or near the beach whom his scouts hadn't located, the error could be fatal. They needed some kind of advantage or a diversion.

"If we wait for dark, our night-vision equipment might give us an advantage," Cray said.

Tower shook his head. "That's at least four hours from now. Colonel Sadiq is sending someone they called 'the Russian.' He could arrive at any time, and we don't know how many people may be coming with him. I think we have to take a chance and do it now."

Cray thought hard. He could ask General Sykes what he thought, but that was just passing the buck. It was Cray's responsibility. The Army paid him to make difficult decisions.

"All right," he said, "we'll do it now. Use your radio. Call Preston. Tell him to come up here with Sergeant Hall. We'll use Grivas and his truck as a diversion. Tell him to give us twenty minutes to get in position and then drive down the road. When he's got their attention, we'll hit them with everything we've got.''

Cray smiled grimly. Grivas was going to earn his pay in the next half hour. They all were.

3

Cray went over it with Preston one last time. "Grivas drives up in the truck. The two guards here stop him. With canvas covers up on the back of the truck, they can't be sure how many men are on the truck. With any luck, their friends will come out to reinforce them. We take them out. Sergeant Blake will take out the two guards to the west and watch out for any more of them coming from that direction. As soon as the area is secure, I'll give you a hand signal. You call Captain Stuart. She flies Dr. Hill in immediately. Got it?"

"I understand, Major," Preston said softly. He seemed a bit pale and subdued. The fact that they were about to be in a firefight against heavy odds made him nervous. That didn't bother Cray. He had been frightened in his first firefight and every one since then. He knew the grim truth that a brave man was not a man who wasn't scared, but a man who got the job done anyway.

"All right. Stick close to Sergeant Hall. If anything unexpected happens, Hall will know what to do."

Preston nodded. It was obvious that he was awed by Sergeant Hall. It was not Hall's appearance that impressed Preston, though the tall, gray-haired sergeant was impressive enough. It was Hall's rifle.

It was the most remarkable rifle Preston had ever seen. It was huge, nearly six feet long, made of dull gray metal and black plastic, and sitting on a metal bipod. Hall was peering through its large telescopic sight. "What kind of rifle is that?" Preston asked.

Hall smiled tolerantly. He was used to questions about his rifle.

"That's a Barrett M82A1 .50-caliber semiautomatic sniper's rifle. It fires .50-caliber Browning heavy machine gun cartridges. It's very accurate out to about eighteen hundred yards. It has about five times the power of a .30-caliber machine gun. It usually gets the job done."

It was time to go. Cray moved quickly but carefully through the stunted trees toward the last bit of cover about sixty yards from the edge of the road. General Sykes and Captain Tower were waiting there, quiet and motionless with their M-16A2 automatic rifles in their hands. The third man with them was Lieutenant Commander Peter Ward, a U.S. Navy SEAL. Cray had never seen Ward in action, but was willing to believe he was competent. Ward was armed with a silenced Heckler & Koch submachine gun. They were as ready as they would ever be.

The seconds crawled by. Cray would have cheerfully sold his soul for some machine guns and mortars, but he would have to get the job done with what he had. This would probably be the only time in his life that he led an attack party that included a brigadier general. The sun was starting down toward the horizon. They didn't have all day. Where the hell was Grivas? He resisted the temptation to look at his watch every five seconds. He was getting a splendid case of premission nerves.

What was that? Cray listened intently. He heard the sound of a truck grinding slowly down the dirt road that paralleled the beach. He glanced to the east. Grivas's old surplus British army truck came slowly into sight.

The two Arab guards heard it, too. They were instantly alert. They had no reason to believe that they were about to be attacked, but Cyprus was a center of smuggling and international intrigue. They didn't like the canvas covers that arched up and over the truck bed. Twenty men could have been concealed in the back of the truck. Actually, it was empty, but there was no way they could know that. One of them shouted, and the two men by the fire moved quickly to reinforce them.

Cray saw movement in the clump of trees near the fire. Tower had been right. Cray watched intently. He knew there were men there, but he couldn't tell how many. The men stayed in the trees, which was normal. They were displaying the average infantryman's passion for cover if he thought a firefight was imminent.

Grivas's truck came slowly down the road. When it was about twenty yards away from the men by the road, one of them stepped forward and held up his hand in the universal signal to stop. The men let Grivas see their weapons now. They didn't point them directly at the truck, but the threat was clear. Grivas stopped his truck and stepped down from the cab. He began to argue, gesturing and swearing fluently. The attention of all four men seemed to be fixed on Grivas and his truck.

Now or never! Cray glanced to his right. Tower was ready. Now to his left. Sykes and Ward were looking through the sights of their weapons, picking their targets. Cray took a deep breath and—

Suddenly something went wrong. One of the Arabs shouted. Cray heard the blast of an AK-47 firing. Grivas staggered and fell. Cray could see blood on his black leather jacket.

The scene exploded into action as the Arabs dived for cover, all except the RPG-7 gunner. The long tube of his launcher was over his shoulder, pointing at Grivas's truck like an accusing finger. Cray swung his sights onto the gunner's chest and pulled the trigger. His M-16A2 spat a 3-round burst. He saw dust fly from the gunner's clothes as the .223 bullets tore through him. He staggered and started to fall, but he pulled the trigger of the RPG-7 as he fell. The rocket whooshed from the launcher and shot toward the truck, trailing gray-white smoke. The rocket struck the truck's radiator, and its five-pound warhead detonated in a blast of orange fire. The truck's engine began to smoke and burn.

Cray swung his rifle, looking for another target, but all four Arabs were down. Cray heard the cracking sound of automatic rifles firing as the men in the trees began to fire. Green tracers whined over Cray's head. The enemy didn't seem to have the Omega Force team precisely located. They were simply firing enthusiastically in their general direction. Cray heard the dull boom of Hall's big .50-caliber rifle firing from above and behind him. That would give the opposition something to think about!

Cray turned and shouted to Tower, pointing to Grivas. Tower nodded and crouched, ready to run. Cray brought his rifle to his shoulder and placed the flat black front sight against the edge of the trees. He shouted "Go!" and fired a series of bursts while Tower ran forward and threw himself down by Grivas's motionless body. Cray snapped a fresh 30-round magazine into his rifle. He looked quickly to his left. General Sykes and Lieutenant Ward were firing steadily. The enemy was pinned down, but their return fire showed no sign of slackening.

Cray thought furiously. The fight was becoming a stalemate. He couldn't afford that. Enemy reinforcements might arrive at any moment. Somehow, he must win quickly and decisively. There were forty or fifty yards of open ground between his position and the edge of the trees. Any attempt to lead a heroic charge would only get them all killed. Cray was prepared to die for his country if it came to that, but he wasn't ready to throw his life away. He needed something to blast them out, mortars or artillery.

Suddenly, the answer came to him. He shouted to Tower to cover him and ran for the truck. He threw himself down beside Tower. There was no time for long conversations.

The truck provided some cover against AK-47 fire, but not much.

"Grivas?" he asked.

Tower shook his head. "He's dead."

Cray looked ahead where the bodies of the four dead Arabs lay sprawled in the road. Smoke from the truck's burning engine was drifting that way. It would give him a little cover. "I'm going to get the RPG-7. Keep their heads down," he ordered.

Tower slipped a fresh 30-round magazine into his rifle. "Any time you're ready," he replied.

Cray didn't want to go out there, but he was running on adrenaline now, full of the strange mixture of fear and fury that close-quarter combat brought. Hearing the crackling snarl of Tower's M-16A2 rifle as he fired his first burst, Cray shot forward. The few seconds it would take him to reach the rocket launcher seemed like forever. He reminded himself not to run in a straight line or at a constant speed, since an erratically moving target was harder to hit.

A few feet behind him the ground exploded in a dozen gouts of dust as steel-jacketed AK-47 bullets struck and ricocheted away. That was dangerous, but they would have to be lucky to hit him, firing long bursts from the shoulder. What would really be bad would be a man who used his sights and took the time to fire one well-aimed shot. But there was no use thinking about it. Ten yards to go, five, two, there! Cray threw himself down beside the body of the RPG gunner. He grasped the long cylindrical launcher in one hand and reached for the gunner's spare rocket pack with the other. He slipped the long, thin, cylindrical rocket motor body down the muzzle of the launcher tube and checked to see that it was properly seated.

A burst of green tracers shot over Cray's head. He didn't have all day. He swung the RPG-7 launcher over his shoulder and peered through the optical sight. He saw AK-47 muzzle-flashes from the edge of the trees. They all seemed to be firing straight at him. He put the cross hairs of the sight in the center of the muzzle-flashes, grasped the pistol grip and pulled the trigger. The ejection cartridge shot the rocket grenade from the launcher. Its fins snapped out, the rocket motor ignited, and it hissed toward the trees, trailing gray-white smoke.

The rocket struck, and its five-pound, high-explosive warhead detonated. Fragments tore through the edge of the stunted trees. Cray slipped in another round and fired again. The second rocket exploded five yards to the right of the first. Cray heard another loud explosion and saw fragments tearing splinters from trees. The AK-47 firing stopped. Cray wasn't particularly vindictive, but he had to make sure. He loaded and fired two more rounds. They struck and exploded. The edge of the woods was silent and motionless. That was just as well. RPG-7 rounds weighed fifteen pounds, each. Even a strong man could carry only five or six. Cray had no rocket grenades left.

He signaled to Tower, and they moved forward slowly and carefully, rifles ready. There might be one or two men still alive who wanted to take an American with them before they died. No shots came. Reaching the clump of stunted trees, they found six dead men. The small trees had provided little protection against the lethal 85 mm RPG-7 warheads.

Tower checked the bodies and collected weapons while Cray turned and waved at Preston. Preston stood up and waved. Signal acknowledged. Good. Now, if Preston was not too excited to remember what the signal meant, they were in business.

Cray glanced at his watch. He was astounded to see that the whole fight had taken less than three minutes from start to finish. If Captain Stuart would get Dr. Hill here, she could perform her scientific wizardry and get the hell out. Cray hadn't forgotten that the party they had just attacked had been expecting reinforcements. He had been lucky so far. He didn't want to chance it again with a second group of terrorists.

The sound of helicopter rotors announced the arrival of Dr. Hill. Amanda Stuart was bringing the MH-60K Black hawk in low and fast, contour chasing at less than a hundred feet. The Blackhawk made a smooth landing, a side door opened, and Cora Hill stepped out. Dressed in a white plastic suit with air tanks in a backpack, she looked like an astronaut or the heroine of a science fiction movie. She was carrying a transparent plastic helmet in one hand and an equipment case in the other.

She didn't look happy, and Cray couldn't blame her. She was the one who had to go on board the Israeli patrol boat. If whatever had killed the Israeli crew were still active, all the courage and skill in the world couldn't save her if her protective equipment did not work.

"The area is clear and secured, Doctor," Cray said. "Are you all ready?"

Doctor Hill smiled thinly. "I'm as ready as I'll ever be. Please help me with my helmet."

She carefully put the breathing mask over her nose and mouth and placed the plastic helmet over her head. With the helmet in place, she wasn't breathing the air around her, but an oxygen-helium mixture from the suit tanks. She checked the suit seals very carefully. She was completely isolated from the environment around her.

"All right, Major, I'm ready to go. Hand me that aluminum box. That's my specimen container. Thanks. Now, that black cylinder. That's CAM, a chemical-agent monitor. I'm going on suit radio now. Can you understand me?"

Her voice was distorted by her helmet and the oxygen-helium mixture she was breathing, but Cray could understand her. He gave her a thumbs-up signal. He could hear her sigh through the suit radio. It was obvious she didn't want to go anywhere near the Israeli patrol boat, but it was her job and she was going to do it or die trying. Cray admired her cold courage. He would rather have faced machine guns than an invisible killer that bullets could not kill.

He watched through his binoculars as she plodded slowly toward the *Gaash,* carrying her equipment. She didn't waste her breath on conversation. All Cray could hear was the rasping sound as she breathed through her mask. At last, she reached the side of the Israeli patrol boat. Cray heard her voice on the radio, high-pitched and squeaking, almost like that of a cartoon character. It would have been funny if it hadn't been, literally, deadly serious.

"All right, Major, I've reached the boat. My CAM doesn't detect any chemical agents. I am ready to board. There is a large piece of cargo netting on the left side of the boat. I'll climb that. I'm starting now."

Cray watched as Hill climbed slowly, planning each move in advance, careful to avoid anything that might puncture or cut her suit. His nerves crawled. They might be attacked at any moment. He wanted her to get it over with so that they could get the hell out of there, but he wasn't stupid enough to try to hurry her. One mistake, and she could be very, very dead. God only knew what they would do if they lost their only expert.

"I'm on the deck. I'm starting my examination. I will be too busy to talk for the next few minutes, but I will report anything important or unusual. Understood?"

"Yes, Doctor."

Cray watched Hill through his binoculars as she moved carefully, inspecting each body that lay sprawled on the deck.

"I have examined all the bodies on deck. I have taken blood and tissue samples and removed the filter canisters from two gas masks. I have sealed them in my specimen container. I have closely monitored the clothes of the crewmen. My CAM seems to be detecting a trace of something, but it is very faint. I am now going to go below.

Whatever it is, it should be present in larger concentrations inside the hull compartments, where it will not have been exposed to the outside air for the last few hours. I'm starting now."

"Good luck, Doctor."

"Thanks, I'll probably need it. One other thing, if I don't come back on deck, don't let anyone do anything stupid. The chances are overwhelming that I'll be dead, and anybody who tries to rescue me will be throwing their life away."

Cray acknowledged her message and watched Hill disappear below. He heard nothing but static. The metal hull of the patrol boat was interfering with radio transmissions. Staring at the boat was accomplishing nothing. There was nothing to see. He looked to his right. Twenty feet away Sergeant Blake was carefully checking high-explosive charges and detonators. Blake was Omega Force's demolition expert. It would be up to him to destroy the *Gaash*.

"How does it look?" Cray asked.

Blake smiled. He was always cheerful when he was about to blow something up. "There's no problem, Major. We don't have any heavy charges, but I'll detonate all six of the boat's missile warheads simultaneously. That ought to take care of things nicely."

Blake's concept of "nice" was different from that of most people, but Cray had faith in Blake. If he said what he was planning would take care of the *Gaash*, Cray knew Blake would blow it to hell. Assuming, of course, that Blake could go on board the Israeli patrol boat and place his charges. Cray didn't know what they would do if Cora Hill failed to come back.

He scanned the deck of the *Gaash* again. It was an eerie sight. Nothing moved. Cray glanced at his watch. Dr. Hill had been below only five or six minutes, but it seemed like forever. He saw a flash of motion as Hill reappeared on deck, the rays of the late-afternoon sun reflecting off her white protective suit. She seemed to be all right.

Cray discovered that he had been holding his breath. He let it out and listened intently as he heard Hill's distorted voice on the radio. "I'm back on deck. I have completed my inspection. They are all dead below. I detected traces of something down there and took samples. My CAM couldn't identify the agent. It must be something new. Whatever it was, it seems to have acted faster than any known agent. I think the entire crew was killed in less than sixty seconds. I'm coming back now. Stay away from me until I have decontaminated my suit. Do you understand?"

Cray shuddered. The thought of an invisible thing that could kill him through a gas mask made his nerves crawl. He didn't want to be anywhere near Hill until she had safely decontaminated her protective suit.

"I understand," he said quickly. "I need to know one thing. Is it safe for me to send people on board the boat?"

"Yes, provided they wear self-contained breathing apparatus. They shouldn't go below. Have them stay on deck or on the bridge. They shouldn't touch anything unless they have to and do whatever they need to do as fast as they can."

All right, it was time to do it. Cray turned to Ward and Blake. "You heard her. Let's go," he said. "Get the boat off the beach and out to sea if you can. If not, blow her up where she is."

Ward and Blake checked their breathing masks and moved quickly toward the patrol boat. They stayed well clear of Dr. Hill as she plodded back along the water's edge. Cray watched as they climbed aboard. Ward went to the bridge as Blake moved quickly toward the missile launchers and began to place his charges. Cray heard a rumbling sound and saw a cloud of gray-white smoke when Ward started the *Gaash*'s four diesel engines. Water bubbled and frothed at the patrol boat's stern as Ward reversed the propellers and tried to back the *Gaash* off the beach. Her two hundred sixty tons shuddered as Ward applied more and more power, and 13,400 horsepower pulled her free.

Blake clambered down the side, gave Cray a thumbs-up signal, and started swimming for shore. The demolition charges were set and ready to fire.

Ward swung the boat around until her bow pointed out to sea. There was nothing more for him to do. He moved quickly off the bridge, dived smoothly over the side, and began the swim to shore. Manned only by dead men, the *Gaash* moved steadily away from the beach.

Cray ordered everyone else on board the Blackhawk. Now, only he, Blake, and Ward were left on the ground to watch as the *Gaash* sailed on. Cray estimated she was a thousand yards from the beach. That would have to do. "All set?" he asked.

"Any time you're ready, Major," Blake said with a grin. Cray nodded. Blake pushed the button on the small radio control box in his hand. Coded pulses flashed invisibly to the detonators on the *Gaash*. Instantly, Cray saw six bright yellow flashes from the patrol boat's missile launchers. Six heavy missile warheads detonated simultaneously. The *Gaash* was blasted and shattered by six huge balls of orange fire. Her torn and smoking hull vanished beneath the waves. The *Gaash* was gone, but not forgotten.

4

Saada Almori sat helplessly in the back seat of the battered Mercedes. She no longer had the slightest idea where she was. The Israeli Intelligence agents had carefully blindfolded her, and the car had made many turns. The three Israelis, two men and a woman, were conversing, but Saada couldn't understand Hebrew. They might be discussing how they would kill her and where to dispose of her body. She told herself that such thoughts were foolish. Whatever happened, the Israelis wouldn't kill her until they had obtained the information she had promised. Her credentials as an international journalist were perfect. She didn't think that even Mossad knew that she worked for Colonel Nizar Sadiq.

The car came to a stop. She heard the door open. The Israeli woman spoke in perfect Arabic. "We are here, Miss Almori. Step out carefully."

Saada felt the Israeli woman's hand on her shoulder, guiding her forward. Her other hand grasped the leather belt of Saada's fashionable dress, making it impossible for her to run if she were stupid enough to try. The Israelis were Saada's mortal enemies, but she had to admit that they were extremely competent. She walked forward. She could hear a door open, then could feel a floor under her feet and some kind of carpeting. They were in a house.

"Very well, take her blindfold off, and let us talk to our guest." It was a man's voice, one that Saada hadn't heard before. She blinked as the Israeli woman behind Saada removed the blindfold. She was in a small room, facing a table. A stocky, balding man in his late forties sat facing her. He was apparently the leader. Two other men stood behind him out of the light. There was nothing remarkable in their appearance. They would go unnoticed on the streets of Beirut.

The leader pointed to a chair. "Sit down, Miss Almori. Miriam, get our guest some tea. We must not be inhospitable." He, too, spoke perfect Arabic. He studied Saada carefully. She was used to men looking at her. Tall and well-built, she had long legs and long black lustrous hair. Her expensive gray dress showed off her excellent figure, but the Israeli was looking at her with cold calculation in his eyes. Saada knew he would order her death in a second if he thought that it was necessary. The fact that she was a woman would not make the slightest difference.

The Israeli woman set a cup of hot tea in front of her and another in front of the leader. Saada hesitated. It might be drugged, some kind of truth serum, perhaps. The Israeli leader smiled. "Drink it, Miss Almori. You are among friends here. It is only tea." Saada shrugged. He might be lying, but it made no difference. She was helpless. If they wanted to drug her, there was nothing she could do to stop them.

She sipped the steaming tea.

"Now that you are comfortable, Miss Almori, let us talk. You are here because you put out the word that you wanted to talk to Israeli Intelligence concerning certain information you have. You said this information was vital to the security of Israel. You were unwilling to come to Israel. You insisted that we meet in Beirut. We took you at your word. We are the Mossad, and we are ready to listen to anything you have to say."

He paused and drew a flat, black, silenced Beretta .22 automatic from under his worn leather jacket.

"I am sure that every word you say is God's truth, Miss Almori, but you do know that, for us, Beirut is hostile territory. There are thousands of people in this city who would love to kill us and laugh to see us die. If by any chance you have set a trap for us, you will be the first to die. As God is my witness, I will put a bullet through your head at the first sign of treachery. Now, time is short. What do you wish to tell us?"

Saada took a deep breath. This was it! She reminded herself that she was a soldier for the Arab cause. If she died fighting for what she believed, it was God's will.

"Very well. First, do you know who I am?"

The Israeli leader smiled again.

"Only a few small details. You are Saada Almori. Born in Basra, Iraq to a well-to-do family. You have relatives in Lebanon and Iraq. You were educated in Iraq and Lebanon. You studied journalism at the University of London. You have a Lebanese passport. You are five feet eight inches tall and measure 35-23-34. You do not use perfume. Your bank balance is 19,400 Lebanese pounds. You are fond of expensive French dresses. Your favorite drink is Scotch malt whiskey. You believe very strongly in the idea of a single, unified Arab nation. For the last seven years you have worked as a free-lance journalist in the Middle East. You have published many articles. I read a few of them while waiting for you."

He paused and shook a finger at her.

"You do have a colorful way with words. I was particularly struck by the phrase 'the bloodstained hands of Zionist imperialism reached out again to ravish the peace-loving nation of Lebanon.' Really, Miss Almori, wasn't that a little strong?"

Saada flushed. "I wrote that after your troops stood aside and let hundreds of unarmed refugees be massacred. You may not like my words, but they are true!"

"Yes, Miss Almori, I am sure that you think that they are. That gives us a small problem. Everything we know about you suggests you are hostile to the state of Israel. How is it that you have suddenly become our friend and rush to tell us that we are in mortal danger?"

"I am not your friend," Saada said sharply. "I would like to see Israel totally defeated and your military power shattered. I will dance and sing the day that happens, but above all else, I do not want to see another war in the Middle East."

She paused for a moment and stared at the Mossad agents. "I have just come from Cyprus. I have reliable evidence that an Arab terrorist base has been established there to launch chemical and biological warfare attacks against Israel. The weapons are new and advanced. Your chemical-warfare protective equipment will be useless against them. Your cities will be struck. Tens of thousands of your people will die."

She certainly had their attention. The Israeli leader was no longer smiling. "Let us assume that what you say is true, Miss Almori. Would you not, as you said yourself, dance and sing to see Israel struck such a blow?"

"Since you know so much about me, you should know that I do not want to see thousands of women and children killed. And I know you will retaliate if attacked in this way. Some of these chemical weapons are being sent to Lebanon and may be used against Israel from there. I know that you have hundreds of nuclear weapons. You will not hesitate to use them if you think Israel is in mortal danger. I don't want to see nuclear war in Lebanon. Its people have suffered enough. I am telling you this only so that you can prevent the attack. You may believe me or not. That is up to you!"

The Mossad agents conversed rapidly in Hebrew. Saada listened intently and caught the words *"Ba'ir"* and *"Gaash"* repeated more than once. She kept her face expressionless and waited. Good! What she had told them fit perfectly with what they already knew.

The leader turned to Saada again. "We understand, Miss Almori. Now, tell us everything you know."

"There is an envelope in my purse. Yes, that's it. Here is a map of Cyprus. The base is here, near the western tip of the island. It is an old, ruined stone fort. It is guarded by a number of heavily armed men. The man in charge is an ex-Iraqi army officer named Kawash."

She continued smoothly, watching the Israeli agents carefully as she spoke. She was sure they couldn't ignore her information. The risk was simply too great. They would have to do something. God is great! The Israelis were taking the bait!

EVERYONE WAS HAPPY in the recreation room of the consulate. It was, after all, a special occasion. The CIA did not wine and dine the leaders of Omega Force every day. Preston had ordered lamb roasted with herbs from what he swore was the best restaurant in Nicosia and produced strong, red, Cypriot wine to wash it down. He and Dr. Kaye were happy. Their plan had succeeded. Washington was pleased. Only Grivas had been killed. Perhaps they felt he was expendable. The members of Omega Force were enjoying the feeling of immense relief of men who have just been in mortal combat and survived.

Cray was considering having another glass of wine when a Marine guard entered the room and move rapidly toward the table where Kaye and Preston sat. The Marine handed Preston an envelope. He read the message, frowned and handed it to Dr. Kaye. Kaye read the message quickly, said a few words to Preston and stalked out of the room. It was obvious he was not amused. Alarm bells began to ring in Cray's head. Whatever was happening, he would have bet a month's pay that he wasn't going to like it.

Preston consulted with General Sykes, then turned to Cray. "Major Cray," he said politely, "there has been a change in the situation. Dr. Kaye would like to speak to you and General Sykes immediately in the briefing room. Please follow me."

In the briefing room Sykes and Kaye were looking at a map of Cyprus.

"I'm sorry to take you away from the celebration, gentlemen, but we have a problem," Kaye said. "We have just received a message from Tel Aviv. Our friends inside Israeli Intelligence have learned of a terrorist base in western Cyprus. It is supposedly to be used to launch chemical or biological attacks against Israel. The Israeli high command is planning to attack this base in the next twenty-four hours. They intend to use air strikes and special operations troops. As you can see, this presents quite a problem."

"Why does that present a problem, Doctor?" Sykes asked. "I assume we want this base destroyed. I wouldn't worry, the Israelis are damned good at that sort of thing. They will take care of it for us."

"I'm afraid you simply don't understand the situation, General. There are two governments on Cyprus. The Republic of Cyprus controls this part of the island. Its citizens are mostly ethnic Greeks. The Turks control the western part of the island. Greece and Turkey fought a limited war over the control of Cyprus in 1974. The Turks occupied the western end of the island then. They have over eight thousand troops there now. The terrorist base is here, in Turkish-controlled territory. If Israel attacks Turkish-controlled Cyprus, there may be a serious international incident, possibly war between Israel and Turkey. Both countries are United States allies. We must prevent this at any cost."

Cray didn't like that phrase. He felt that he might be called on to pay far more of that cost than Dr. Kaye. Still, he wasn't paid to make foreign policy, just to execute it.

"Do we have photographs of the base?" he asked.

FIVE HOURS LATER Cray and Sykes were concealed in a clump of bushes, studying the scene in front of them through their night-vision AN/PVS-7 goggles. It looked like the right place, four or five run-down buildings surrounded by a low stone wall. Several men were sitting by a small fire in front of an open gate. If there were more on the other side, they were keeping quiet and out of sight. Something about it bothered Cray. He couldn't put his finger on exactly what was wrong, but he wasn't about to ignore his feelings. He was alive to lead Omega Force because he had paid attention to things like that in the past.

Dave Tower came quietly back to the bushes, having crept within twenty-five yards of the men at the fire. "I count eight men at the front gate, and three or four at the back," he reported. "They all have AK-47s or submachine guns. No one else is in the compound. No sign of any heavy weapons or night-vision equipment. None of them are dug in. No sign of any scouts out, and nobody is patrolling. It looks like a walkover. I don't like it. It's too damned easy!"

Tower considered the matter carefully. "There are several other things that don't seem right. I got close enough to hear them talking. None of them sound like Iraqis to me. Hell, some of them don't even sound like Arabs! They don't look like experienced soldiers, either. If this is the terrorist base, we killed twelve of their people less than twenty miles from here a few hours ago. They should be alert and ready to fight, not sitting around drinking coffee and telling jokes. We're either in the wrong place, or it's a trap. I didn't see anybody in the buildings, but there could be two hundred men in there. Maybe they're just waiting for us to waltz in, fat, dumb and happy, so they can blow our heads off! I don't like it!"

Cray thought it over. Tower's words echoed his own sentiments. He didn't believe they were in the wrong place, though. The buildings and the low wall around them looked exactly like the photographs he had studied in Nicosia. There simply could not be a nearly identical place guarded by armed men, but everything that Tower said seemed right. Cray had fought Colonel Sadiq's men before. Most of them had been in the elite Iraqi Republican Guard or the Iraqi Special Forces. They weren't superhuman, but they were experienced soldiers, veterans of Iraq's eight-year war with Iran and the Gulf War. They would be ready for combat. These men were not. Perhaps the real terrorists had gone and taken their chemical weapons with them. The men left behind might be the second team, good enough to guard the base, but not first-rate soldiers.

It was a pretty theory, but it didn't change the fact that they had to get inside and find out. If chemical weapons were stored there, Dr. Hill had to examine them, and if they were going to destroy the base, Blake had to set his charges. Decisions were easy when there was only one thing you could do. Of course, that thought may have occurred to the man who'd led the charge of the Light Brigade. Cray did not like that thought and he put it out of his mind.

"All right," he said quietly, "we're going in. Ward and Hall are in place. They take out the guards in back. We'll take care of this lot. We'll use the M-203s."

Tower nodded. Each of them had one of the wicked little 40 mm grenade launchers clipped under the barrels of their M-16A2 rifles. The 40 mm high-explosive grenades might not be heavy artillery, but they were extremely effective at close range.

"Pass the word. We go in three minutes. I need to talk to Preston."

Cray moved carefully back about twenty yards. The CIA man was crouched by the radio with his 12-gauge shotgun in his hands. Cray was careful not to startle him. Preston wasn't used to night raids, and a misdirected friendly blast of buckshot would kill you just as dead as one fired by your mortal enemies.

Cray gave the password and crouched by Preston's side. Preston looked nervous. Perhaps his CIA academy instructors had never told him there might be days like this.

"We're going in. You will hear a lot of automatic-rifle fire and some explosions. Sit tight. We can take the people we can see, no sweat. But there may be more inside. If there is a big counterattack, we break contact and get the hell out of here. If that happens, you call Captain Stuart and tell her to bring the Blackhawk to the extraction zone. Got it?"

Preston nodded. "To the extraction zone."

Cray vanished back into the darkness. A moment later he was back beside Tower and the others. They were waiting tensely. Cray checked his rifle and his grenade launcher and turned on his infrared sight. To the naked eye, nothing was happening; with his infrared night-vision goggles Cray saw a glowing spot that showed exactly where the bullets from his rifle would strike. He studied the greenish images of the guards in his night-vision goggles. One of them was standing with his AK-47 ready. Cray took aim and saw the invisible spot of light appear on the guard's chest.

He began to count softly, "Three, two, one, fire!"

Cray squeezed his trigger and fired a burst of high-velocity .223 bullets. He could hear three other M-16A2s snarl into life. The men around the fire were caught in one of the most appalling situations imaginable, totally unexpected blasts of automatic-weapon fire out of the dark. Some of them went down and lay still. Others dropped to the ground and fired long ineffective bursts that sent green tracers streaking high over the Americans' heads. Cray sneered. They were a bunch of damned amateurs! He felt almost sorry for them as he pulled the trigger on his grenade launcher.

Four 40 mm grenades struck around the fire and detonated in less than three seconds. Through the team's night-

vision AN/PVS-7 goggles, the explosions were dazzling.
Cray heard fragments whining through the air. The return
fire stopped instantly. The seconds crawled by. Cray stared
through the gate and listened intently. He saw and heard
nothing. If there were others inside, they were doing absolutely nothing.

He could not wait any longer. He slipped another 40 mm
round into his grenade launcher and motioned Tower and
Blake forward. They moved cautiously toward the fire, rifles ready. Nothing happened. Tower kicked the weapons
away from the victims sprawled on the ground and quickly
checked the bodies. Blake moved past him and peered
through the open gate. He scanned the buildings, keeping
his rifle ready. After a moment he set down his rifle and
began to study the gate itself.

Tower motioned Cray forward. Cray pointed inquiringly at the bodies of the guards. Tower shook his head. He
had found nothing. Cray was still nervous. It was just too
damned easy! Every instinct told him something was
wrong. He motioned to Tower to follow him and began to
move cautiously toward the gate. He was almost there when
Blake suddenly threw up his hand in an abrupt gesture to
stop. Cray froze, literally not moving a muscle. Blake was
not only Omega Force's demolition expert, but he also
knew more about bombs and booby traps than anyone
Cray knew.

Cray looked at the ground in front of him, searching for
a trip wire or a suspicious patch of earth that might indicate a mine. He saw nothing. Blake motioned for Cray to
come closer, pointing to a spot just a little ahead of him.
There were few things Cray hated worse than mines and
booby traps, but it was obvious that Blake wanted to show
him something. He moved forward and looked over Blake's
shoulder. Blake pointed carefully at something about two
feet above the ground. At first Cray could see nothing.
Then he saw a pale, narrow, almost invisible line of light

stretching across the opening. He looked inquiringly at Blake.

"It's a beam of infrared light, Major, invisible to the human eye. We see it only because we're wearing night-vision goggles, the same way we see the targeting spots from our infrared sights. This is the source, here. That thing on the other side that the beam is shining on is an infrared detector. If the beam is interrupted, the detector will send an electrical signal, and something will sure as hell happen."

"Can you disable it or shut it down?" Cray asked quickly.

Blake shook his head. "I could, Major, but I don't think you want me to. If anything shuts off the signal from that detector, it will be the same as if someone broke the beam by passing through the gate. That will trigger something. It could just be an intrusion detection device, but I don't think so. That doesn't make any sense if you have guards on the gate. I think it's hooked up to something extremely nasty. The whole place is probably mined and booby-trapped. You don't want to go inside, Major."

Blake was right. The last thing in the world Cray wanted to do was go inside those buildings, but he had no choice. "I hear you, but we've got to go in," he said quietly.

Blake shrugged. The Army paid Cray to make hard decisions. "All right, Major, just be damned sure you and Captain Tower step over that beam."

Blake took his own advice. Cray and Tower followed him carefully. Cray scanned the buildings again through his goggles. There was no sign of life. The buildings appeared dark and deserted, but he didn't relax. Colonel Sadiq's men might be gone, but they could have left some very unpleasant surprises behind. The nearest building was smaller than the others. It had several windows and a single door. He pointed to it and followed Blake to the door. Blake checked the door slowly and carefully. Cray resisted the temptation to ask questions or tell him to hurry. Distracting Blake while he was working could be suicidal.

It seemed to take forever, but at last Blake was satisfied. Standing carefully to one side, he eased the door open an inch or two. There was no reaction. Blake raised one hand. Cray and Tower pointed their weapons, ready to rake the room with automatic-rifle fire. With coordination that a ballet star might have envied, Blake brought his hand down, shoved the door hard with the muzzle of his rifle and threw himself to the ground.

The building contained one large room. Cray scanned it quickly. No one was home. The room had been used as an office or a headquarters. He saw a battered desk, a table with a few chairs, and a pair of filing cabinets. Whoever had been there seemed to have left in a hurry. There were papers on the desk and some cups and plates on the table. Blake entered and produced a small black box from his pack. He used it to scan the dark room.

"I don't detect anything, but be careful," he said. "This little gadget will detect almost anything that uses electricity, but it won't see something old-fashioned, like a simple mechanical pull fuze. Before you pick anything up, let me check it first."

Tower went quickly to the desk, took out his flashlight and examined the papers. Cray couldn't help him since he couldn't read Arabic. He took out his own flashlight and searched the walls. A large map with printing in Arabic was taped behind the desk, outlining Cyprus and the coastlines of Lebanon and Syria to the east. There were hand-drawn lines and notes on the map that might be important. Cray took it off the wall and handed it to Tower, who added it to the stack of papers he was putting in his pack.

"No bombs," Blake announced. "It looks like they were using this as their headquarters. They wouldn't have wanted it booby-trapped while they were using it. And since they probably left in a hell of a hurry, they didn't have time to rig anything.''

That made sense to Cray. He glanced at Tower, who seemed to have everything he wanted. If there was anything more to find, it would be in the other buildings. He glanced at his watch. They were taking far too long and had to speed things up, even if it meant taking a few more chances.

He turned to Tower. ''Get Ward and Hall from the back gate. Have them rejoin General Sykes. Ask the General to have Captain Stuart land the Blackhawk on the road close to the gate. Tell her to be ready for an emergency takeoff. We may be in a hell of a hurry when we leave. Blake and I will check out the other buildings.''

Tower nodded and was gone.

The nearest building was noticeably larger than the building they had just investigated. It was windowless and had a single door that looked big enough to allow trucks to pass. It was probably a warehouse of some kind. Blake risked using his flashlight as they approached the door. There were many tire tracks and footprints in the soft ground. There had been a lot of activity here in the last few hours.

Blake pointed at the door, which was standing open. A pale thin beam shone across the entrance. Blake examined it carefully. ''It's the same kind of device that was on the gate, but it's hooked up differently. It's attached to something that is either a timer or a counter. Several wires run out of that, and I think they go to the other buildings. If this device activates, I think it's going to trigger a number of things.''

Wonderful! But there was still no choice. They had to go in.

''All right. Put on your mask. We're going in.''

Blake grimaced as he reached for his M40 gas mask. His fondness for destructive devices didn't extend to poison gas or unpleasant viruses. The masks were a compromise. Cray had discussed the question with Cora Hill. Wearing the gloves, hoods, suits and boots of full chemical-warfare equipment would have slowed them down too much. There are gases that can kill by being absorbed through the skin, but it took far longer than if you breathed them. Cray slipped his M40 over his head and carefully checked the seal. The feel of the mask against his face was reassuring. Some chance is always better than none! Dr. Hill had lent him her Chemical Agent Monitor, which he activated carefully and watched the display. Nothing—as far as the CAM could tell, the area was clear.

Blake was ready. Cray scanned the inside of the building through his night-vision goggles. He saw no sign of life, but there were three stacks of something piled against the back wall of the building. Cray used his flashlight. Bingo! The objects were silver cylinders, about three feet long. They looked like oxygen tanks, but Cray would have bet his last dollar that, whatever they held, it wasn't oxygen. It was risky, but he decided to take one if he could. It would probably be invaluable to Dr. Hill's people if it contained the new agent. Better have Blake check it before he touched it, but where was Blake?

Cray turned and saw Blake moving toward the back wall. He was using his scanner and his flashlight, searching for something. He came to a pile of crates and cylinders that were different from the others. The crates seemed to be strapped together and connected with a jumble of wires.

"Good God Almighty!" Blake exclaimed, his voice distorted by his gas mask. Cray moved carefully to his side and stared at the stack of crates, sacks and cylinders. He shook his head. All he saw was what looked like a pile of junk. It was obvious that Blake saw something that he did not.

"What is it?"

"It's a bomb, Major!"

Cray looked again. He saw nothing in the pile that looked like a bomb, but Blake was the expert. "I don't see a bomb. Where is it?" he demanded.

"You don't understand, Major. The whole damned thing's a bomb! Those crates are full of dynamite. The sacks are full of a powdered explosive, probably hexogen. The cylinders are fuel, propane or butane. There must be eight or ten tons of high explosives, and when they blow, the fuel cylinders will enhance the detonation. It will be the damnedest explosion you ever saw."

Lovely! They were standing less than three feet from one of the most powerful nonnuclear bombs in history. Cray told himself not to panic. Dead was dead. The bomb couldn't kill him any deader than a well-aimed hand grenade. Somehow that thought was not particularly comforting.

"Just how powerful is it? Will it destroy the entire building?"

"Major, there won't be any building when that thing fires, and that's not all. There are wires running to the walls. There must be bombs in the other buildings. When one goes, they'll all go. There won't be anything left at all!"

"Can you put a charge on it and detonate it by remote control?"

Blake nodded. "I'll use a timer to give us five minutes to get clear." He took a small, black device from his pack and attached it to one of the explosive crates. "All set."

One more thing. Cray pointed to the stacks of silver cylinders. "I want to take one of those for Dr. Hill. Check them out before I touch one."

Blake took out his scanner. "No electrical activity," he reported. He looked at the stack of cylinders carefully. "I don't see anything, but if there is something on the bottom of the cylinder, I won't be able to see it until we lift it. If we want it, we're going to have to take a chance."

Cray understood. Lifting the cylinder was taking a chance, but an intact cylinder of the agent that had killed the Israelis could be the key to the whole mission. He wouldn't ask Blake to take the chance, but he was willing to take it himself.

"Stand back," he commanded. Blake moved back ten feet and pointed his scanner.

Cray took a deep breath and lifted a cylinder clear. He heard a soft popping sound. Almost instantly Blake shouted, "Fuze action! Multiple fuze action!"

Cray dropped the cylinder back into place as if it were red-hot, but it was too late. Blake's scanner was a miracle of modern technology, but it had been defeated by a simple mechanical device. The weight of the cylinder had been compressing a small, spring-loaded plunger. As the weight of the cylinder was removed, the spring drove the plunger upward and closed the fuzing circuit.

He heard pop after pop, and gas began to flow out of the cylinders with a menacing, hissing sound. The room began to fill with an almost invisible cloud of vapor. Cora Hill's chemical-agent monitor was slung over Cray's shoulder. It emitted a piercing howl. Cray held his breath and snatched a quick glance at the CAM's display. The small red letters read, "Warning! Blood gases. HCN and CNCL." Cray knew what HCN was, hydrogen cyanide. A modern gas mask would protect you for a while, but it was slowly absorbed through the skin, and the results were fatal. Time to get the hell out!

He turned to Blake who was staring at his scanner. Small red lights were flickering on its display. "The bomb's activated! It's releasing its fuel gases!" Blake shouted.

Cray had the distinct impression that someone, somewhere, didn't like him. The room was filling with poison gas, and he was within twenty feet of the mother of all bombs. Cray had his faults, but not being able to make up his mind was not one of them. "Run!" he shouted as he turned and sprinted out the door. He didn't understand why the bomb had not gone off, but he was not going to stay around and discuss it. He and Blake ran as fast as they could toward the gate.

It was brutal work, since gas masks only filter air; the lungs have to supply the force to breathe in and out through the filters. Almost instantly Cray was gasping and straining for breath. Only the sight of the helicopter sitting outside the gate with its rotors turning kept him going. Thirty yards, twenty, ten. Tower was holding the side door open. Cray threw himself inside. A fraction of a second later, Blake landed on top of him.

Tower didn't ask questions. He shouted, "Go!"

The whine of the turbines changed to a shrieking howl as Amanda Stuart went to full power. The Blackhawk lifted off in an emergency takeoff that would have given its designers heart failure.

Cray glanced at his watch. They had been in the air for more than a minute. The Blackhawk was doing nearly two hundred miles per hour as Amanda flew at top speed and stayed as low as she dared. They were moving away from the base at better than three miles per minute, but there was no way to know when the bomb would fire. He looked behind them.

Suddenly, there was an immense yellow flash, like a giant bolt of lightning, then another and another. For twenty seconds, nothing seemed to happen, then the Blackhawk bucked and shuddered as the shock wave from the blast struck. Behind them a huge pillar of hot gas and dust was rising into the sky. Cray smiled grimly. You couldn't argue that Omega Force had not accomplished its mission. The Israelis would be happy. The terrorist base was completely destroyed.

5

Cray was finishing the debriefing. "So we made a dash for the helicopter and got the hell out of there. The terrorists' own bombs detonated, and the base was totally destroyed. Washington and the Israelis should be happy about that."

Dr. Kaye smiled. He had already called Washington and declared victory. "Thank you, Major Cray, for that excellent description. Is there anything else you have to tell us? Anything you have concluded from the operation?"

Cray considered the question. "Well," he said quietly, "the people we were up against were real pros. If we hadn't been wearing night-vision equipment, their bombs would probably have gotten us. If we take them on again, we're going to have to be extremely careful. Any mistake is likely to be our last. We were lucky that our gas masks protected us. I don't understand that, though. The Israeli gas masks didn't save them, and I thought ours weren't any better."

"I think I can answer that," Cora Hill said quickly. "They didn't use the same thing. The CAM shows exactly what Major Cray reported. It was exposed to high concentrations of hydrogen cyanide and cyanogen chloride. Both are blood gases and kill quickly. Hydrogen cyanide is quicker, but cyanogen chloride attacks and breaks down key elements in a gas mask's filters. Had you stayed in the building too long, your gas masks would have failed. Neither of those gases is new, but their use in combination is significant. Whoever set that trap has a sophisticated knowledge of chemical warfare. As you said, Major, a real pro. Possibly our friend, the Russian. Is the CIA any closer to identifying him?''

Kaye frowned. "We're running a computer check on all known Russian chemical- and biological-warfare experts, trying to see if any of them left Russia or any of the other republics in the last year. There are a lot of names to check. Washington will inform us as soon as they learn anything."

"Why didn't they use the same stuff that they used on the Israelis?" Cray asked. "It killed them in seconds. It would have killed us. Why did they use these blood gases?"

"They were too smart to chance that you might have disarmed their traps," said Dr. Hill. "If we had captured a full cylinder of their new agent, it would have been a real breakthrough. Our people back in the States are working night and day to analyze the samples from the Israeli patrol boat. They are hampered because they have only extremely small samples. With a large quantity, the analysis would go much faster. We don't have a prayer of developing a defense until we have completed our analysis."

"Anything else?" Kaye asked. He seemed impatient to end the meeting.

"Yes," Dave Tower responded. "The map Major Cray found at the terrorist base has three routes from western Cyprus to the coast of Lebanon marked on it. There are some notes written in Arabic that refer to times of departure and arrival, but they don't really tell us much. At a guess, the map shows the plan for moving weapons from Cyprus to Lebanon by sea."

He paused, and then continued slowly. "Those are the facts. This is what I think. I don't like it. It's just too damned convenient! That map tells us what we want to know, and somehow it just got left behind, taped to a wall where we couldn't miss it. If we go to the places shown on the map, we had better be ready for anything."

Cray was about to say that he agreed completely when a Marine guard entered the room and handed Dr. Kaye an envelope. He opened it, read a short message, then frowned and read it again. His expression and tone of voice seemed to become nervous, tense, perhaps even afraid as he said, "Thank you, ladies and gentlemen. The briefing is concluded. Will General Sykes, Major Cray, and Mr. Preston stay for a moment?"

Kaye waited until the others left. "Gentlemen, there is a major new development. Our people in Lebanon have been contacted by an Arab woman named Saada Almori. She says that she has extremely important secret information concerning terrorist plans for a major attack on Israel. She is unwilling to reveal her information to Israeli Intelligence or the Lebanese government. She demands a face-to-face meeting in Beirut with a senior U.S. Intelligence official and guarantees of her personal safety in exchange for her information. The meeting must take place in the next forty-eight hours."

"Do we believe her?" Preston asked dubiously. "There are a lot of crazies in Lebanon. It could be a hoax or a trap."

"I think we have to go. Some of the things she said are very convincing. She mentioned advanced chemical and biological weapons. She says she has met with Israeli Intelligence agents in Beirut and told them about the base here on Cyprus. We have checked with our people in Tel Aviv. That appears to be true. No, it would be stupid to trust her, but I think we have to talk to her."

"It's too great a risk for you to go to Beirut, Doctor. You stay here. I'll go to Beirut and talk to her."

Kaye smiled bleakly. "Thank you, Preston. I appreciate that. Beirut is an extremely dangerous place for American Intelligence and military personnel, but Almori specified a senior CIA officer. I don't think you would satisfy her. I have to go. I would appreciate it if you would go with me and coordinate the operation. Please make provisions for a party of eight for covert travel to Beirut as soon as possible. Arrange for covert shipment of arms and equipment.''

General Sykes stared at Kaye. ''I thought you said you were going to Beirut and talk to a woman, Doctor. It sounds like you and Preston think you're going to war!''

''That's correct, General, and you had better think of it that way. Do you have any idea what the situation is in Lebanon?''

''I've never been briefed on it. I know what I've seen on television. The Muslims and the Christians have fought for control of the country. The Israelis went in in 1982 and ran the PLO out. There's some kind of UN peacekeeping force there. That's all I know.''

Kaye's usual superior smile was back. ''I only wish it were that simple, General. I was there during the civil war in 1976. It was the most remarkable thing I ever saw. The Christians fought the Muslims, the Muslims fought other Muslims, and the Christian factions fought each other. The Syrians helped first one side, then another. It's still like that. Even though the Syrians have gained overwhelming political superiority, there are more than fifty factions and groups in Lebanon. Any of them still maintain militias, and they are armed to the teeth with automatic weapons and rocket launchers. Some of them even have tanks. Some of them dislike Americans; most of the rest hate us intensely.''

Sykes was impressed. Kaye had the air of a man who knew what he was talking about. If half of what he said was true, Lebanon was a very dangerous place indeed.

''All right, Doctor, you've convinced me. Omega Force will be landing on Cyprus in an hour or two. It sounds like the action will be in Lebanon. Shall we contact the Lebanese government and get authorization to divert them to a base in Lebanon?''

Kaye looked astounded. "That is completely out of the question! The Lebanese government only fully controls the larger cities. The various factions control parts of the countryside. To openly introduce U.S. troops into Lebanon would create an international crisis, and your men would be immediately subjected to terrorist attacks."

"All right, Doctor, if we don't do that, what do we do?"

"I want your people to go with me to Lebanon. Nobody knows them there. If we have to, we can pass them off as military advisers to the Lebanese military. In the meantime, the CIA is going to contact Israeli Intelligence. We are going to convince them we are the good guys. We'll tell them we discovered a plot against our Israeli allies and that we destroyed the terrorist base on Cyprus to protect them. We'll say we want to move Omega Force into a base in northern Israel to be ready for action in Lebanon. You will be the senior U.S. military representative to coordinate operations. Dr. Hill will accompany you. The Israelis will be told that she is there to coordinate research on analyzing and perfecting defenses against the new agent. If you wish, I will contact Washington and ask that the Joint Chiefs of Staff authorize these actions."

Sykes smiled. "That won't be necessary, Doctor. Omega Force is committed to this mission, and we will carry it out. As for your terrorists, do you know the Rangers' unofficial motto?"

Kaye looked blank. Cray laughed. "It's very unofficial, Doctor. It goes, 'Travel To Exotic Places, Meet Interesting People, And Kill Them.'"

CRAY CHECKED his security arrangements again. The flight into Beirut and the drive into the central city from the airport had been sobering. The sights along the way had convinced him that Kaye had not been exaggerating. Parts of the city were as modern and peaceful as a prosperous city in Europe, but other areas looked like a war zone, devas-

tated by rockets and artillery. Whether you called them
factions, terrorists or militias, it was obvious that the people who controlled that kind of firepower would be formidable enemies. Cray knew his people were good, but they
weren't invincible, and there were only six of them. If this
were a trap, and the mysterious Saada Almori showed up
with a few dozen friends, the Americans would be in a lot
of trouble.

A light blinked on Cray's low-probability-of-intercept
tactical radio. Sergeant Hall was on the roof. He must have
spotted something. "Major," Hall said softly, "a cab just
stopped at the corner. One woman got out. She seems to be
alone and has no visible weapons. She is headed toward
you."

Cray turned to Tower. "Our friend seems to be on the
way. Go put out the welcome mat."

Tower chuckled and said something in Arabic. The tall
Special Forces captain was wearing local clothes. A red *ke-
fiyah,* the traditional Arab headcloth, was wound around
his head, partially concealing his face. Cray didn't think
that Tower looked particularly like an Arab, but at a distance he might get by. He had a loaded AK-47 slung over
his shoulder. That should discourage casual questions from
strangers. Tower stepped out the door of the safe house.
Cray heard the click of a woman's heels. Tower spoke in
Arabic. The woman replied.

The safe house was a shop that sold brassware and ori-
ental rugs. Cray had left a few lights on. To an observer, the
woman would appear as a shopper looking for a bargain.
The door opened and Tower showed the woman in. She
glanced casually at Cray. She didn't seem to be alarmed at
the sight of his automatic rifle. If you were a journalist in
Beirut, you were used to the sight of men with guns.

Tower ushered the woman to the back room of the shop.
Kaye and Preston were waiting there, sitting at a table.
Blake stood nearby, holding an object shaped like a small

wand. Kaye greeted the woman in Arabic. The lights were brighter in the room. Cray looked at Saada Almori carefully. Tall and well-built, she was worth looking at.

Kaye switched to English. "If you would stand there for a moment, Miss Almori. It is a mere formality, but we would like to check something." He motioned to Blake, who stepped forward and ran the wand over her body. He didn't touch her but moved the wand carefully, scanning her from head to toe. Blake's wand emitted a soft chime, and a red light began to flicker on its handle.

Blake smiled. "She has a weapon in her purse and something else, probably an electronic device which is not activated."

Saada Almori also smiled and handed Blake her purse. He reached inside and drew out a small flat automatic pistol, no bigger than the palm of his hand. "A .25-caliber Beretta." He checked it carefully. "It's loaded and ready to fire, and—" he reached into her purse again, "—a tape recorder. There is a tape inserted, and it is ready to record."

Kaye raised one eyebrow. "You seem very well equipped for a peaceful and friendly meeting, Miss Almori."

Saada Almori's smile broadened. "I notice a number of automatic rifles in the room. You should not be afraid of my little pistol. My brother gave it to me. He thinks I need protection when I am in Beirut. As for the recorder, I am a journalist. It is a tool of my trade. You may keep them both until I leave if you wish."

"Perfectly logical, Miss Almori. We do not imply that we don't trust you, but we must be careful. Please be seated. Now, you said that you had important information concerning advanced chemical and biological weapons that have been brought into Lebanon. You asked for a face-to-face meeting with a senior U.S. Intelligence official. I am Peter Kaye from the Central Intelligence Agency. Here are my credentials. I hope that I am satisfactory."

"Perfectly satisfactory, Dr. Kaye." Saada Almori handed them back and with a slight sneer. "You are well-known in Lebanon, but not well-loved. Very well. I have information concerning chemical and biological weapons that were smuggled into Lebanon. They are controlled by Colonel Nizar Sadiq and his Arab Nation Movement. They intend to use these weapons against Israel. Their objective is to destroy the peace process by provoking a war between Israel and Syria. Colonel Sadiq believes that this will advance his cause. He doesn't care how much blood is shed. Believe me, he will do anything to create a single, unified Arab nation."

"Why give this information to us, Miss Almori? Why not take it to the Israelis? They are capable of defending themselves."

"Are you testing me, Doctor? You know the answer to that. If I give my information to the Israelis, they will either invade Lebanon or launch massive air strikes. There are thirty thousand Syrian troops stationed in Lebanon. If the Israelis launch an attack, there will be war between Israel and Syria. Colonel Sadiq will have achieved his objective. You have friendly relations with Syria. They sent troops to fight on your side in the Gulf War. The Israelis are your allies. If anyone can stop a war, it is the United States. I don't like your country, but at the moment you have more power and influence in the Middle East than any other country. That is why I have come to you. I have no other choice."

"You are right, Miss Almori. The United States will do anything in its power to prevent war between Israel and Syria. Now, may we have your information? Where are the weapons stored? How are they protected? Can you guide us to them?"

Saada Almori smiled. "You have forgotten one thing, Dr. Kaye. Perhaps it isn't important to you, but it is to me. I asked that you guarantee my safety in exchange for this information. I must insist on that. I am an Arab woman. If people learn that I gave information to the CIA, they will call me a traitor, and my life will be worth nothing. You must protect me."

Kaye smiled broadly. He reminded Cray of a shark about to bite. "Of course, Miss Almori, that goes without saying. The CIA will protect you. If necessary, we will get you out of Lebanon and take you anywhere you want to go. If necessary, we will give you asylum in the United States. You have my word."

"Very well. Take me to a safe place and I will tell you all I know."

Kaye nodded. "Agreed. Preston, take Miss Almori to the alternate safe house. This place may have been compromised. Major Cray, may Captain Tower and Sergeant Blake accompany Preston and provide additional security? Perhaps Captain Tower could act as Miss Almori's special friend."

Cray agreed. He watched until Saada Almori and her escorts reached the front door of the shop. "What do you think, Doctor? Can we believe her?" he asked softly.

Kaye sneered. "Don't be naive, Cray. She said the right things and she had the right answers. I believe that she has something she wants to tell us, but don't trust anyone here. If you do, you will end up dead."

Dave Tower and Saada Almori stepped out into the street, walking arm in arm. To a casual observer, they might have appeared to be close friends. Tower scanned the street. "All right, it looks clear. Let's walk to the car, slow and easy, as if we don't have a care in the world."

A HUNDRED YARDS AWAY Jamal Tawfiq stared intently through the telescopic sight of a 7.62 mm Dragunov sniper's rifle. Its cross hairs were centered on Dave Tower's chest. It would be an easy shot, but he would have to be careful. Saada Almori was closer than he liked. He wasn't fond of her, but Colonel Sadiq would be irritated if Tawfiq killed his best agent by mistake. Tawfiq took up the initial pressure on his trigger. He spoke quietly to the other men waiting tensely at his side.

"Remember, do not fire until I give the order."

He looked through his telescope, feeling the tension build. Saada Almori lifted her free hand and stroked her hair twice. It seemed like the casual gesture of a young woman who was vain about her appearance.

"Hold your fire!" Tawfiq snapped. "God is great! That is the signal. The Americans believed Saada's story. The colonel will be pleased."

The sniper to Tawfiq's left sighed as he pushed on the safety of his Dragunov.

"I do not question your orders, Major, but these Americans are our enemies. Why do we not kill them now?"

Tawfiq smiled. Ibrahim was a good man, always eager to kill the enemies of the Arab Nation Movement. Tawfiq liked that. "It would be a good thing to kill them, but there are only five or six here for us to kill. Do not worry. The colonel has plans. Saada will send their entire group into our trap. As God is my witness, we will kill this Omega Force to the last man."

6

Cray and his officers sat around a table, sipping coffee and studying maps of Lebanon. Whatever else that could be said against Lebanon, the coffee was excellent. Cray poured another cup and waited as Dr. Kaye and Preston entered.

From the look on Kaye's face, it wasn't a social call. He went straight to the point. "I've been talking to Washington. They are extremely concerned about the situation. They want us to take action as soon as possible. Major Cray, you've had time to evaluate the information Miss Almori provided. What do you think?"

Cray frowned. "It's good as far as it goes, but it doesn't go nearly far enough. She's given us a location in southern Lebanon. She says she has been told that Colonel Sadiq's people have a base there, but she's never seen it. She says she doesn't know exactly what's located there or how many people are guarding it. We can't stage a raid with that kind of information. We need to know the layout of the base, the number of people there and some idea of how they're armed. If we go in blind, we could be ambushed and wiped out. We have to get close to the place and scout it out."

"That won't be easy," said Kaye, pointing to the map. "It's about forty miles southwest of here, on the edge of Syrian-controlled territory. To get there, you have to pass through areas controlled by the Druze or Hezbollah. Neither group tolerates strangers in their areas, particularly Americans. Could aerial reconnaissance provide the information you need?"

Cray shook his head. "Aerial photographs would be helpful, but we need more information than aerial reconnaissance can supply. There is no alternative, Doctor. We have to go there and look."

Kaye frowned. "You're the military expert, Major. But what you want is very difficult and extremely dangerous. If you are killed or captured en route to Sadiq's base, the whole mission will be jeopardized. It would take days to replace you."

Cray was touched by Kaye's concern for his safety, but this wasn't the time to exchange insults.

"What about the two groups you mentioned, Doctor? Could we strike some kind of deal with one of them to take us there?"

"Certainly not with Hezbollah," Kaye said. "That is the Party of God group. They are Shiite Muslims, armed and controlled by Iran. They are the ones who bombed our embassy in Beirut and blew up our Marine headquarters in 1983. They hate Americans. As for the Druze, I don't know. They are a clannish and secretive Muslim sect. Orthodox Muslims regard the Druze as heretics and nonbelievers. They have been a persecuted minority for one thousand years. They are on nobody's side but their own. They will switch sides in a minute and do whatever they think will help the Druze survive. If we could convince them that helping us will help the Druze, fine, but that won't be easy."

"There's a third possibility," Tower said. "Saada Almori or her contacts. Perhaps we could persuade them to guide us to the base."

"Possibly. Preston, would you ask Miss Almori to join us?"

Cray glanced at his watch. Like most commanders in a combat zone, he spent most of his time worrying. Unless things moved very rapidly, there wasn't much chance of attacking the terrorist base tonight. Tomorrow was the best he could do.

Preston led Saada Almori into the room. She shook her head at the question. "No, Dr. Kaye, for two reasons. I've never been in southern Lebanon. I would be a poor guide. You need someone who knows the area."

She looked around the table. "Also, it would be dangerous for me to guide you in the south. Dangerous for me and dangerous for you."

"Why?"

"You should know, Doctor. Hezbollah controls much of the south. I am a Sunni, an orthodox Muslim, and an Iraqi. They are Shiites and controlled by Iran. To Hezbollah, I am an enemy. If they find me in their territory, they will think I am a spy. My life will be worth nothing. I am not prepared to take the risk."

"Do you know anyone who could guide us?"

Saada Almori shook her head. "No. I am a journalist. I have informants, but I don't control anyone. But have you considered the Druze? I could introduce you to their leader in Beirut. If they let you pass through their territory in the Shouf Mountains, you will save time, and there are no better guides in the back country than the Druze."

"An interesting suggestion, Miss Almori, but why should the Druze help us?"

"Because there is nothing more important to them than the survival of their people and their religion. Most Druze live in southern Lebanon or across the border in northern Israel. If there is a war and it is fought with chemical and biological weapons, they will find themselves in the middle, no matter who wins. Their people could be killed by the tens of thousands. Convince them that they are in danger, and they will help you. I will go with you. I have dealt fairly with them in the past. They trust me as far as they trust anyone who is not a Druze."

Kaye turned to Cray. "What do you think, Major?"

Cray shrugged. "It sounds like that's the only card we have. Let's play it."

"Very well, Miss Almori. Take us to the Druze. Where will the meeting be, and how soon can you arrange it?"

"It will be here in Beirut. Exactly where and when is up to the Druze. I must make one phone call." She smiled at Kaye. "You are welcome to listen, of course."

Kaye stood up. "Miss Almori and I will make the arrangements, Major. Assume that we will leave in an hour. Take everything you think you'll need. We may not come back here."

Cray turned to his officers. "You heard the man. Check out all the weapons and radios. Put fresh batteries in the night-vision goggles. Let's get ready to go!"

AN HOUR LATER they were driving back toward west Beirut. Amanda Stuart drove the lead vehicle, a small BMW. Saada Almori rode with her. Both women were wearing dresses and had no visible weapons. They appeared harmless, two friends out for a morning shopping tour. There was no reason for anyone to stop them. Kaye and Preston followed in an old Mercedes sedan. Cray and the rest of the team took the rear in a battered yellow Volkswagen van. If the lead vehicles were stopped and couldn't talk their way through, Cray would provide the firepower to shoot their way out.

Cray didn't like the idea of going into combat in a civilian vehicle. He would have preferred a Bradley Infantry Fighting Vehicle, but he had to admit that the CIA had done a good job of modifying the van. The body had been armored with Kevlar panels, and the windows and sun roof were hinged for instant removal. In an emergency, four weapons could be firing in two seconds. Two loaded RPG-7s lay on the seats. If they encountered a barricade or had to deal with hostile vehicles, their high-explosive warheads would come in very handy.

Tower, who was driving, was varying the speed and the interval between the van and the Mercedes, so as to avoid looking like a procession of three cars. They crossed the Green Line that divided Christian-controlled east Beirut from the Muslim-controlled west. Cray had supposed the Green Line was an actual line painted on the pavement marking the boundary, with policemen checking passes and directing traffic. It was nothing like that. The fighting had raged so fiercely along the border between the two halves of the city that a green band of plants and weeds had grown up among the rubble. He no longer felt that Dr. Kaye suffered from paranoia. Beirut was beginning to affect Cray the same way. It was ten o'clock in the morning. The sun was shining brightly. People were going quietly about their business. The scene appeared perfectly normal and peaceful, but it didn't seem that way to Cray.

He couldn't forget that any vehicle on the street might be filled with armed men about to attack. There might be an ambush at the next corner. The peddler they were passing might have an RPG-7 in his cart. The rusty truck parked at the curb might contain a ton of explosives, waiting to be detonated. It was enough to make the bravest man paranoid.

They were moving deeper into west Beirut now. Ahead, Amanda Stuart turned into a narrow side street, and Preston followed her. They were passing through a district of shops and warehouses. Suddenly, a large black sedan screeched out of a side street and roared toward them. The van shuddered as Tower swerved frantically to avoid a collision. The black sedan missed the van by inches and shot ahead until it was alongside Kaye's Mercedes. The sedan's windows were open and the barrels of two automatic rifles protruded, pointing like accusing fingers at the CIA car. Yellow flashes danced around their muzzles as they opened fire and poured burst after burst into the Mercedes.

Tower slammed on the brakes, and the van skidded to a halt. The left side of the van was exposed to the action. Cray couldn't risk firing past Tower. He threw the right-hand passenger door open, jumped out, rolled and brought his rifle up ready to fire. The black sedan had pulled ahead of the Mercedes and was forcing it toward the curb. Cray got his sights on and squeezed the trigger, sending a series of short controlled bursts into the rear of the black sedan. He saw the yellow-white flashes of bullets striking metal, but it seemed to have no effect. The fast, light .223-caliber bullets from his M-16A2 were lethal against people, but lacked the capability to tear up a vehicle.

Cray heard several dull, booming roars. A series of red dots flew toward the black sedan as Hall opened fire with his big rifle. Several .50-caliber armor-piercing incendiary bullets struck the sedan and tore through it. As the sedan shuddered to a halt, its doors flew open and men jumped out, clutching automatic weapons. One of them ran toward Preston and Kaye in the stalled Mercedes.

Cray swung his rifle smoothly, applying the lead necessary to hit a running man, and squeezed the trigger. A 3-round burst struck the running man. He fell hard, his AK-47 dropping from his hands. Cray heard the shriek of tearing metal as bullets struck the van a foot above his head and ricocheted. A second attacker, crouching behind the hood of the sedan, fired a submachine gun at the van. Cray fired back.

Tower had jumped out the driver's door and was firing at the men behind the sedan. The snarling crackle of automatic weapons firing echoed from the building walls, punctuated by the roar of Hall's big .50-caliber rifle. Bullets shrieked and whined as they ricocheted from the building's stone walls.

It was a stalemate. The attackers were pinned down, but so were Cray and his men. Anyone on either side who left cover would be committing suicide.

Sensing movement, Cray looked behind him and saw Blake crawling toward him, using the side of the van for cover. Even in the middle of a firefight, he wore his usual cheerful smile. Cray could see the slender tube of an RPG-7 launcher over Blake's shoulders. There was no need for Cray to give orders. Blake was a professional and knew what had to be done. He crouched at Cray's side, peered through the RPG-7's optical sight, and pulled the trigger.

The rocket hissed from the launcher and streaked toward the sedan, trailing gray smoke. It struck the sedan's hood, and detonated in a ball of orange fire. The high-explosive warhead tore the engine compartment to pieces. The man behind the hood fell and lay still. Flames began to lick up from the shattered engine compartment. Two men burst from behind the burning car and made a dash for the door of a nearby building. Tower cut them down with two well-aimed bursts.

For a few seconds there was silence. Cray's ears rang from the repeated noise of muzzle blasts at close quarters. Then, he heard the boom of Hall's big rifle firing repeatedly. Hall was not a man to waste ammunition and he wouldn't be firing if he didn't have targets to shoot at, but who was he firing at?

"Heads up, Major!" Hall shouted. "They're coming up behind us."

Cray rolled to the back of the van and peered around a rear tire. A truck was stopped at the corner of the side street and another one was behind it. Heavily armed men were moving up the street, firing as they came. They were not in uniform, but they were all wearing pale blue *kefiyahs* wound around their heads. Cray aimed his rifle and sprayed them with several short quick bursts. He could hear the crackle of another M-16A2 as Tower joined in. The enemy's advance slowed but it didn't stop. They moved carefully from door to door, taking advantage of every bit of cover, firing as they came. There were too many of them, twenty or thirty, at least. Four or five weapons were not going to stop them

Cray was trying to come up with a plan when he saw windows in the buildings along both sides of the street fly open. Flickers of yellow light danced in the windows as dozens of automatic rifles raked the street. For a heart-stopping moment Cray thought he was a dead man. Then he realized that the men in the buildings weren't firing at him. They were firing withering bursts at the men in the blue *kefiyahs*. The attackers were caught in a lethal cross fire. They had no chance. Man after man went down and lay still. The men in the buildings stopped firing when there was no one left alive for them to shoot.

"Americans! Do not fire. I am your friend. I am coming to talk to you."

A door in one of the buildings opened, and a man came out and walked slowly toward the van. Cray hoped the man was telling the truth when he said he was friendly. Cray had seldom seen a more warlike sight. The man was six feet tall, strongly built, with a black curly beard and a jagged white scar on one cheek. A Russian RPK light machine gun was slung over his shoulder and two big automatic pistols were in holsters on his belt, which was festooned with spare magazines and hand grenades. He moved to the van, careful to make no sudden moves. He was smiling broadly.

"I am Yusef. Kamal has sent me to escort you to our meeting. I am sorry these Hezbollah dogs annoyed you. We must teach them to stay away from Druze territory. I am glad to see you. It is well we knew you were driving a yellow van. Be sure that we are your friends. Will you come with me?"

Tower laughed, and replied in Arabic. Yusef chuckled. "You speak with a tongue of silver. Follow me. My men will take care of your vehicles."

Tower and his men followed Yusef down the street. Climbing out of their Mercedes, Kaye and Preston looked pale and shaken but otherwise all right. Cray glanced behind him. The Druze were efficiently stripping their enemies' bodies of weapons and ammunition and clearing the street.

"What did you say to Yusef, Dave?" Cray asked.

"I just quoted an old Arab proverb. 'The enemy of my enemy is my friend.'"

Cray smiled. It did seem appropriate.

They collected Kaye and Preston and followed Yusef to the front door of a large warehouse. It looked like any other building, but there were armed men at the doors and on the roof. If they hadn't been with Yusef, their welcome would have been far less friendly. Yusef led them into the dim interior to a small back room. Cray's attention was instantly drawn to a small, thin man sitting at a table, one of seven men in the room. He was in his late fifties, with spots of gray in his beard and hair. There was nothing remarkable about his appearance, but he radiated authority and Yusef and the other Druze treated him with great respect. Cray had no doubt that this was Kamal.

There was a quick conversation in Arabic. Kaye and Saada Almori sat at the table with Kamal. Yusef led the rest of the party to a table in a corner. One of his men produced a large brass tray with a pitcher of hot tea and a plate of small sweet cakes. Cray hated tea and he despised small sweet cakes, but he knew the critical importance of giving and receiving hospitality in the Middle East. He sipped tea and nibbled a cake and kept a big smile on his face.

Kamal and Saada Almori began to talk rapidly in Arabic, and Kaye joined in. Cray, who could not understand a word, looked inquiringly at Tower. "They're being polite," Tower said softly. "Kamal is very happy that Yusef wiped out the Hezbollah party without losing a man. That's a strong point in our favor. 'The enemy of my enemy is my friend.' Now Kaye is laying out the situation and explaining what we want the Druze to do. Kamal is thinking it over.

Now he says yes. Yusef and some of his men will take us. We must show them anything we find. Now, they're being polite again."

Kamal left the room. The meeting was apparently over. That was just as well. Yusef, an attentive host, kept refilling the Americans' cups and passing the plate of cakes. Cray had faced death for his country more than once, but he didn't think he could force down another cup of tea and keep smiling.

Finally Yusef stood up. "We go together. Are you ready? Good! We will leave in half an hour. I go to make preparations."

Kaye and Saada Almori came to the table. "Congratulations, Doctor. Your diplomacy seems to have worked perfectly," Cray remarked. Kaye seemed lost in thought.

"What? Yes, the Druze will help you. I will not be going with you. Kamal says the Hezbollah attack was clearly aimed at me, not the rest of us. I must stay here where he can protect me." Kaye smiled bleakly. "I will be his insurance policy. If you and Yusef do not return, he will conclude that this was a trick, and things will become, shall we say, rather difficult. I would appreciate it if you make every effort to come back."

Cray smiled. "I promise you we'll do our damnedest. You can count on it."

"Very well. Preston must stay with me. Could Captain Stuart take Miss Almori back to the safe house and stay with her? I don't want her left alone."

Cray thought for a moment. Amanda Stuart was a superb helicopter pilot, but a ground raid wasn't her thing. "Certainly, Doctor. No problem."

"Everything is settled, then. Good luck, Major."

"Thanks. We're probably going to need it."

7

Saada Almori drove her BMW slowly and carefully back to east Beirut. Amanda Stuart sat beside her in the passenger's seat, watching her and the traffic. Amanda was nervous and tense. She was a captain in the U.S Army, and she had flown assault troops into Iraq during the Gulf War, but that had been something she understood and had been trained to do. Now she was alone in a strange city, armed only with Saada Almori's tiny .25 pocket pistol.

She wished she had her own .45 Colt automatic, but there was no place she could carry it concealed, dressed the way she was. She couldn't speak the local language, and she didn't trust Saada Almori. The situation made her nerves crawl. She would be glad when they reached the safe house.

Saada Almori also seemed quiet and tense. Amanda didn't blame her; the Hezbollah attack had been frightening. Apparently the attackers had not connected the BMW with the CIA Mercedes and had not considered the two women a worthwhile target. Thank God for that. If they had chosen to spray their unarmored car with rifle bullets, she and Saada Almori would have been dead. And it wasn't comforting to realize that any passing car might contain men with automatic rifles.

Amanda tried talking to Saada Almori, but she wasn't interested in conversation. She answered any question Amanda asked but volunteered nothing. She seemed to be frightened, perhaps regretting ever having wanted to talk to the CIA. Amanda looked around. She thought she recognized the street they were on. They should be getting close to the Green Line. Once they were in east Beirut, she could relax a little.

Suddenly Saada gasped and twisted the wheel, desperately trying to avoid a car that had shot in front of them. She spat something in Arabic and stood on the brakes. The BMW shuddered to a stop, tires squealing. Only Amanda's seat belt kept her from going through the windshield. The doors of the car in front of them flew open, and four men with AK-47s jumped out. Two of them moved to each side of the BMW. For a second Amanda thought about drawing Saada Almori's pistol from her purse but froze as she saw the black muzzles of two AK-47s pointed straight at her face. Trying to fight two automatic rifles with a tiny pocket pistol wouldn't be brave; it would be suicidal.

One of the men snarled something in Arabic, and Saada Almori began to get out of the vehicle. The two men on Amanda's side opened her door. One of them snapped an order. Amanda shook her head. She didn't understand. The man prodded her brutally in the side with the muzzle of his rifle. Amanda froze. One of the other men laughed and spoke to Saada Almori.

"He is the leader. He says tell the red-haired whore to get out of the car if she wants to live. Put your hands behind your head and get out quickly. They will kill us if you don't," Saada reported.

Amanda, hearing the fear in Saada's voice, got out of the car as quickly as she could. One of the men beside her prodded her with the muzzle of his rifle, while another cruelly and efficiently tied her hands behind her. The leader grasped a handful of Saada Almori's long black hair and pulled her head back. He looked at her face for a second, then stared at Amanda.

"Yes, they are the ones we want, this naked-faced whore who has betrayed her people and her red-haired friend.

Bring them." He was speaking English now, perhaps for Amanda's benefit.

Without warning, he slapped Saada Almori's face. It was an open-handed blow, but he struck with all his strength. Saada was knocked flat on her back and lay there moaning. The leader kicked her in the side. She gasped as the air whooshed out of her body. He grasped Saada by the hair and jerked her back to her feet again. She shrieked in pain and began to sob.

"Please, please, do not hurt me," she gasped.

The leader laughed cruelly. "We have not even begun to hurt you, whore. You are going to learn what pain is. You will find out how we deal with traitors. Gag them both and put them in the car."

Amanda gasped as a wad of cloth was forced into her mouth and tied in place. The leader inspected her for a second. He smiled as he reached out and pinched her cheek. "Don't be jealous because your friend is getting all of the attention," he said. "Your turn will come. You will find that we know how to deal with spies as well as traitors."

FORTY MILES TO THE SOUTH Cray lay concealed in a fold in the ground screened by some scrubby bushes. If Saada Almori had told the truth and the map was right, the terrorist base was about a mile ahead, behind a low rocky ridge. He glanced at his watch. It was about half an hour before sunset. It had taken them longer to get there than he had planned. They had traveled south from Beirut, past the international airport and up into the Shouf Mountains. They had gone by way of winding back roads, and the two trucks the Druze had provided weren't particularly fast.

The Shouf Mountains were a stronghold. A dozen times they had passed groups of heavily armed Druze guarding the roads. With Yusef to vouch for them, they had been waved on through. That was just as well. It would have taken a brigade of troops to move through the mountains without the Druze's permission, and Cray wasn't sure they would have made it if the Druze had decided to fight.

Once they came down from the mountains and began to move farther south, Yusef grew cautious. He stopped the trucks frequently and sent scouts ahead. At times they waited for half an hour or more to avoid contact with traffic ahead. Yusef's explanation was simple but convincing. They were near the southern end of the Bekaa Valley and close to the Litani River. The Syrian, the Israeli and Hezbollah troops that occasionally patrolled the area all shared the lamentable tendency of shooting first and asking questions later. Avoiding contact with unknown groups was the only sensible thing to do.

Tower and Blake had gone ahead to inspect the base. They couldn't get close during daylight, but a careful examination through field glasses could obtain a lot of information. Yusef had politely but firmly insisted that two of his men go along. Cray knew why. Yusef wanted to keep the Americans under observation at all times. The Druze trusted no one but themselves. For his part, Cray didn't trust them either. For the moment, there was no reason the Druze should betray Omega Force, but the situation could change rapidly. Being on a mission with people he didn't know and couldn't trust made Cray nervous.

Yusef pointed toward the ridge as Tower and one of the Druze were returning. Tower sat down beside Cray, took out his canteen and drank a few swallows of lukewarm water. Crawling through the bush could be thirsty work. Cray looked at him inquiringly. "There's something there," Tower said softly, "but it's not what I expected. There are six run-down buildings. There's a road to the east, another one to the north, and one to the south. One of the Druze said he thinks it's an old construction camp. People were looking for oil here years ago."

"Anyone there?"

"Yes. I saw six or seven. There could be more inside the buildings. Everyone I saw had an AK-47, but I'm not sure that means anything. Half the people in Lebanon have AK-47s. There are a couple of trucks, and there's at least one machine gun placed to cover the road to the south. I could see a lot of tire tracks. There's been a lot of traffic through there."

Tower considered this. "I don't know. It's not an operational base. It's too small, and there aren't enough people, but look at the map. If you were trying to move things from the coast north into the Bekaa Valley or south into Israel, it's an ideal location. The roads are dirt, but they're good enough for trucks. The people there are alert and they look ready to fight. They're waiting for someone, but that doesn't say they're Colonel Sadiq's men. They could be the local drug dealers, waiting for a shipment."

Cray smiled grimly. "There's only one way to be sure, Dave. As soon as it gets dark, we'll have to pay our friends a visit. Invite Yusef and his merry men to the party."

Yusef had no objections. He left two men to guard the trucks. Slowly and carefully the Omega Force team and the rest of the Druze moved to just below the crest of the ridge. Cray crawled the last few yards to the top and scanned the valley beyond with his field glasses. It was starting to get dark, but he could see enough to confirm Tower's report. He glanced up at the sky. There were a few clouds, but basically it was clear. A crescent moon was starting to shine wanly as the sun went down. That was good, since Omega Force's night-vision goggles were light-amplifying devices and worked better with a little background light.

Cray realized that an attack as soon as it was completely dark, would be a problem since the Druze had no night-vision equipment. The chances for confusion and casualties from friendly fire were high. He signaled Tower and Yusef to join him. Tower always had good ideas, and Yusef would have to agree to any plan that involved the Druze. They scanned the area with their binoculars.

Cray reached into his pack and took out his helmet. It was the new model, made of Kevlar. When it was first issued, the troops had derided the idea of a plastic helmet and called it the Fritz because it looked like the famous German World War II helmet. The Kevlar helmet actually provided far better protection than the old steel model. It had saved many lives in Panama and the Gulf War. No one thought it was funny anymore.

Cray's night-vision goggles were attached to his helmet. He swung them down and turned them on. The goggles converted the scene to images in green and black. Cray scanned the target again. Sometimes you could see things through night-vision equipment that you do not see with the naked eye. He looked carefully, but nothing seemed to have changed. It was dark enough. Time to do it.

He turned to Yusef and Tower. Tower had his helmet and night-vision goggles on. Yusef stared at the two Americans in amazement. The AN/PVS-7 goggles gave them an appearance of aliens from space. Cray smiled, and pointed to his goggles.

"These are special glasses. They let us see in the dark. We have special sights on our weapons that let us aim in the dark."

Yusef was impressed. He had heard that the Americans had remarkable equipment. He was ready to believe it. If Cray had told him the Americans could walk through walls, he would almost have believed it. Cray saw that his prestige had gone up and he decided to use it while it lasted.

"We must make a plan, but we must be careful. Your men and mine have never fought together. We must make sure that there is no confusion. No one must be killed by friendly fire."

Yusef nodded. It was hard to disagree. Any experienced soldier knew that confusion in a night raid could be deadly. "What do you suggest?" he asked.

"Move your men to the road that leads to the northeast, into the Bekaa Valley. I will attack with my men. If any of the enemy escape, I think they will use that road. Make sure none of them escape. If any reinforcements arrive during the raid, ambush them and give me time to withdraw. I will not move toward the road. I will attack from here and fall back to here if I must. Anyone moving on the road will be hostile. Attack without warning. If I secure the base, I will signal with a flashlight, two short, three long."

Yusef thought it over. "Very well, it will be as you say. Give me fifteen minutes, and I will be in position. God be with you."

There was nothing for Cray to do now but wait, and he hated waiting. Sergeant Hall was in position, ready to cover the attack with his big .50-caliber sniper's rifle. Cray, Tower, Ward and Blake would be the assault party. Cray knew they would be heavily outnumbered. They would have to depend on speed, skill and surprise.

Cray checked his equipment. He had a 30-round magazine in his M-16A2 rifle and a 40 mm high-explosive grenade loaded into the M-203 grenade launcher clipped under its barrel. He had six M67 hand grenades attached to his web equipment, and his .45 automatic was ready in his holster. None of this was for show. He might need every weapon he had in order to live through the next few minutes.

He glanced at his watch. It was time to go. Upon his signal, the small attack party started quietly down the ridge. Blake and Ward, who went first, carried silenced Heckler & Koch 9 mm submachine guns. The M-16 rifles that Cray and Tower carried were impossible to silence. Their bullets cracked at three times the speed of sound. The submachine guns were loaded with heavy bullets that never went faster than the speed of sound. They were impossible to hear ten feet away. If the Omega Force team ran into anybody as they worked their way in, the submachine guns could take them out silently.

They moved forward slowly, careful to avoid making noise. The buildings were about fifty yards away. Cray was scanning the area carefully when the world blew up. The scene in his night-vision goggles suddenly changed to a featureless, bright green glare as its photocathode overloaded. He had to see. Instantly, with the reflexes that come from long training, Cray pushed his goggles upward. The night was illuminated by brilliant white lights floating in the sky. Someone had fired flares!

Cray dropped to the ground and rolled. If he could see with his naked eyes, so could other people. He heard the ominous rattle of a light machine gun opening fire, then another. Green tracers crisscrossed through the air as another machine gun fired back. The firing was to the northeast. Something had gone wrong. Yusef was in trouble. Men were running from the buildings. Cray aimed at the nearest group and pulled the trigger of his grenade launcher. He heard a dull bloop as it fired and saw an orange flash as the 40 mm grenade detonated, sending lethal fragments shrieking through the air. He heard shouts and screams and the snarl of AK-47s firing as the enemy shot back. Green tracers streaked in his direction, but since his grenade launcher had almost no telltale muzzle-flash, they were simply spraying the landscape.

A second grenade exploded as Tower fired. Cray had no time to load another round in his grenade launcher. He squeezed the trigger of his rifle and sent burst after burst of high velocity .223 bullets at the enemy. To his left he heard the snarling crackle of another M-16A2 as Tower joined in. The enemy was pinned down, but they were still firing back. As long as the flares were still burning, neither side could move.

Blake and Ward were closer. Cray caught a flicker of motion as they threw hand grenades. He saw two orange flashes as their grenades detonated. The enemy fire suddenly stopped. Against men fighting in the open without protective cover, the M67 grenades were utterly lethal. Blake and Ward moved toward the door of the closest building, holding fresh grenades. Yellow flashes flickered as someone just inside the door opened fire. Ward fell heavily and lay still. Cray fired at the muzzle-flashes as Blake threw a grenade through the door. There was a muffled boom as the grenade exploded, then the firing stopped.

The flares flickered and burned out. It was suddenly very dark. Cray could see nothing. He flipped his night-vision goggles back into position and prayed that their sensitive detectors were not still saturated. He had apparently been living right. He saw from the scene around him the familiar green-and-black images displayed by his goggles. Eight or nine bodies lay sprawled on the ground in front of the building, still and lifeless. Blake threw another grenade inside and ducked as it exploded. There probably was no one still alive inside, but Blake intended to make sure.

Cray motioned to Blake to check Ward. The SEAL officer wasn't moving, but he might still be alive. He moved quickly to the corner of the building and took a look around. Two light machine guns were firing steadily. Their tracers were bright, streaking balls of fire in his night-vision goggles. Both weapons were firing toward the northeast. Yusef was in trouble. Cray signaled to Tower and loaded a grenade in his M-203 launcher.

Tower moved forward and indicated that he was ready. Cray pointed to the left-hand machine gunner. Tower signaled that he understood and aimed his weapon. Cray put his sights on the right-hand gun. "Three, two, one, fire!" he counted, and pulled the grenade launcher's trigger. He and Tower fired together. Cray saw two bright flashes as the

40 mm high-explosive grenades struck and detonated. Both machine guns stopped firing abruptly.

Cray slipped a fresh round into his grenade launcher and waited tensely. Nothing happened. Tower slipped forward, staying low, and threw a hand grenade into each of the two machine-gun positions, in case either gunner had been playing dead. Cray and Tower scanned the area. Nothing moved. The fight was over.

Tower shouted in Arabic. Cray heard Yusef reply. "Tell him to bring up the trucks," Cray said. "We have to search this place and get out of here."

Cray moved quickly toward the two parked trucks. He checked the back of each truck. The first one was empty. The second had rows of metal cylinders, carefully stacked and strapped in place. Remembering the cylinders on Cyprus, Cray looked carefully, then called to Blake.

Blake swung his night-vision goggles upward and used his flashlight to examine the cylinders closely. "This is it, Major. They are the same design as the ones we found on Cyprus, but there's something different. These have decals on them, some in Arabic and some in Russian. I can't read Arabic, but the Russian ones are warnings. They say that the contents are dangerous as hell, only qualified chemical-warfare personnel are to handle them, and standard protective equipment will not be effective if the contents are released. They must be what we're after."

Cray remembered the trap on Cyprus vividly. "Check them out, he said. Check the truck, too. If we can use the truck, we'll take it all. If not, I want to take at least two cylinders. Make sure they both have the special warning decals."

"Right away, Major," Blake said. "I checked Lieutenant Commander Ward. He's alive but he's shot through the chest. I slapped a bandage on and gave him a shot to kill the pain, but he should have medical attention soon."

Cray felt a twinge of guilt. He had been concentrating on the mission to the point where he had almost forgotten Ward. Still, there was nothing more that they could do but get Ward to a doctor as soon as possible. The sooner they could leave this place, the better. "Do it as fast as you can, but don't take any chances."

Blake took out his scanner and began to check the truck and the silver cylinders. Cray provided security for Blake while he worked, scanning the area carefully, keeping his rifle ready. He saw movement to his left. Tower and Yusef were approaching. Cray was surprised. Was something wrong? Where were Yusef's men?

Tower did not wait to be asked. "Yusef had two men killed and one wounded. He sent this other man to bring up the trucks. I told him we want to get out of here as soon as possible. He agrees."

Yusef nodded. He didn't seem cheerful. "I am sorry," he said. "Those sons of Satan had trip flares set. One of my men stumbled over one. I lost two good men. I hope you have found what we came here for."

"We did. We're getting ready to take some of it now . We will go as soon as we can. We thank you for your help. We couldn't have done it without you and your men. I'm sorry that two of your people were killed."

Yusef shrugged. "We are Druze. We do not fear death. When a Druze dies, he is reborn again as a new Druze. We say that dying is no more than changing your shirt. That is the way it is with us. I don't know if it is the same for others. What do you believe?"

Cray didn't have an opinion on reincarnation, and Tower said, "God knows. We do not."

Yusef smiled. It was a suitably pious remark. He was glad to learn that the Americans had some respect for religion, though of course, their understanding was limited. They weren't Druze.

Blake appeared at Cray's side. "That truck is shot, Major. Something's wrong with the engine. I got two of the cylinders out and some kind of handling equipment. I'm ready to load them on the Druze trucks as soon as they get here." He glanced at the small tactical radio clipped to Cray's equipment. "Your radio is blinking, Major," he said.

Cray saw that the green incoming-message light was blinking steadily indicating that someone wanted to talk to him immediately. He had set the radio for silent operation at the start of the attack. He pushed the switch and heard Sergeant Hall's voice.

"Major, I'm still in position on the ridge. Everything seems secure locally, but I see lights on the road to the northeast. It looks like about nine or ten vehicles with their headlights on. They're coming this way, and they're in a hell of a hurry."

Cray had no friends in the Bekaa Valley, and he knew that anyone coming rapidly from that direction was bound to be hostile. He was beginning to understand why most of the generals he knew had gray hair.

"How long until they get here?"

"Ten, maybe fifteen minutes at the most. You want me to delay them, Major? I can hold them up for a while."

Hall wasn't joking. His big M82A1 sniper's rifle could hit a truck at over a mile, and the heavy armor-piercing incendiary bullets could tear through a truck and set it on fire. But the vehicles might not be trucks. They could be armored cars or armored personnel carriers. Good as Hall was, he could not stop armored vehicles with a rifle.

"Not this time, Sam. Come on down. We're getting the hell out of here."

Cray heard engines and saw the Druze trucks approaching. They had what they'd come to get. There are times when the only sensible thing is to avoid combat. This was one of those times.

Things were moving rapidly. Blake and Tower loaded the cylinders, one on each truck. If one of them didn't get through, the other might make it. They also loaded Ward. It would be a hard ride for a wounded man, but Cray wouldn't consider leaving him behind. The people they were fighting didn't treat prisoners kindly, wounded or not. When Yusef signaled that he was ready, he and Cray climbed into the cab of the lead truck. Hall arrived and swung on board. Yusef shouted an order. The engine roared and the truck lurched forward.

The Druze were driving with their headlights on and as fast as the road allowed. It wasn't stealth but speed that counted now. If they couldn't get to the southern edge of the Shouf Mountains before the people behind them caught up, they would be in a lot of trouble. Cray looked out the truck window. To the northeast he could see the flickering glow of headlights. He touched Yusef's shoulder.

"They're coming fast," Cray said. "Can we beat them to the mountains?"

Yusef shrugged. "God knows," he said.

Cray figured that perhaps their two RPG-7s could be used for a delaying action. It might work, but the men who stayed behind to fight wouldn't get out alive. Cray was certain of that. "We'd better come up with a plan, then," he said.

Yusef smiled. "That will not be necessary. God protects pious men against evildoers."

Though Cray was baffled, he was not given time to worry. Yusef suddenly pointed ahead and snapped an order. The truck shuddered as the driver slammed on the brakes. Yusef reached for the dashboard and blinked the headlights on and off in a rapid pattern. Someone by the side of the road ahead returned the signal with a flashlight. Yusef gave another order. The driver stepped on the gas, and the truck shot forward.

Cray snapped down his night-vision goggles. He saw men carefully positioned on each side of the road, many men. He could see the ominous shapes of rocket launchers and machine guns. It was a classic ambush. Anyone who drove into it without knowing the signal would be lucky to get out alive.

Yusef's smile grew broader. "Kamal trusted you, of course, but you aren't Druze. We are a friendly people, but we take no chances with new friends. If you had betrayed us and come back without me, you wouldn't have reached Beirut alive. These men are commanded by my cousin. They will entertain the sons of Satan who follow us. We shall relax and enjoy the drive."

Cray could think of nothing to say to that. He sat quietly while the two trucks roared on through the dark, back to Beirut.

8

Amanda Stuart sat in a chair in a small, dingy room. She was tied to the chair, her hands were tied behind her back. She was shaking with anger and shame. The strip search she had been subjected to was the most humiliating experience in her entire life. They hadn't hurt her, but to stand bound and helpless before five laughing, jeering men while they prodded, pinched and probed her naked body was worse than anything she had ever imagined. They had enjoyed her fear and humiliation and laughed at every gasp and moan they had forced from her gagged mouth. Even worse was the knowledge that she was utterly helpless. They could and would do whatever they wanted to her, and she could not stop them.

Now they were working on Saada Almori. They were treating her in a far more brutal fashion than they had Amanda, twisting her arms behind her back, slapping her repeatedly and pinching the sensitive parts of her body until she shrieked through the gag in her mouth. They taunted her while they probed and prodded, calling her a whore who sold herself to the CIA and betrayed her people for American dollars. Saada was sobbing helplessly when they finished.

The leader laughed. "Save your tears, whore," he said cruelly. "You don't know what it is like to be hurt, but you are going to find out. We will teach you. Take her to the interrogation room."

Sobbing and trembling, Saada bent to pick up her dress. The leader slapped her several times until her head rocked on her shoulders. "Leave it, whore. You won't need clothes for what's going to happen to you now."

One of the men laughed. "Shall I bring the redheaded whore? I am sure she would enjoy the party."

"Leave her here—her turn will come." He smiled cruelly at Amanda. "We will leave the door open so that you can hear your friend. You will not be bored. You can imagine what it will feel like when we start on you. Stay and watch her, Umar. We would not want our guest to feel lonely."

Amanda shuddered as they led Saada Almori into the hall. She had to do something. She couldn't just sit there waiting to be tortured, but what could she do? She was helpless, bound and gagged, and guarded by a man with an AK-47. All she could do was wait. Perhaps her captors would make a mistake. She had to be ready to seize the slightest chance if it came.

She heard sounds from the next room. They must have removed Saada Almori's gag. Amanda could hear her begging.

"Please. Please don't hurt me. I have done nothing. I am a journalist. I don't work for the CIA. Please don't hurt me."

"Do not think you can deceive us, you lying whore. You came here from Cyprus to report to your CIA masters. Tell us what you told them. Tell us now!"

Saada Almori screamed again and again, long, wordless shrieks of agony.

Amanda's guard laughed. "Listen to her. They are teaching the traitorous bitch to sing. It will be interesting to hear the noises you make when it is your turn."

Amanda trembled. She couldn't help it. Her guard smiled at her look of fear.

It went on and on, the harsh repeated questions and Saada Almori begging and screaming. Amanda would have covered her ears if she could, but all she could do was sit there and listen. At last it stopped. They carried Saada Almori back into the room and threw her into a chair. Amanda shuddered. Saada's hips and thighs were streaked with thin, raised weals, and her naked body was mottled with bruises. She was moaning with pain and sobbing brokenly. They tied her in the chair.

"We will eat now, but we will be back for you in an hour, whore. Then we will start again," the leader said. He looked at Amanda and smiled. "Or perhaps it will be your turn. Your friend cannot have all the fun. We will see if you can scream louder than she can."

Tower DROVE the yellow van slowly and carefully toward east Beirut. The van had some interesting fresh bullet holes that might be a little difficult to explain if they were stopped, even in Beirut. Cray still felt tense. They had made it back to Beirut without any trouble, and the Druze had released Kaye and Preston. The two mysterious cylinders were no longer his responsibility, since Preston had taken them. The CIA would smuggle them out of the country. All they had to do now was to collect Amanda Stuart and Saada Almori at the safe house and exit the country.

The hard part was over, but still Cray couldn't relax. Any car they passed could be full of men about to attack. Yusef seemed relaxed, but Cray noticed that he never stopped scanning the streets, and his AK-47 was ready across his knees.

Cray saw lights flashing in the rearview mirror. A car behind them was blinking its headlights on and off rapidly. Tower started to step on the gas.

Yusef held up his hand. "That is a Druze signal. Stop at once," he said quickly.

Tower pulled the van over and stopped. A battered blue pickup truck pulled ahead of the van and stopped. The back of the truck was full of boxes and sacks. Cray had seen a dozen like it on the streets. The driver, a middle-aged woman dressed in traditional Arab dress, got out quickly and hurried to the van. As she spoke to Yusef in Arabic, Cray had a cold feeling in the pit of his stomach. Whatever the news was, it wasn't going to be good.

When the woman finished, Yusef turned to Cray and Tower. For once he wasn't smiling. "Something unfortunate has occurred. Kamal assigned this woman to follow the two women who were with you when you came to speak to us. To be frank, he wished to know where you were staying in Beirut. They never arrived. They were stopped and kidnapped by five men. She followed them. They were taken to a house in west Beirut."

"Can she lead us there?" Cray asked.

Yusef stroked his beard. "Yes, she can, but think carefully, Major. How did someone know where your two women could be found? For that matter, who told Hezbollah you were coming to see the Druze? Someone knows far too much about you and what you are doing. This may well be a trap."

Cray didn't hesitate. Yusef could be right, but Cray was not the kind of man who would abandon any of his people while there was a chance they could be saved.

"That's a chance I have to take. Ask her to lead us there immediately."

Yusef shrugged. "As you wish, but you may be too late. She couldn't see into the house where your women were taken, but she was close enough to hear women screaming. They may both be dead by now."

AMANDA STUART WAS still tied to the chair in the small room. Two men were guarding her. They had untied Saada Almori and were making her wait on them. The marks on her body from being beaten were livid. Saada was still sobbing softly as she served the food. The two men were looking at the two women, pointing and laughing. Amanda couldn't understand Arabic, but from the horrified look on Saada Almori's face, she knew that what they were saying was unpleasant.

The men finished eating. They laughed again as they moved toward Amanda. They hadn't tied Saada Almori to a chair, so there was a chance she could grab a gun if they got careless. However, Amanda wasn't optimistic. Saada seemed broken by what the men had done to her. If anything was going to be done, Amanda would have to do it herself.

One of the guards moved behind her chair. Amanda felt a flicker of hope as he untied the ropes that held her, but her hands were still tied behind her back. He spoke to her in accented English.

"Stand up, whore, and let us look at you."

Amanda started to stand up. She moved slowly, because her legs were almost numb from being tightly bound for so long. She didn't move fast enough to suit the guard. He grasped her by her hair and jerked her upward. When she shrieked, the man laughed cruelly.

"We must see to the comfort of our guest, Umar. See, she is flushed and sweating. It is a hot night. She will be much more comfortable if we take her clothes off."

Umar smiled. "You are right. It is a kind thing to do. Besides, she is much more attractive when she is naked."

He grasped the neck of Amanda's dress and ripped it open to the waist.

Looking over Umar's shoulder, Amanda saw the door of the room open slowly. Two menacing figures stood in the doorway. They were wearing flat black nonreflective clothes, and carried automatic weapons. Their faces were stained with camouflage paint. Amanda felt a wild surge of hope as she recognized the silenced 9 mm Heckler & Koch submachine guns in their hands.

The two guards concentrated on Amanda. That was their mistake. The taller of the two in the doorway yelled something in Arabic. The two guards whirled, reaching frantically for the AK-47s slung over their shoulders. Amanda was no longer in the line of fire. She heard the hiss as the silenced submachine guns fired and bursts of 9 mm bullets tore through her guards. They fell heavily and lay still.

The two men in black stepped into the room and swept it with the muzzles of their weapons, but there was no one left to shoot. Amanda recognized Tower and Blake. Blake moved swiftly to her side and cut her hands free with his fighting knife. She ignored the pain in her wrists and immediately pulled her dress together as best she could.

Saada Almori shrieked and ran to Tower. She threw her arms around him and hugged him tightly. Tower was startled. He had been on a lot of combat missions since he joined the Green Berets, but he had never been embraced by a naked woman in the middle of a raid.

He patted Saada on the shoulder awkwardly.

Sergeant Hall stepped through the door. "The house is secure Captain. I've searched the place. The two you shot are the only ones here. I found some papers, nothing else." He smiled at Tower and Saada Almori. "If you and the lady are ready, I think we should get the hell out of here."

Tower flushed. He had a feeling he was never going to live this down. He pried Saada loose and led her toward the door. Saada said something sizzling in Arabic and kicked Umar's body. Amanda couldn't understand what she said, but she was sure she shared her feelings. Amanda followed Tower and Blake from the house. All she wanted was to get out of Beirut and back to a world she understood.

COLONEL SADIQ LOOKED UP as Jamal Tawfiq entered the room. He smiled and motioned Tawfiq to a chair. Tawfiq was the first man Sadiq had recruited when he started his Arab Nation Movement. There were few people in the world Sadiq trusted, but he would trust Tawfiq with his life.

"What word from Beirut, Jamal? Does the plan go well?"

"I think it does, Colonel, but there have been unexpected developments."

Sadiq frowned. A superb planner, he tried to be prepared for any eventuality, and he didn't like unexpected developments.

"What has happened?"

"Kawash kidnapped Saada Almori and the red-haired American whore as we planned. We intended that Saada should appear to escape with the American woman after both had been beaten. They would take the papers from the house and deliver them to the Americans as you wished. All was proceeding according to plan. Kawash left the house, leaving two men as guards. Saada was supposed to seize a weapon loaded with blanks while the guards were raping the American whore and pretend to kill them. But when Kawash returned to the house, he found his two men dead and the women gone. The guards had been killed with automatic weapons. Somehow the American sons of Satan found where we were holding them and rescued them."

Sadiq's frown deepened. "Do you think the plan is ruined?"

"No, Colonel. I don't think the Americans will suspect Saada. Kawash beat her severely. He says she was covered with bruises. She wasn't permanently injured, of course. She will be fine in a week or two, but she will look like hell. There is no reason that the Americans should believe that the kidnapping was staged. I am sure the redheaded whore believes it. And the Americans have the papers. Since they killed the guards and took the papers themselves, I think they will believe them."

Sadiq smiled. "God is great! Where are the Americans now?"

"They drove south from Beirut and were picked up by a helicopter two hours before dawn. The helicopter flew south, toward Israel."

Sadiq's smile broadened. "Excellent. God is delivering them into our hands."

9

General Jim Sykes stood on the dock and watched the Israeli defense force sailors swarm about their boats. What appeared to be mass confusion was actually grim preparation for battle. The Israeli squadron was going out on a combat mission within the next half hour. They expected to have to fight, and every man knew his life might depend on just how well his boat and its equipment worked during the next twenty-four hours. That thought kept everyone's attention concentrated on their job. Sykes hoped every man knew his job perfectly. When the Israelis sailed, he was going with them.

The idea didn't make him happy. Sykes was an expert on special operations, but he knew nothing about naval combat. He was going because the Israelis had insisted that an American officer accompany their squadron. The U.S. government had agreed, and at the moment Sykes was the highest-ranking U.S. military officer in Israel. Like it or not, he was the man.

He stared at the nearest missile boat. Except for the number 341 painted on the bow, it was an exact duplicate of the *Gaash*. That thought was sobering. They were going out to intercept a ship carrying chemical-warfare weapons to Lebanon. The *Gaash* had gone on a similar mission and hadn't come back. Sykes could not help remembering the *Gaash*'s crew, every man dead at his station. The Israelis had issued him protective equipment. Their gear was good, but it hadn't saved the crew of the *Gaash*.

Someone called from the deck of the boat and motioned for him to come on board. Sykes recognized Captain Bron, the Israeli squadron commander. The stocky, sun-bronzed Israeli seemed eager to get under way. Sykes could understand that. Waiting for a mission was sometimes harder than the mission itself. He stepped on board the *Herev* and followed Captain Bron to the bridge. Bron was wasting no time. Sykes heard the rumble of engines starting, and the *Herev*'s hull began to vibrate as all four of her high-performance diesels came on-line. Two of the crew cast off the lines that held her to the dock, and the two-hundred-sixty-ton missile boat moved away from the dock. Behind her, two sister ships followed her out to sea. The small squadron was headed west, into the setting sun. Captain Bron gave an order, and the rumble of the diesels became louder as the *Herev* picked up speed.

Sykes was glad the sea was calm. Boats sometimes made him seasick. He had taken a motion-sickness pill half an hour before, so as not to get seasick. If he looked a little pale, perhaps the Israeli sailors would think it was merely precombat nerves.

The three missile boats moved steadily west, increasing speed as they cleared the harbor. Captain Bron gave orders and received reports, in Hebrew, and Sykes had no idea what they were doing, but he asked no questions. At last the bustle of organized confusion died away. Bron turned to Sykes.

"All is well, General. We are under way. All three boats are operational and ready to proceed with the mission. We will turn north as soon as it is completely dark and proceed toward the intercept area. If the information your people brought from Beirut is correct, we should intercept the target ship in three hours. My orders are to stop it and bring it into a port in Israel. If it will not stop, my orders are to sink it. I will follow my orders, but I will take no chances. We have already lost one boat from this squadron on a similar mission. I don't intend to lose another. Do you understand?''

Sykes nodded. Bron was in the difficult position of having orders based on political considerations that clashed with the military realities of the situation. Sykes had been in that bind many times. Bron's interpretation of his orders seemed reasonable to him.

Bron continued softly, "One other thing, General. I don't wish to be rude, but I must make this clear. You are a senior officer and will be treated with courtesy, but you are here as an observer. This is my command. I must make all the decisions, and I will probably not have time to consult with you. Do we agree on this?''

"Certainly, Captain. I'm not dumb enough to try to tell you what to do. I do have one question, though. Your government insisted that a senior American officer be here as an observer. Just what the hell does that mean? What am I really supposed to do?''

Bron smiled. "Your role is extremely important, General. There is a great deal of pressure on Israel from your government to support the Middle East peace process. Many people in your State Department think Israel is the obstacle to peace. They suspect that we might create incidents with our Arab neighbors. You are here in case we encounter any Arab warships. You will be able to say what we did, and if there is a battle, you can say who fired first. We ask nothing of you but that you tell your government the truth.''

Bron's smile grew wider. "You can see that this makes you very important. I must bring you back alive at all cost. You can be sure I will do my best.''

There was nothing to say to that. Sykes could only hope that Bron's best was good enough. He found an unused chair in a corner of the bridge and sat down. Despite the fact that he was in the middle of a combat mission, he was bored. He was almost dozing as the *Herev* and her sister ships sailed steadily on. An hour passed, then another. Then things changed. Sykes sensed an air of excitement and tension as men began to move purposefully on the *Herev*'s bridge and deck. Something was about to happen.

Bron motioned Sykes to the bridge and pointed to a display on the commander's console. "We are going to battle stations. We are approaching the intercept area and are running under complete electronic emission control. Our radar is not operating, and we will send no radio messages until we make contact. We are listening intently for hostile radar or radio traffic. So far, we have heard nothing."

Sykes glanced outside. Except for a faint crescent moon, it was pitch dark. He couldn't see the other Israeli missile boats. "How are you going to find the ship we're looking for without using radar?" he asked.

Bron smiled. "Israeli ingenuity and a little advanced technology. Look aft."

Sykes saw three Israeli sailors moving away from a rail along the *Herev*'s port side. Something was sitting on the rail, perhaps some kind of missile. Bron snapped an order, and there was a bright orange flash as a small rocket motor ignited. The thing shot off the rail and climbed skyward. In the glare from the motor, Sykes saw that they had launched something that looked like an airplane, too large to be a toy but much too small to carry a man. "What the hell is that?" he asked.

Bron had the air of a man performing a magic trick. He pointed to what looked like a television screen. The screen flickered, then cleared to show a picture of the *Herev* from the air. A crewman moved a control, and the other two Israeli boats moving through the dark came into view. Every detail was visible as though it were broad daylight. It was obvious that somehow Bron had an eye in the sky, one that could see in the dark.

"Are you getting that from a helicopter?" Sykes asked.

"No. It is from our air force. That was an RPV, a remotely piloted vehicle, we just launched. That is a fancy way of saying it is a small airplane without a pilot. We are controlling it from this console. Its infrared sensor can see in the dark. It picks up the heat from anything it sees and converts it into visible television pictures. It doesn't radiate, so no one will be able to detect it."

Sykes was impressed. It was a damned clever idea, but he thought he could see one problem. "Can't they detect the RPV with radar?"

"Not likely. Most of it is made of radar-transparent plastic. That gives it a very small radar cross section. Unless they are—"

One of Bron's officers interrupted. There was an urgent tone in his voice. Whatever was happening, it wasn't good. He pointed to a red light on the console that was blinking steadily. He and Bron exchanged a few quick words. Bron frowned.

"We are being illuminated by a radar operating in the search mode. The electronic warfare officer is trying to classify it, but it isn't one of ours. It cannot be from a ship—it's moving too fast. It must be mounted on a plane or a helicopter."

Another light began to blink on the electronic warfare console. Bron's frown deepened. "Two more radars, Soviet Square Tie fire-control radars in the missile-targeting mode. They are carried by Soviet Osa II missile boats. I am afraid we have been detected. They carry long-range SS-N-2 antiship missiles. They are preparing to fire. We are flying the RPV in the direction of the radars. Our Gabriel missiles are ready to fire, but we must locate the targets before we can launch."

Sykes glanced at the picture from the RPV. It showed nothing but water. Now it changed. He could see three white lines moving slowly together at the edge of the picture, the wakes of three ships, one much larger than the others. The Israeli officer pushed a button. The RPV sensor zoomed in, and the image of the three ships filled the screen.

Bron snarled. "Two Osa II missile boats and a freighter. The freighter is what we are looking for. The missile boats must be Syrian. They are preparing to fire. They wouldn't be operating their radars if they were not. To hell with your State Department. I'm not going to sit here, waiting to be sunk. I am going to fire!"

Sykes wasn't about to argue. It was certainly possible for a missile to roar out of the dark and sink the *Herev*. And if the *Herev* was sunk, he was going down with it. Bron barked an order and the weapons officer began to push buttons on his console. Sykes watched as a row of green lights blinked on. The *Herev*'s missiles were ready to launch.

He glanced at the RPV display. The unmanned aircraft was continuing to track the targets. Sykes suddenly saw a bright flash, then another. Something large flew from one of the missile boats, trailing a long column of pale flame. There was another flash, and another. Sykes needed no explanation. The enemy's SS-N-2 antiship missiles were headed for the *Herev* and her sister ships. Bron said something sizzling in Hebrew. The weapons officer pushed the firing button, and the *Herev* was suddenly illuminated by a series of immensely bright yellow flashes as her Gabriel missiles shot from their launchers and streaked toward the west. There were more flashes to the left and right as her sister ships fired.

Bron pointed to a display. At its center Sykes could see the symbol that marked the position of the Israeli boats. To the left, another symbol showed the location of the targets. A green line connected the two markings. Green arrows were moving slowly along the line. Bron pointed at the incoming arrows on the display.

"Those are SS-N-2s headed our way. They are big missiles. One hit will sink one of my boats. However, if they sink us, I don't think they will live to brag about it. We have twelve Gabriels on the way."

That was nice, but it was the incoming missiles that bothered Sykes. "Can we shoot down the SS-N-2s?" he asked quickly.

Bron shrugged. "Probably not. We have only our guns for missile defense. Perhaps we can jam them. We shall see. Their missiles will be here in two minutes."

He seemed singularly calm for a man facing death and destruction, but there was really nothing he could do. This was a high-tech battle between machines. The skill of the electronic-warfare officers might influence the outcome, but superior technology would decide who lived or died. Still, Bron must do everything he could. He gave a series of orders, and the *Herev* began to vibrate as all four of her engines went to full power. Her 76 mm gun rotated and pointed to the west, ready to fire. Alarms sounded as her antimissile decoys were prepared for firing.

Bron looked through his binoculars and pointed to the west. Sykes looked through his binoculars. He saw four pale yellow dots coming over the horizon as the SS-N-2s headed for the *Herev* and her sister ships. The electronic-warfare officer threw switches and pushed buttons. To the human eye, nothing seemed to happen. The electromagnetic spectrum, however, was a different story. The sky exploded as the *Herev*'s jammers flooded the attacking missiles' radars with blasts of noise and false targets. The SS-N-2s radars were confused and lost their targets, but their Russian designers had known that this might happen. Their guidance units steered them toward the area that seemed to contain so many delightful targets, and their infrared homing sensors flicked on. Radar jamming had no effect on infrared sensors. Only three radar targets showed them matching radar and infrared targets. The missiles changed course slightly and headed for those three.

White water boiled around the *Herev*'s hull as she began to twist and turn in an intricate pattern. Her decoy launchers fired flares that emitted bright, blinding infrared flashes and shot floating decoys into the water behind her. The deck slanted alarmingly as the hostile missiles closed in and the helmsman put the rudder hard over. The *Herev*'s 76 mm gun began to fire rapidly, sending a burst of fourteen-pound high-explosive shells at the incoming missiles. One shell scored a direct hit, and one SS-N-2 vanished in a huge ball of fire as its warhead detonated.

Sykes could see the incoming missiles now. They were huge, more than twenty feet long, their blunt fuselages and stubby delta wings illuminated by the pale yellow fire from their rocket motors. Now that they were close, they no longer seemed to be moving slowly. Sykes stared, hypnotized, as the closest missile began its terminal dive toward the *Herev*. It seemed to be coming straight at him. His infantryman's reflexes screamed at him to take cover, but there was no place to hide.

The missile roared over the *Herev*'s bridge and crashed into the water in her wake. The *Herev* shuddered as the 2,200-pound warhead detonated, and her hull shook as if she had been struck by a giant sledgehammer. A gigantic fountain of water shot skyward and cascaded down on the deck.

A second missile streaked by. Something had hit it, perhaps fragments from a 76 mm shell. The missile was trailing smoke and bright orange flames. It tried to turn toward the *Herev*, but it was no longer responding correctly to guidance commands. It struck the water and skidded away from the *Herev*, like a rock skipping across a pond.

The bridge crew was cheering. The SS-N-2s were formidable missiles, but they were based on outdated technology. The modern Israeli countermeasures had been too much for them. Sykes discovered he had been holding his breath. He was glad the attack was over. He was used to fighting against men. This cold-blooded combat of machine against machine wasn't his kind of war.

Bron shouted something Sykes couldn't understand, but he could hear the elation in the Israeli captain's voice. Bron was pointing at the RPV display. The screen was lit with flash after flash. The Gabriels had arrived. The Syrian guns stopped one or two, but the Israelis had launched twelve. The defense was saturated and overwhelmed. One Osa II exploded in a giant ball of fire as an Israeli missile detonated an SS-N-2 that was still in its launcher. The second missile boat was burning and exploding from three quick hits. The freighter was a much larger target than its escorts, and it attracted the attacking Israeli missiles like a magnet. Six Gabriels struck and detonated in less than sixty seconds. The freighter's hull was torn open. Spouting flame and smoke, it keeled over and began to go down.

Bron gave an order. The *Herev* and her sister ships turned away from the shattered burning hulks and headed east, back to Israel. Sykes was surprised. "Aren't you going to pick up survivors?" he asked.

Bron shook his head. "I am not going to risk my crews and my boats trying to save men who were bringing weapons of terror to destroy Israel. We are going home."

10

The morning sun was slanting through the windows as Cray led the Omega Force officers into the improvised briefing room. The room was Spartan, holding only a battered table and a few chairs. The Israeli military did not believe in luxurious facilities. The only decoration was a large map of Israel and Lebanon pinned to a wall.

General Sykes was already there, waiting with Dr. Kaye. He motioned to them to be seated. Cray noticed that the general looked tired. Apparently his night with the Israeli navy had been exciting, but hardly restful.

Cray sighed. There was tea on the table but no coffee. The Israeli army appeared to run on tea. He poured himself a cup since it was better than nothing. Preston entered and handed Kaye a folder. The young CIA man looked tired and rumpled. Cray knew he didn't look fresh himself. They were all beginning to show the strain of continuous action and rapid movement.

Kaye read the papers in the folder and frowned.

"These are the latest signals from Washington," he said. "We have trouble, gentlemen, real trouble. The Syrians are complaining to the United Nations. They accuse Israel of an unprovoked attack on Syrian warships on the high seas. They say a North Korean freighter carrying medical equipment to Syria was also sunk. They are threatening military retaliation."

Kaye turned to Sykes. "You were there, General. Are you absolutely certain that the Syrians fired first?"

It was Sykes's turn to frown. He wasn't used to having his word questioned, by the CIA or anyone else. "Absolutely, damn it! Absolutely!"

"There was no incident, no Israeli provocation, before they fired?"

"I'll tell you one more time, Kaye," he said angrily. "There was no incident or Israeli provocation. They fired antiship missiles as soon as they detected us. I saw them do it. If the Syrians were on a peaceful mission, they were awfully damned quick on the trigger. The Israelis didn't launch their missiles until the Syrian missiles were on the way. Those are the facts."

"I'm certainly not questioning your word, General, but I must be certain before I report to Washington. There is another problem, you see. It appears that the Israelis sank the wrong ship."

"I don't see how that's possible, Doctor. We acted on the information from the papers we captured in Beirut. That freighter was exactly where it was supposed to be. How can it have been the wrong ship? The CIA surely doesn't believe that nonsense about medical equipment."

Kaye sneered. "Hardly, General. Give us some credit for intelligence. We aren't naive enough to believe that a shipment of medical supplies was escorted by two heavily armed warships. The facts indicate that the North Korean freighter was carrying advanced Scud missiles to Syria. The missiles were probably intended for use against Israel, perhaps with the chemical weapons we are trying to destroy. But there was a second ship, and it got through. Here!"

Kaye took several photographs from the folder and spread them on the table.

Cray studied the pictures quickly. He saw nothing remarkable. They showed a small freighter anchored in a cove surrounded by low hills. There were three or four small buildings clustered together on the shore. Several trucks were parked nearby.

"The pictures show a place on the coast of Lebanon," Kaye continued. "It's not a commercial port. It's primarily used by smugglers. The local officials have been bribed to look the other way. The Israelis have an agent in the area and he reports seeing a number of silver cylinders being taken off the ship and loaded on trucks. I think there can be no doubt. This is the ship we are looking for. It is our target."

Cray didn't miss the word "target." He no longer wondered about the purpose of the meeting. "You want us to attack the ship?" he asked.

"Yes. If we don't, the Israelis will. One more clash between their forces and the Syrians, and there will almost certainly be war. Preventing a war in the Middle East is our mission. There is no other choice. What is your capability? How soon can you be ready to go?"

Cray glanced at Sykes. The general nodded. He didn't like it, but he had to agree with Kaye's logic. "We have our entire force here and enough Blackhawks to carry them," Cray said. "We will check out our equipment and the helicopters and be ready to leave as soon as it gets dark."

Kaye frowned. "That is nine or ten hours from now. Can't you do it sooner?"

"No," Cray said flatly. "We need time to get ready." He looked at the map. "This place is fifty miles from here, and forty miles of that is over Lebanon. If we go in during daylight and get bounced by a few Syrian fighters, we won't come back. It has to be tonight."

"Very well, Major. You're the military expert. But make sure that the mission is a success. Washington will be extremely unhappy if you fail."

Cray smiled faintly. That was the least of his worries. He and Kaye didn't live in the same world. If the mission wasn't a success, the odds were overwhelming that he would be dead.

NINE HOURS LATER Cray and Tower stood inside a hangar door and watched the helicopter crews make their final checks. Amanda Stuart was moving slowly around the closest MH-60K. It was the same special-operations Blackhawk they had used on Cyprus, but it didn't look the same. U.S. Army Blackhawks normally carried only defensive machine guns. This MH-60K had sprouted short stubby wings and rocket pods, underneath which missiles had been installed. The wings were the ESSS, the external stores support system. Four of the special-operations Blackhawks carried the ESSS. They had never been used in combat, but Cray was glad they had them.

The flight crews were finishing their checks. The assault teams began to load, eleven men to each helicopter. They moved slowly and carefully, every man weighed down with weapons and equipment. Cray glanced at the last helicopter. Blake was finishing loading his equipment. Cray was happy he wasn't riding in that Blackhawk. He had the utmost faith in Blake, but he didn't want to go into combat sitting next to several thousand pounds of high explosives.

Everyone was on board. "Let's do it," Cray said to Tower. "I'll take off with the main force three minutes after you and Stuart. Maintain radio silence unless something is really wrong when you get there."

Tower nodded. He knew what to do. There was nothing more to say. He climbed on board the lead Blackhawk. Cray heard a whine as Amanda Stuart started her engines. The Blackhawk taxied slowly out of the hangar. The whine of its twin turbine engines rose to a shriek as Amanda went to full power, and the Blackhawk lifted into the air and headed north toward Lebanon.

AMANDA STUART FLEW her MH-60K low and fast through the darkness. The infrared picture on her MFD, multifunctional display, clearly showed the ground ahead. The radar altimeter indicated that she was maintaining a constant hundred feet, following the contours of the ground. Her warning system read all clear. No radar was tracking her right now, but she was still nervous. At the moment no one was trying to kill her, but that would probably change when she reached the target. No use thinking about that. She had better keep her mind on her flying. As long as she didn't make a mistake and fly into the ground at one hundred twenty miles per hour, it was a piece of cake.

She glanced at the moving map display. The glowing green dot was approaching the target. Tower was sitting to her right in the copilot's seat. He hadn't said anything since they took off. If you wanted to live to collect your pension, you didn't distract your pilot when she was flying fast and low at night.

"Target area in two minutes," Amanda announced.

Tower began to arm the weapons systems. He threw a series of switches, and power flowed to the weapons racks on the ESSS. A row of green lights on the weapon control console came on. The 2.75-inch rockets and Hellfire missiles were ready to fire. Amanda checked the .50-caliber machine gun she controlled to make sure it was loaded and the safety on. They were as ready as they would ever be. She checked the picture on the MFD. They were moving toward a low-lying hill ahead at one hundred twenty miles per hour.

The hill seemed to grow and fill her screen as the Blackhawk flew toward the crest. She kept her eye on her altimeter, seventy-five feet, sixty, fifty. She eased back on the controls as the Blackhawk shot over the top of the hill. Instantly the picture on the MFD changed. There it was, the freighter, the buildings and a few vehicles. Amanda smiled. She was proud of her flying. She had flown fifty miles in total darkness and hit the target right on the button.

She swung the Blackhawk out to sea and circled the cove, keeping one hand near her countermeasures controls. The Blackhawk was painted a flat nonreflective black. No one on the ground should see it in the dark, but they would hear the whine of the engines and the noise of the rotors. If they weren't expecting friendly helicopters, they were likely to become belligerent.

Amanda saw two lights suddenly flicker on one of the trucks. She pulled the Blackhawk into a hard right turn as streams of glowing green tracers streaked by its nose. Tower keyed the laser designator and fired back. An AGM-114 Hellfire missile shot from its launcher and flashed toward the truck. It was overkill. The Hellfire had been designed to destroy sixty ton main battle tanks. Its effect on the truck was spectacular. A white-hot jet of gas and molten metal struck the truck's gas tank, and the truck exploded into flaming fragments.

The MFD showed a dozen flashing lights from the deck of the ship. Automatic rifles were being fired at the weaving, twisting Blackhawk. That didn't worry Amanda. If anyone hit her firing a rifle in the dark, it would be pure dumb luck. But missiles worried her. She saw a flash of fire from the freighter's deck, and a long, slender shape shot toward the Blackhawk, trailing a plume of fire. Instantly she pushed her countermeasures switch. The Blackhawk's ALQ-144 jammer began to emit immensely bright pulses of infrared light. She triggered the flare launcher, and six infrared flares flashed and burned behind her helicopter.

The missile was a Russian SA-7. Its guidance unit lacked the sophistication of an American Stinger. Confused and blinded, it lost lock on the Blackhawk and flashed harmlessly by. They might not be so lucky next time. Amanda swung the Blackhawk's nose toward the ship and pulled the trigger, spraying the freighter's deck with bursts of armor-piercing .50-caliber bullets. Tower threw a switch, and a dozen 2.75-inch rockets streaked at the ship. He saw a series of bright yellow flashes as the rockets struck, their five-pound, high-explosive warheads detonating spectacularly. They couldn't sink a ship with just machine guns and rockets, but anyone on the freighter's deck was vulnerable to that deadly hail of fire.

The air was suddenly full of helicopters as the main body arrived. Amanda was busy avoiding a collision. The other armed Blackhawks were spraying the ship and the truck with rockets and machine-gun fire as the assault helicopters touched down and the Omega Force troopers poured out.

Tower saw a multitude of flickering, flashing lights as dozens of automatic rifles and machine guns opened fire. The firefight was quick and sharp. The defenders fought bravely, but they had been taken totally by surprise. Outnumbered and outgunned, their defense collapsed. Now Omega Force's men were mopping up and searching the area.

Tower waited tensely as Amanda circled the area. He was out of the picture until he heard from Cray, who was on the ground commanding the attack and probably very busy. Tower wasn't about to bother him with questions.

Amanda circled again. Tower kept his eyes on the sensor displays, but there was nothing for the armed Blackhawks to shoot at. He saw no sign of a counterattack. Tower felt satisfied. Their mission appeared to be a complete success. Then he heard Cray's voice in his headphones. Something was wrong. He could tell by the tone of Cray's voice.

"All Omega Force units, stand by to load and leave the area. Do not fly over the ship or the buildings. We are rigging charges for demolition now."

Tower wasn't sure he understood. He keyed his transmitter. "Roger, Omega Lead, what is the situation?"

Cray was furious. He did not bother with call signs. "It's a bust, a goddamned bust! We haven't found a thing but some damned papers! The stuff was never here, or it's long gone. Cover the withdrawal. We're getting out of here."

Tower felt a cold knot in the pit of his stomach. Somehow, the enemy always seemed to be a step ahead of them. Omega Force seemed to be winning the battles but losing the war. Someone had a lot of questions to answer when they got back to Israel.

11

Cray was finishing the debriefing. He was still angry. If looks could kill, Kaye would have died on the spot. "Tactically the mission was a complete success, but we didn't accomplish a damned thing. Our Intelligence was wrong. Either there never were any chemical weapons there, or they had been moved out long before we got there. All we did was blow up the ship and a few buildings. We're not even sure that the people there have anything to do with Colonel Sadiq. I lost three good men for nothing."

Kaye shook his head. "I understand how you feel. I'm sorry you lost three men. But it is premature to say that the mission was a total failure. Preston and the Israelis are examining the papers you captured. You may have brought back some very valuable information."

It was the right thing to say, but Cray was not sure that Kaye was sincere. He couldn't help feeling that Kaye would sacrifice Omega Force to the last man to accomplish his objectives.

Kaye went on in his cool, precise way. "It is not correct to say that our Intelligence was incorrect. The ship was there. Perhaps the weapons were simply moved before you got there. It may simply have been bad luck."

Cray glared at Kaye. Kaye stared back. He didn't care if Cray liked him or not. To him, Cray was merely a useful tool.

"Does anyone else have something to say? If not—"

Tower got to his feet. He didn't think anyone would be pleased with what he was about to say, but the Army paid him to think as well as fight, and he had been thinking hard. "I think we need to step back and take a long hard look at the whole operation. I did a tour with British Special Operations three years ago. They have a saying when things go wrong. 'The first time it's happenstance, the second time coincidence, but the third time, it's enemy action.'"

Kaye glared at Tower. "That's interesting, Captain, but what do you mean?"

Tower wasn't easily intimidated. He wouldn't have been in Omega Force if he could be frightened by a hard look. "Just this. From the start Colonel Sadiq and his people have been ahead of us. Think it over. The Israelis got word that the *Ba'ir* was carrying weapons. They intercepted it and lost the *Gaash* and its crew. We went to Cyprus and raided their base. It was deserted and full of high-tech booby traps. We were lucky to get out alive. But when we were there, we found a map which someone just happened to leave on a wall where we couldn't miss it. We went to Lebanon because we found the map. We thought we had located their main base there and we raided it. It turned out to be a truck stop, and we just got out alive by the skin of our teeth. Then we captured those papers in Beirut, but somehow they led us to the wrong ship. Then there was this affair tonight. If this is all coincidence, it's the damnedest set of coincidences I've ever seen. I think it's enemy action, Doctor."

Kaye looked grim. One of the worst things that could happen to an Intelligence organization was to be deceived by false information planted by the opposition.

Tower continued coolly. "That's not all. Think about it. The other side knows too much. They know what we are planning to do before we do it. Not every time, but too often for it to be pure luck. Unless Colonel Sadiq has a crystal ball, I think that our security has been broken. I don't see any other explanation."

Kaye turned pale. The absolutely worst thing that could happen to an Intelligence organization was to be infiltrated by an enemy agent. Each person in the room looked at the person sitting next to him. Few things were more unnerving than the thought that one of the people you were working with was one of the enemy.

"It can't be Preston," Kaye said quickly. "He has been cleared repeatedly at the highest levels by the CIA. What about your people, General?"

Sykes noted that Kaye considered himself above suspicion, but he didn't comment on that. God help them if Kaye were an enemy agent.

"Everyone in Omega Force is cleared for top secret and has an extended background investigation before being assigned to the unit."

"What about Captain Stuart? Technically, she isn't a member of Omega Force."

"She went through the same procedures. Besides, I know her father and have known her since she was a young girl. It's impossible for me to believe Amanda is an agent for a group of Arab terrorists."

Kaye smiled bleakly. "So we are all beyond suspicion. Yet Captain Tower's logic is extremely persuasive. Any one of the incidents he mentioned could be chance or bad luck. Put them together, however, and the pattern is ominous. We can't take a chance. I will contact Washington and have a counter-Intelligence team put on it at once."

"We may be overlooking someone," Sykes said. "What about Saada Almori?"

Kaye thought for a moment. "I don't know. The information she has given us and the Israelis has been basically correct. She hasn't been in our planning meetings, but she has been in a position to pick up a lot of information. We investigated her once, but we will do it again."

He stopped and stared coldly at everyone in the room. "If there is an enemy agent, we will find who it is, and believe me, that person will wish he or she had never been born."

MAJOR JAMAL TAWFIQ waited tensely in his ambush position, repeatedly scanning the road to the south. He was looking for the Israeli army. He had never fought the Israelis, but their reputation was fearsome. When they came, they were going to be in a very bad mood. If Tawfiq's plan didn't work, he was probably not going to live through the next hour. He checked his position through his field glasses and was pleased to see that his men were carefully concealed, their missiles and machine guns ready.

He checked his watch. It would be dark in an hour. Kawash should have attacked the Israeli border patrol by now. God grant the Israelis took the bait and pursued him into Lebanon. Tawfiq scanned the road to the south again and saw a cloud of dust, indicating a group of vehicles moving rapidly. Kawash was coming. Tawfiq watched impatiently as the vehicles came closer. He saw six jeeps, driving rapidly. Now he could see the men in the jeeps. They were wearing the distinctive multicolored camouflage uniform of the Syrian army's elite commandos.

Tawfiq stood up and shouted loudly. "Hold your fire! It is Captain Kawash. I will personally kill anyone who fires before I give the order!"

Five of the jeeps roared through Tawfiq's ambush position. The sixth skidded briefly to a halt and Kawash leaped out, ran toward Tawfiq and threw himself down beside him. Tawfiq didn't have to ask Kawash how it had gone. The look of glee on Kawash's face told Tawfiq he had been successful.

"God is great!" Kawash exclaimed. "We took the damned Israelis by surprise! There must have been thirty men in their patrol, and we killed half of them. It was complete success. I didn't lose a man. The Israelis will be furious."

Tawfiq smiled. Good. The Israelis weren't invincible. They could be defeated and killed like other men. "God is great! You have done well. Do they pursue you?"

Kawash smiled broadly. "Oh, yes, Jamal. They are very eager to catch me. There is a column of tanks and armored personnel carriers, at least ten of each, close behind me. They will be here in minutes. We must be ready."

They were ready, but Tawfiq didn't like the word "tanks." He had fought tanks before. He knew they could be stopped, but they could be incredibly lethal against men on foot. He didn't have time to brood over it. The jeeps had roared on to the north, the Israelis in hot pursuit. Tawfiq heard the sounds that could freeze any infantryman's blood, the rumble of diesel engines and the dry squeak and clack of tank treads.

There was a bend in the road about six hundred yards away. As Tawfiq watched, a menacing shape rounded the bend and began moving forward. His field glasses showed every detail, the smoothly rounded hull turret and the long-barreled 105 mm cannon which seemed to be pointing straight at him. Tawfiq instantly recognized an American M60. The U.S. Marines had used them in Kuwait. It wasn't the latest model, but it was still sixty tons of steel and firepower. A second tank rounded the bend, then a third.

Tawfiq looked at his nearest missile team. They were armed with a French MILAN missile launcher. In the Iraqi army Tawfiq had been told the MILAN was one of the finest antitank missiles in the world. He hoped devoutly that this was true. The launcher was loaded and ready to fire. The gunner kept his eyes glued to the launcher's optical sight. His assistant was watching Tawfiq, for the signal to fire. The temptation to give the order was overwhelming, but he waited grimly until the rest of the Israeli armored column clanked around the bend.

He knew not to wait too long. Like most guided missiles, the MILAN had a minimum range, a dead zone in which the guidance unit didn't have time to function. Tawfiq could wait no longer. He gave the order, no stirring words, merely the simplest possible command that could not be misunderstood, even in the heat of battle, "Fire!"

The MILAN gunner pushed the firing button. The missile shot from its launcher and rocketed toward the leading tank, trailing two thin wires. The gunner watched as the missile flew and moved his controller to adjust his aim. Guidance commands flashed along the trailing wires from the launcher to the missile.

The Israelis were stunned, caught totally by surprise. Before they could react, the MILAN struck the tank's turret and detonated. A jet of white-hot gas and molten metal penetrated six inches of armor plate and sprayed the interior of the tank. After a second or two the ready rounds for the 105 mm cannon began to explode like a string of giant firecrackers. Gouts of flame and smoke poured from the M60's shattered hull.

Tawfiq heard the MILAN crew cheering as they loaded another missile into the launcher. He quickly scanned the rest of the Israeli column. He had eight MILAN launchers. He must not get enthralled in watching one of them. It was up to him to direct the whole battle. God is great! His men were doing well. At least two more Israeli tanks were hit and burning, and three of their smaller, more lightly armored M113 personnel carriers seemed to have been knocked out.

Tawfiq's men had won the first round, but now the Israelis had time to react. Tawfiq ducked as a thirty-pound, 105 mm shell struck and exploded close to the nearest MILAN launcher. Rocks and steel fragments whined through the air. Israeli machine gunners opened fire and began to spray both sides of the road with .30-caliber bullets. The rear doors of the M113 armored personnel carriers clanged open, and Israeli infantrymen poured out, diving for cover at the sides of the road. Tawfiq's machine gunners sprayed them with bullets. Tawfiq could see the yellow flashes as their bullets struck the M113's armor and ricocheted away.

His missile crews reloaded and fired more MILANs at the Israeli tanks. The Israelis fired back, but they were exposed on the open road. Tawfiq's missile launchers were carefully concealed, detectable only when they fired. The odds were too great. Gray smoke began to shroud the Israeli tanks as their drivers turned on their smoke generators. Tawfiq's gunners quit firing. The MILANs, like any wire-guided missiles, were useless when their gunners couldn't see their targets.

The cloud of smoke spread until Tawfiq couldn't see the Israeli column. He waited tensely. Would the Israelis counterattack? He didn't think so. They had thought they were pursuing a hit-and-run terrorist force and had run into a well-organized antiarmor ambush. The MILANs had been a lethal surprise. They had no way of knowing how many men and missiles they were up against. The only logical thing for them to do was withdraw, but Tawfiq had been in enough battles to know that combat wasn't always logical.

The firing stopped and the sound of engines faded away toward the south as the Israelis retreated. The colonel must know. Tawfiq pushed the button on his radio, broke radio silence, and poured out his report to Colonel Sadiq.

"It was a complete success, Colonel. Your plan worked perfectly. We destroyed several tanks. They must have suffered heavy casualties. They are retreating across the border into Israel. I am preparing to withdraw."

"God is great!" Colonel Sadiq exclaimed. "You have done well, Jamal, very well indeed. Our Syrian friends will be impressed. I will start the next phase of the plan immediately. Be careful as you withdraw. The Israelis will be very angry.''

Tawfiq smiled. Those words from Colonel Sadiq meant more to him than a chestful of medals. But the colonel was right. The Israelis would retaliate for this major attack out of Lebanon. The next time they came north, it wouldn't be just a company or two. They would send whole brigades and divisions. It wouldn't be wise to be there when they came.

CRAY AND TOWER HAD BEEN waiting outside the door for two hours. They hadn't been invited to the high-level meeting that was raging inside the Israeli base's main briefing room. Only Sykes and Kaye were meeting with the Israeli general from Tel Aviv. Cray didn't know how Tower felt about it, but he was just as happy to be outside. From the angry voices he could hear inside and the look on the face of the Israeli general when he and his staff went in, it would not be the kind of meeting Cray enjoyed.

The door of the briefing room flew open, and the Israeli general stalked out. He was obviously furious. Cray stood up and saluted. He wasn't a stickler for military politeness, but he was a guest of the Israeli army. The general returned Cray's salute as he swept by, but if looks could kill, Omega Force would have needed a new commander. General Sykes didn't look happy, either, when he emerged from the briefing room. It was obvious that whatever had happened inside hadn't advanced the cause of American-Israeli friendship.

"If you gentlemen will follow me to my quarters?" Sykes said curtly. Cray and Tower followed him immediately. When they were inside his room and the door was closed, Sykes went immediately to the point. "All hell's breaking loose. An Israeli border patrol was hit by an attack out of Lebanon. They thought it was a guerrilla group and pursued them across the border with a mechanized force. They ran into an ambush. Whoever it was knew their business. They used antitank missiles and gave the Israelis a bloody nose. They lost six tanks and two dozen men.''

"Who did it?" Tower asked.

"The Israeli soldiers say the men who attacked them were wearing very distinctive camouflage uniforms, of the type that Syrian army commando troops wear. Israeli Intelligence says the Syrian First Commando Group is in the Bekaa Valley. They are one of the Syrian army's elite units. But it doesn't really matter who did it. The balloon is going up. The Israelis are mobilizing. Unless we can talk them out of it, in forty-eight hours they will invade Lebanon. The only question is whether they'll go all the way to Beirut. Kaye says that doesn't really matter. If Israel goes into Lebanon in force, the Syrians will fight. It will be an all-out war, and that's what we're here to prevent.''

Cray had heard more cheerful news. "There's something I don't understand, General. The Israelis seem to be mad as hell at us. What did we do? They seem to feel it's our fault.''

"Maybe it is. Not yours or mine, but the fault of the U.S. government. The Israelis used to occupy southern Lebanon. We pressured them to pull their troops out. The Israeli army wanted to reoccupy Lebanon when they first heard about the chemical weapons on Cyprus. Our government talked their leaders out of it. The Israelis say they were told Omega Force would take care of it. They don't think we've done a very good job.''

Cray was livid. "Damn it, General, with all due respect, that's the craziest thing I've ever heard. My people are good, but we have less than two hundred officers and men and only sixteen helicopters. We can't protect all of Israel.

Sykes sighed. "You know it and I know it, Major. But we're preaching to the choir. Try and tell that to the politicians in Washington and Tel Aviv. They seem more interested in who's responsible for the situation than in solving the problem.''

Cray resisted the temptation to pound his fist on the table and swear. International policy was decided at a much higher pay grade than his. He must concentrate on Omega Force. It was his command and his responsibility.

"All right, General. I don't like it, but I understand. What happens next? What should we get ready to do?"

"The Israelis have to call up their reserves before they will be ready to go. That will take at least forty-eight hours. If there's going to be a war, I think Washington will order us out. They won't want us involved in fighting between Israel and Syria. If Intelligence can locate the weapons, we'll probably go back into Lebanon and try to take them out. Alert your people. Either way, we may have to move on extremely short notice."

Nothing Cray heard made him happy. If Omega Force was evacuated, they had failed to accomplish their mission. To go back into Lebanon, with Colonel Sadiq's people alerted for trouble and the Syrians getting ready for war, sounded ominously like a suicide mission. Either way, they were in a lot of trouble, but there was no use complaining to General Sykes. He wasn't calling the shots.

"Right away, General. We'll be ready, either way," he said.

12

Cray was enjoying the deep, dreamless sleep of the exhausted when someone called his name. He reached for his knife with the intent of doing someone grave bodily harm and awoke with a start when he couldn't find it. He opened his eyes. Tower was standing at the foot of the bed. He was too old a hand to risk shaking the shoulder of a sleeping man who had spent his career in the Rangers.

"Wake up, Major. Something's up. There's a briefing in ten minutes."

Cray made a few sizzling remarks about briefings and people who called them in the middle of the night. Then he pulled on his boots and followed Tower to the briefing room. Kaye and Sykes were already there. An Israeli officer Cray had never seen before was sitting at the table. His beret and the silver jump wings on his chest indicated that he was a paratrooper. He stared at Cray. No one offered to introduce him.

Cray and Tower sat down. There was a knock on the door, and Preston came in. A tall attractive woman in her late thirties with prematurely gray hair was with him. She was Cora Hill, but for a moment Cray didn't recognize her. She no longer looked elegant. Her clothes were wrinkled, her eyes red. She looked as if she hadn't slept for a week. Things seemed to have been busy in advanced chemical and biological warfare.

"Dr. Hill has something important to tell us, gentlemen." Preston said, then gestured toward the Israeli officer. "I'm sorry, Doctor, but is this officer cleared?"

"This is Colonel Dror of the Sayret Mat'kal, the reconnaissance unit of the Israeli General Staff," said Kaye. "I will vouch for his clearance and his need to know. He may be briefed on any information concerning the mission."

That got the adrenaline flowing. Cray had heard of the Israeli colonel's unit. They were the most secret special-operations unit in the Israeli army. Rumor had it that it was totally ruthless and totally competent, the unit the Israeli government called upon when the chips were down. If it was involved, things were really going to get exciting.

Kaye continued smoothly. "Colonel Dror, this is Dr. Cora Hill of the U.S. Army's chemical and biological research center. Dr. Hill is an expert in advanced chemical and biological warfare. She has been working closely with our scientists and yours. I believe they have made important discoveries. Could you please brief us, Doctor, in simple terms we laymen can understand. Have you determined what killed the crew of the *Gaash?*"

Kaye might be able to intimidate some people with his superior airs, but not Cora Hill. "Certainly, Dr. Kaye," she said coolly, wearing a thin smile. "In layman's terms, our analysis indicates that they were killed by cobras. Not ordinary cobras. Perhaps I should say 'super mutant cobras.'"

There was a moment of silence as everyone stared at Hill. Kaye frowned. "I realize that you have been working long hours and have been under a great deal of strain, Dr. Hill, but we are engaged in serious business. Your joke is not funny!"

Hill stopped smiling. "I wish I were joking, Doctor, but I'm not. We have examined the tissue samples from the crew of the *Gaash,* analyzed the contents of the two cylinders Major Cray captured in Lebanon and conducted tests on laboratory animals. The agent is a form of elapid venom. Elapids are a class of venomous snakes with grooved fangs. They include Asian and African cobras, mambas, coral snakes and the Australian death adder. Their venom is a complex mixture of toxins and enzymes. The venom causes severe pain, nerve damage, respiratory paralysis and eventual paralysis of the heart. Once the victim has been bitten, death is almost certain unless an appropriate antivenom is administered immediately. Death will occur within six to forty-eight hours, depending on the part of the body bitten and the amount of venom injected."

Kaye stared at Cora Hill. Apparently she was serious. "Very well, Dr. Hill. You're the expert. We must accept your analysis. But what did you mean when you said 'super mutant cobras'? Surely that was an attempt at humor on your part."

"I wish it had been. Perhaps those words were not scientific. What I meant to convey is that, while the agent is clearly based on cobra venom, it is not cobra venom in the ordinary sense of the word. Someone has altered it, using advanced genetic-engineering techniques to create something far more powerful and far more lethal than any cobra venom found in nature. A cobra must bite its victim and inject its venom through its fangs. Here the agent has been altered into the form of a gas. It can enter the victim's body through the lungs or penetrate the skin, like a nerve gas. Ordinary cobra venom takes hours to kill. This agent takes only seconds."

She paused, then continued quietly. "Perhaps that's just as well. Cobra venom causes severe pain. To judge by the reactions of test animals, the agent is worse, much worse. At least the agony is over quickly."

Sykes's eyes narrowed. "Who the hell would make a thing like that?"

"Almost certainly the Russians," she responded. "Before 1989 they had extensive programs investigating genetic engineering to create advanced biological weapons.

And we know they were interested in snake venoms. They purchased large quantities of cobra venom from Africa and India. They appear to have investigated all possible aspects of their use. It would seem that they got further than we thought."

"Are you saying that the Russian government is involved in this operation?" Kaye asked.

"That's impossible to say, but it's clearly their technology. The warning markings on the two cylinders we investigated are in Russian. The machine that Sergeant Blake discovered in Lebanon is a standard Russian military device. It is used to transfer chemical agents from their storage cylinders to rocket or missile warheads shortly before use. Remember that Captain Tower overheard one of Sadiq's men talk about someone he called 'the Russian.' That person was apparently on Cyprus when the agent was delivered. My opinion is that one or more Russian scientists have given or sold the agent to Colonel Sadiq."

Kaye frowned. "It would be better if it were the Russians. We have a considerable amount of influence with their government. We could put immediate pressure on them to call off the operation. There is nothing we can do to influence Colonel Sadiq. He is a fanatic. Threats or bribes will not stop him. Nothing matters to him but his cause."

"You're right, Doctor," Sykes said somberly. "Everything we know about Sadiq says he will stop at nothing. He has gone to a great deal of trouble to move this stuff into Lebanon. He won't hesitate to use it against Israel, and we are sitting in the probable target area."

That wasn't a happy thought. Cora Hill's information was fascinating, but she hadn't told Cray the one thing he had to know. "I have a question, Doctor. If this agent is a gas, why won't our gas masks and suits protect us?"

"It's because of the way a gas mask works. When you put one on, you seal off your face from the outside air, but the gas mask does not supply you with air. It can't because it doesn't have an air supply. You have to breathe the outside air, but it passes through the gas mask's filters before it reaches your lungs. The filters absorb or neutralize chemical warfare agents in the air before you breathe it. If they do their job properly, you are safe. Our army uses the M40 mask. It is an excellent design, meant to protect against any known chemical-warfare agent. Against something entirely new, it may fail, as it did with the crew of the *Gaash*. The same with the suit. It was designed to protect from all known chemical agents that attack through the skin, but it may fail against something new."

"Can't you modify the filters so that no gas can get in?"

"We could do that, Major, but you don't want us to. Remember, air is a gas, a mixture of oxygen and nitrogen. If we made your gas mask filters gas tight, you would die of suffocation."

"So there's no defense? Nothing you can do, at all?"

"Not at the moment. We are working on it twenty-four hours a day. So are the Israelis. We will find something, I'm sure, but it may take weeks to find a defense, modify our equipment and test it. I'm sorry, but that's the way it is."

Cray had no further questions. He didn't like what he had heard. Poison gas couldn't kill him any deader than a bullet, but at least he had a chance against men who were trying to shoot him. If he were attacked with this stuff, he had no chance at all.

Cora Hill stood up to leave. Kaye stopped her with a question. "Dr. Hill, do you think Colonel Sadiq's people are manufacturing the agent? Or have they simply obtained a supply from some Russian source?"

"I don't believe they can make it. It would require a highly specialized production facility and some well-trained people. However, don't underestimate the Arabs. Some of them are brilliant scientists. With technical assistance from Russian experts, they could set up a production facility. For all we know, they may be working on it right now. For the moment, though, I believe their capability is limited to the supply they brought into Lebanon."

"Thank you, Dr. Hill. An excellent briefing," Kaye remarked. "Well, gentlemen, there appears to be only one possible course of action. We must destroy Colonel Sadiq's supply of this weapon. But in order to do that, we must locate it. Any suggestions?"

Cray snarled quietly. Kaye had an extremely annoying way of stating the obvious as if it was the divinely revealed word of God. Still, he was right. If they were going to do anything, they had to locate the target.

Colonel Dror, the Israeli officer, had sat silently during Cora Hill's briefing. Now he stood up and moved to one end of the table. "Perhaps I have the answer to that problem, gentlemen," he said in flat, precise English. He dimmed the lights and turned on a slide projector.

Cray stared at the screen. The picture showed a group of huge stone walls and old weather-beaten buildings, partly in ruins. They seemed to be located on top of a mountain.

"This is Beaufort Castle," said the Israeli colonel. "It was built in the 1100s by the Crusade leader, Simon de Beaufort. It is located in southern Lebanon, on the Litani River. It is an immensely strong position, built on a small plateau some twenty-two hundred feet above sea level. It was built to dominate southern Lebanon, and it still does. From the castle you can observe most of southern Lebanon and most of the Galilee region of Israel, as well. It is ideal for artillery observation, intelligence gathering, and as a base for launching raids into Israel. It was a major Palestine Liberation Organization base until we went into Lebanon in 1982 and cleaned them out. We captured the castle then. It cost us many casualties."

He paused and looked around at the grim faces in the room.

"We would still be occupying it if the United States government hadn't forced us to withdraw from Lebanon. I recall that they said our withdrawal would ensure peace and the safety of Israel."

He showed a second slide. "For obvious reasons, we keep Beaufort Castle under continuous observation. This is a view from the air, taken from one of our remotely piloted vehicles. The picture was taken at night, using an infrared camera. Look at this road winding up the side of the mountain. It is the only road in or out of the castle. Here is a photograph taken with a zoom lens. You will note there are a dozen trucks moving up the road toward the castle. We have other photographs which show that the castle has been occupied by a force of fifty to sixty men. It is obviously being used as an active base again."

"Why are you sure that these trucks are the ones we're after?" Tower asked.

Dror smiled bleakly. "I will not bore you with the details of Israeli Intelligence operations. I will merely say that we have tracked these trucks from the coastal port, where you attempted to destroy them and failed. No, gentlemen, we are certain that these trucks carried the terrorist's weapons, the ones that your Dr. Hill just described. Now they are in position to be used against Israel, while you sit here and talk."

Cray didn't like Dror's choice of words or his tone of voice. "You might remember that we are here to try and protect Israel," he said curtly. "Something seems to be bothering you, Colonel. Don't be polite, just spit it out!"

"Very well. We are in this situation because of interference from you Americans. You seem to be determined to pursue your stupid, so-called peace policy even if it kills every man, woman and child in Israel! If it had not been for pressure from your government, we would have sent planes to destroy those trucks before they reached Beaufort Castle. Now we are waiting for you to decide if you are willing to do anything while this damned Sadiq plots to slaughter thousands of Israelis. We don't need your famous Omega Force to protect us. If it were not for your damned interference, my unit would have already stormed Beaufort Castle and destroyed the terrorists and their filthy weapons.''

Cray choked back a hot reply. Dror was obviously upset, and a shouting match would gain them nothing.

Dror took a deep breath. ''I am sorry, gentlemen. I allowed myself to become emotional. I don't mean to insult you, but my sister's family lives in Kiryat Shmonah, near the border. She has four children. They are the only relatives I have. I can picture them dying in agony. We must do something, but your government has blocked Israel from taking action for forty-eight hours. Forty-eight hours! Anything can happen in forty-eight hours! Something must be done, and done at once.''

General Sykes spoke calmly. ''We understand how you feel, Colonel. We are soldiers. We don't make policy—we just try to carry it out. You can rest assured we don't intend to sit here and do nothing. As you're aware, our instructions are to do anything possible to protect Israel from these terrorists, and we'll do our damnedest to carry them out. Your Intelligence seems to say that Beaufort Castle is the key. Very well, we are authorized to operate in Lebanon. Omega Force will assault it. What more can you tell us about the castle? What's the best way to attack?''

Dror smiled in relief. ''I am glad to hear that, General. I can tell you quite a bit about Beaufort. That, in fact, is one of the reasons I am here. I was in the attack force when we took it in 1982. It is a very strong position. The castle is divided into an an upper and lower fortress. The road from the valley leads to a gate house. Once you get in there, you must go through an underground tunnel and then climb a steep and narrow path to the gate house of the upper fort. Inside its walls is the citadel, a large stone tower. It is surrounded by a maze of chambers and passages. Many places in the castle have been converted to fighting bunkers. It took us six hours to capture it in 1982. The PLO defenders were brave but not particularly skillful. If Colonel Sadiq's men are experienced soldiers, it will be worse this time."

Cray didn't like what he had heard. Beaufort Castle seemed like a place that could stand off an army. It sounded like any attack was likely to be a bloody failure. There must be some way to do it successfully, but he couldn't see how.

"Is there anything you can suggest, Colonel? The place must have some weak points. Can we blow down the walls and blast our way in?"

Dror shook his head. "The walls are immensely thick and strong. Of course, heavy artillery or many large bombs might batter the castle to rubble, but that would take days, and we don't have days. The only chance we have is to achieve surprise, but I don't see how. Helicopters cannot make an assault landing. There is only room for one or two to land at a time inside the walls. And unless the defenders are asleep, they will hear the engines, and you will be cut to pieces before you hit the ground. If you to try to come up the road, you are bound to be detected, and it will take you hours to fight your way in. I am sorry, but I have no answer."

Cray thought hard. He wasn't an intellectual, but he was an excellent military planner. There must be an answer, but what? The men who had built Beaufort Castle eight hundred years ago seemed to have planned for every eventuality. Wait a minute, that was it! They had planned for anything they could imagine, but in the 1100s, men flew through the air only in fairy tales.

"That's it, by God, that's it!" he almost shouted. "We'll take them by surprise. They'll never know what hit them."

The others looked at Cray. "I am sorry, Major," Dror said, "but I do not understand. What is the answer?"

Cray smiled. "Have you ever jumped HAHO, Colonel?"

13

Captain Dave Tower sat in one of the web seats in the cargo compartment of the Israeli C-130H Hercules. The big four-engine transport had been climbing steadily since it left the runway. They should be reaching thirty-two thousand feet at any moment. Tower listened to the harsh sounds of his own breathing through his oxygen mask. The C-130's aft compartment couldn't be pressurized. The high-altitude high-opening, jump would require opening the tail door and if the pressure inside didn't match that of the thin outside air, a hurricane of air would blast through the compartment the instant the door was opened. That meant Tower and the assault party must breathe oxygen, first from the plane's supply until they jumped, then from their individual bailout bottles until they were down.

He told himself to settle down and relax. A HAHO parachute jump is not the safest thing in the world, but everyone in Omega Force was trained for it. He would have been happier if there had been more time to rehearse their plan. The past four hours had been hectic as their HAHO equipment had been unloaded from the C-5, checked transferred to the Israeli C-130 and checked again. That was just as well. There were no unimportant details in HAHO jump. Small mistakes could kill you.

The droning whine of the C-130's four turboprop engines changed as the pilot throttled back and leveled off. Cray came slowly down the aisle, breathing from an oxygen bottle on his back. He would act as the jumpmaster.

Tower smiled wickedly, recalling a previous conversation. It was a good thing that his oxygen mask still hid his face. Cray had planned to lead the HAHO jump in person, but General Sykes had vetoed that. A force commander shouldn't be the pointman. Cray had argued long and hard, but majors seldom won arguments with generals. Instead, Tower had been elected. He was a veteran of more than two thousand jumps, and he was the only officer in Omega Force who could speak fluent Arabic. There were times Tower thought learning Arabic had been a mistake. This was one of them. He smiled again. He always felt frightened just before he jumped, but he always went anyway.

Tower was just as happy that Cray would control the jump. He had done more HAHO jumps than anyone in Omega Force, and he kept his head when things got tense. Cray gestured upward with both hands. The eight-man assault team rose to their feet, gave their oxygen masks one last check and disconnected them from the C-130's oxygen supply. Tower and his men were breathing oxygen from their bailout bottles now, the individual oxygen tanks that would keep them alive until they were below ten thousand feet.

The four minute warning light was on. Cray gave each man the last equipment check. He looked to see if each man's head and face was covered by his helmet and oxygen mask. Boots, gloves and insulated jumpsuits protected the rest of their bodies. It was sixty degrees below zero outside, and the air would be howling past the C-130's fuselage at one hundred thirty knots when they jumped. It would be like stepping into an icy gale. Any unprotected skin risked instant frostbite. Each man gave the thumbs up signal. Cray nodded and pointed toward the tail door.

Slowly, careful not to tangle their equipment, they moved toward the door. They would jump at ten-second intervals. Tower as the jump leader, the low man, would go first.

Blake would jump next. As usual, he was carrying more high explosives than seemed humanly possible. Sergeant Hall would be the last man out. If anything happened to Tower during the jump, Hall would take command.

The two-minute warning light came on. Tower and his men were standing at the end of the cargo compartment now, facing the C-130's tail door. When the door opened, there would be nothing below them but thirty-two thousand feet of air. The Israeli pilot was waiting until the last moment to open the door. Cray signaled for the final oxygen check. Red warning lights came on, and Tower heard the high-pitched whine of hydraulic motors as the tail door was lowered and locked open in the horizontal ready position. Ice-cold air filled the C-130's cargo compartment.

The one-minute warning light blinked on. Tower made a thumbs-up gesture at his team. Each man returned the gesture. Good. No one was having breathing problems or trouble with his equipment.

The thirty-second warning light came on. There was a sudden change in the roar of the engines as the Israeli pilot throttled back. He was holding the C-130 as close to stalling speed as he could in order to reduce the strength of the airflow around the big plane's fuselage. When he was satisfied, he would push the ten-second warning light. Unless he or Crazy called an abort, they would go.

The big C-130 began to shake and vibrate as its speed dropped to within a few knots of stalling. Satisfied, the Israeli pilot pushed the button. The ten-second warning light came on, the standby order, the last warning before the jump. Tower felt a quick surge of fear and adrenaline. There was nothing left to do now but pray.

Suddenly the "go" light went on. Tower took two long running steps along the ramp and dived through the open door into the dark. Instantly he was in free-fall. Looking up, he could see the huge wings and fuselage of the C-130 glinting in the pale moonlight as it pulled away. Tower used his arms and legs to turn his body and assume a facedown position. He was counting to himself without thinking as he glanced quickly to the left and right. All clear. Eight, nine, ten!

Tower pulled the rip cord. His pilot chute deployed, pulling the special high-performance, ram-air canopy from its pack and into the air. The canopy blossomed, and Tower felt a hard jolt as it filled with air and slowed his fall. Quickly he slipped his hands into his steering loops, ready to maneuver if he had to. A collision with one of his men could ruin the jump. Quickly he looked around and counted, five, six, seven. He felt a surge of relief. Everyone's chute had opened. Their special chutes could be flown like hang gliders, allowing them to fly down at angles as great as forty-five degrees if they had to. They should all be able to reach the castle and come down close together on the assembly point.

Things seemed almost peaceful. The pale crescent moon and the stars were shining and the night air was clear. The whining roar of the C-130 faded away into silence. All Tower could hear was the sound of his demand-regulated breathing and the air sighing through his parachute's suspension lines. Looking down, he saw southern Lebanon spread out beneath him. From this altitude, it looked quiet and peaceful. Tower had a dismal feeling it would not be that way when he landed. There wouldn't be a friendly welcoming committee waiting at Beaufort Castle. He smiled as the tension of the jump drained away. That was the problem with a HAHO jump; it left you far too much time to think. It would be more than fifteen minutes before Tower and his men hit the ground.

It wouldn't do to get too relaxed. It was time to head for Beaufort Castle. Tower scanned the ground below through his night-vision goggles. He could see the plateau in the distance and the massive stone walls and towers of the castle. He pulled on his steering loops and tilted his canopy in a slow turn to the left, toward the castle. He was going down at a forty-five degree angle, the wind whistling past his canopy as he flew through the dark, trading altitude for speed and distance. He pushed the button on the tactical radio clipped to his harness.

"High man, give me a check."

"Wait one, Leader. I see seven chutes, all guiding on you. Estimate the maximum dispersion at twenty yards," Hall said in his soft southwestern drawl. Tower was glad he had Hall and his big .50-caliber rifle with him. The team was following him perfectly. He had better start concentrating on his landing. It wouldn't do to lead them all to the wrong spot. He was an experienced HAHO jumper, but he had never tried to land on top of a castle at night.

Beaufort Castle was looming larger and larger in Tower's night-vision goggles. He could see the details of the walls and buildings. Tower glanced at the altimeter on his wrist. He was at eight thousand feet now. He unsnapped his oxygen mask. He could feel the warm, dry air on his face below his goggles. There was little or no low-altitude wind. Good. The critical thing was to get down and take the enemy by surprise.

He checked his altimeter again, six thousand feet. Time seemed to be crawling by. What the hell was taking them so long? He glanced at his altimeter again—four thousand feet. He was directly over the castle now. He pulled down on his steering loops and went to full brake. Tower lost all forward thrust from his canopy and hung on the edge of a stall. As he lost forward motion, his rate of descent increased. The surface of the plateau and the castle towers seemed to shoot upward toward him.

Tower thought of the landing on hard stone. He knew he could easily break a leg. Beaufort Castle was directly below him. He went to half brake and turned to the right. He wanted to land directly on top of the citadel tower. He completed his turn and went to full brake. Now he went straight down.

At one hundred feet, Tower pulled the release and felt his equipment pack drop away and dangle below him. The top of the tower came rushing up to meet him. Suddenly he saw movement. There were two men on the top of the tower. They must have been sitting quietly, but now they were on their feet. One of them was pointing to the east. They seemed more astonished than alarmed, but they must have seen something. Tower glanced quickly to the left. Blake was lower than he should be. The extra weight of the explosives he was carrying had pulled him down. He was overshooting and turning back toward the tower. He must have been silhouetted by the moon as he turned.

There was no time to think or draw a weapon. Tower pulled hard on his steering loops and dropped toward the two men like a stone. He was going down feet first. The heels of his jump boots smashed into one man's back. Tower weighed one-ninety, and he was carrying seventy pounds of weapons and equipment. The impact was terrible. Tower felt the jolting shock in his bones, but it was far worse for the man he hit. He was slammed into the stone roof with brutal force and lay there, dead or unconscious.

The second man whirled around. They were ten feet apart. Tower could see the look of utter astonishment on his face. It must have seemed to him that Tower had appeared from nowhere, flying down out of the dark like some kind of evil spirit. Time seemed to slow down to a crawl. The man was reaching frantically for the AK-47 slung over his shoulder. Tower bounced, hit the roof and rolled. He reached desperately for his pistol and tried to twist into a firing position, but his parachute was pulling him off balance.

Something came down out of the sky and seemed to swallow the guard up. The nonreflective gray canopy of Tower's parachute was almost invisible at night. It dropped on the guard, enveloping him in clinging plastic cloth like a ghostly shroud. Tower sprang forward and slammed the flat steel slide of his .45 Colt automatic against the guard's head, once, twice. The guard dropped and lay motionless, still covered by the parachute cloth.

Tower pulled his quick-release handles and slipped out of his harness. He was in the open, on top of a building, with no time to bother with his chute. He opened his equipment bag and pulled out his silenced Heckler & Koch submachine gun. There was a round ready in the chamber. He pushed the safety off and set the selector lever for full automatic. Tower believed in powerful weapons. If he had to shoot someone with a 9 mm, he was damned well going to shoot them more than once. He heard a thump behind him as Blake hit the roof and rolled. Tower looked up. The rest of the assault party was coming in, floating down out of the darkness like giant gray bats.

Tower glanced at Blake. He was out of his parachute harness and had his silenced submachine gun in his hands. Blake seemed to be staring at him. Suddenly, he swung his weapon up, and Tower found himself looking into the cold, black muzzle. Blake shouted "Down!"

Tower didn't stop to think. He threw himself down and to the right as Blake pulled the trigger, and a burst of 9 mm bullets tore through the space where Tower had been half a second before. Tower rolled and twisted, trying to bring his weapon around. He knew something was going on behind him. Blake wasn't given to firing at shadows. He heard the soft hiss of the silencer as Blake fired again.

Tower swung the muzzle of his Heckler & Koch around. The man he had struck when he landed was on his feet again. He was swaying as if stunned or wounded. There was an AK-47 in his hands. Tower could see the dot of his own weapon's laser sight centered on the man's chest. He pulled the trigger and hammered the guard with a 6-round burst. The AK-47 dropped from the guard's hands and struck the stone roof with a clang. Its owner fell on top of it and lay still.

Tower waited tensely. No one inside the tower could have heard the silenced submachine guns firing, but the metallic clang of the falling AK-47 had seemed loud enough to wake the dead. He saw the flash of something moving. A large wooden trapdoor built into the roof of the tower slammed open. A man's head and shoulders appeared in the opening.

The man spoke in Arabic. "In God's name, Ibrahim, what is happening? What is all this noise?"

It was a reasonable question, but Ibrahim was in no condition to answer. Tower aimed at the man and hesitated. Should he risk a reply? His Arabic was excellent, but he had no idea what the guard's voice sounded like. Tower's sights were on. He could shoot, but there might be other men behind the man he could see. A body falling back into the room below would certainly give the show away.

Tower heard a thump behind him as another member of the assault team hit the roof and rolled. The man in the door didn't have night-vision goggles, but the moonlight was strong enough to let him see a blur of motion. He shouted something and reached for the AK-47 slung over his shoulder. Tower pulled the trigger. The Heckler & Koch vibrated against his shoulder as it fired. The opening of the door was suddenly empty as the man fell back into the room below. Tower heard shouts of surprise and fury from below.

No use worrying about making noise now! He snatched a grenade from his belt and pulled the pin. He stayed prone and rolled toward the edge of the door. Someone down there had quick reflexes. Tower heard the snarl of an AK-47 firing, and a long burst of .30-caliber bullets shot through the door. If he had been stupid enough to stand up and look down through the doorway, he would have been dead.

Time to return the compliment. He let the safety handle of the grenade fly and heard the pop as the striker hit the primer. He heard the reassuring sizzle as the fuze ignited and began to burn. He didn't want anyone below to have time to pick up the grenade and throw it back. He counted silently, then dropped the grenade into the room below. He heard a muffled boom as the grenade detonated and lethal fragments shrieked through the air below and glanced off the stone walls. He heard shouts of pain and fury. Someone fired another long burst through the opening. Tower hugged the stones of the roof as green tracers streaked by, inches from his head.

One grenade hadn't been enough. Tower figured the room below had to be a big one. He reached for another grenade but stopped as he felt Blake's hand on his arm. Blake pointed to a nylon web container in his other hand. A satchel charge! He looked inquiringly at Tower.

The rest of the team was coming in. Tower knew that the results were likely to be fatal if they were trapped on the roof. No matter what it cost, they had to take the tower.

"Throw it!" he yelled. Blake pulled the pin and pushed the satchel charge through the trapdoor. Tower couldn't see Blake's face in the dark, but he would have bet his last dollar Blake was grinning. Blake loved to blow things up.

The charge detonated. It contained five pounds of high explosives, compared to the few ounces in a grenade. The blast shook the roof, and the whole tower vibrated. The firing from below stopped abruptly. Tower rolled over the edge of the door and dropped into the room, landing with an experienced paratrooper's crouch and roll. Behind him Blake fired through the opening, spraying the big room beyond Tower with bursts of full-metal-jacketed 9 mm bullets. Tower swept the room with the muzzle of his submachine gun, but there was nothing moving but wisps of smoke from the satchel charge. The defenders were dead or unconscious. Nobody was playing possum after a blast like that.

Tower snapped a fresh 30-round magazine into his Heckler & Koch and listened intently. He could hear men yelling and shouting below and the sounds of AK-47s firing. The enemy sounded confused and disorganized from the shock of the sudden surprise attack. But Tower knew they were probably veterans, experienced in combat. If some sergeant or lieutenant kept his head, they would organize a counterattack. He had to hit them before they could do that. There was a wooden door in one side of the room. It must lead below, down into the bottom of the tower. No other choice—they would attack through there.

"Come on!" he shouted. "Go, go, go!"

Blake dropped through the door and moved to Tower's side. Another man followed him. Tower wasn't sure who it was, but he recognized the SAWS in his hand. Good, the deadly little .223-caliber light machine gun would give them some desperately needed firepower. Tower stood to one side and pointed to the door. He took a grenade from his belt and slipped a finger through the safety pin ring.

Blake moved to the door. He was careful not to stand in front of it. The SAWS gunner aimed his weapon at the door. Blake turned the handle. The door wasn't locked. He kicked it hard, and it started to swing open. Tower heard the ripping snarl of a light machine gun firing a long burst. Gouts of splinters flew as steel-jacketed .30-caliber bullets tore through the door, ricocheted off the walls and screamed around the room. Tower resisted the impulse to try to dig a hole in the stone floor and crawl into it.

The splintered door slammed open against the wall. Tower snapped a hand signal at the SAWS gunner, who pulled his trigger and sent long, raking bursts of suppressive fire through the doorway. The SAWS fired from a 200-round belt carried in a plastic box clipped to the weapon.

While those two hundred rounds lasted, the SAWS could put out a tremendous amount of firepower. Tower pulled the grenade's pin, released the safety lever and threw the grenade through the door in one fluid motion. Quickly he reached for another. He had learned long ago that grenades were better weapons than rifles or machine guns inside a building.

The grenade flew through the air, bounced down the stone steps and detonated. The firing from below stopped. Tower dropped to the floor and risked a quick look around the edge of the door. He saw a narrow stone stairway leading down one wall of a large hall. They must be thirty or forty feet above the floor. Damn! The stairway had no side wall or railing. There was no cover. It was completely exposed to fire from the floor below, but there was no other way to go.

Tower thought furiously for a few seconds. There must be a dozen men above him in the upper tower now, but there was no way he could deploy them and bring their weapons to bear. He and Blake were neither superhuman nor bulletproof, but they were in the lead. They would have to make the initial attack with whatever help they could get from the squad automatic weapons. He signaled Blake to move forward to the door. Blake took a fast look around the corner, jerking his head back as a burst of AK-47 fire came from below.

Tower didn't waste time on long explanations. "We've got to go down those stairs and clean them out," he said. Blake nodded. He was an experienced soldier and understood the situation as well as Tower. Decisions were easy to make when there was only one thing you could do. He took more satchel charges from his pack and checked the fuzes. Tower took the SAWS from the gunner. There was a fresh 200-round belt clipped to its side. He didn't have time to switch magazine pouches. If he couldn't get the job done with two hundred rounds, he wasn't likely to get it done at all.

Blake had a satchel charge in one hand, ready to start the fuze. Tower would have liked to say something inspiring, some ringing words that would live in history, but all he could think of was "Let's go. Now!"

Blake shot through the doorway, flew down half a dozen steps, and hurled the charge into the hall below. Tower followed, pausing only to snap a short burst at the flickering muzzle-flashes at the foot of the stairs. Bullets smashed into the wall above his head and screamed away, scattering stone chips and dust. Someone down below was shooting too damned well. Tower swore briefly but fluently and fired again. If he didn't hit anyone, the blasts of .223 bullets from his SAWS would spoil their aim.

Suddenly the world seemed to explode as the satchel charge detonated with a blinding flash and a deafening roar. The blast shook Tower and the huge hall vibrated. The firing stopped. Blake moved quickly down the steps, taking them two at a time, another satchel charge ready in his hands. He skidded to a halt and threw the satchel charge. Tower plastered himself against the wall as the second blast seemed to rock the huge stone tower on its foundations.

Now or never! Tower hurled himself down the remaining steps and onto the stone floor. Blake was close behind. Drifting smoke and the acrid smell of burning high explosives filled the hall. Dim shapes loomed up a few feet in front of him. Any friends Tower had in Beaufort Castle were behind him. He triggered the SAWS and sprayed the room with a series of fast, short bursts. He heard men yelling and running as he fired again. Someone was yelling behind him. Blake was shouting "Down!"

Tower threw himself to the floor. From above and behind, he heard the crackling roar of M-16 rifles and SAWS opening fire. Omega Force's men were moving down the stairs now, raking the hall with bursts of fire. The fight went out of the enemy. Some threw down their weapons. Others ran desperately for the door that led outside. The assault party swept past Tower, firing as they went.

Blake appeared from nowhere. "All secure, Captain. This place belongs to us," he said. Tower found that he was shaking from reaction. That annoyed him. It always did. He told himself it was merely that he was flooded with adrenaline.

"Damned good work," he said. "Find the radio operator and send a message to the general. 'Assault successful. Send in the main body.' Tell them to be careful. The opposition is still in the lower part of the castle. They may be in a bad mood."

Blake was on his way. The smoke was clearing. Tower glanced around the huge stone hall. He had never been in a medieval castle before. It must have been a splendid sight eight hundred years ago. He smiled, then began to laugh. The men of the assault party looked at him strangely. Had their commander cracked under the strain? That made Tower laugh harder. He didn't think he was hysterical, but he couldn't stop thinking. What would Simon de Beaufort make of the fight that had just raged through his citadel?

AMANDA STUART SAT tensely at the controls of her Blackhawk. The dull black special-operations helicopter was checked out and ready to go. General Sykes sat next to her in the copilot's seat, listening to the radio. They had received the "go" message fifteen minutes earlier. The assault party had jumped. Now there was nothing to do but wait. She had a great deal of faith in her friends in Omega Force, but a HAHO jump into hostile territory was a very dangerous operation, and once you jumped, there was no way back. Once you hit the ground, it was do or die.

A green light began to flash on the communications control panel. A message was coming in. Sykes listened intensely for a few seconds, then keyed the transmitter.

"Roger, Omega Six, message received. I confirm Jackpot. Payoff. I say again, Payoff."

Amanda felt a surge of relief and a flood of adrenaline. "Jackpot" meant that Omega Force's assault party had seized their objective. "Payoff" meant that the main body was going in. It wouldn't be easy. She was going to lead a high-speed, low-altitude flight in total darkness. A dozen helicopters would be following her. She checked her instrument displays. She was ready to go. She poised her hand over the starting switches and looked at General Sykes inquiringly.

Sykes got up and started toward the passenger compartment.

"All right, Captain Stuart. I'll send up Colonel Dror. Takeoff in sixty seconds."

He turned back to Amanda and frowned. She thought she knew what was coming next. Sykes was a good commander. He wasn't going to tell her how to do her job, but was sure as hell going to tell her what he wanted done.

"Get us there as fast as you can," he said, "but get us there in one piece. Understand?"

Amanda nodded. It wasn't a detailed technical description of a helicopter mission profile, but she understood perfectly. Flying helicopters was what she did, and she was leading the mission not because of her good looks and charm but because she was the best MH-60K Blackhawk pilot available.

"I understand, General. Be sure everyone is strapped in back there. The ride is likely to be a little rough."

She pushed the engine starter switches and felt the Blackhawk vibrate as its twin turbine engines whined to life. Colonel Dror slipped into the copilot's seat. Amanda was not happy about flying without a copilot, but she hadn't argued. Dror had been to Beaufort Castle. He had to be where he could see and speak to Amanda instantly in case the plan had to be changed. The whine of the engines deepened to a howl as Amanda went to full power and lifted off. Almost instantly the dim runway lights of the Israeli base vanished into the darkness.

Amanda was extremely busy for a few seconds. She checked her displays. Both engines were running smoothly, her speed was one hundred twenty miles per hour, and the radar altimeter indicated ninety feet. A number of lights were blinking on and off on the survivability-systems display and control panel. Amanda glanced at the display. It indicated heavy radar activity to the south, in Israel, and to the north, in Lebanon. Colonel Dror pointed to the panel. "Are we under attack?" he asked.

Amanda shook her head. "No, those are air-defense surveillance radars. They are making a general search of the area. If a fire-control radar locks on, we'll get an audible alarm and I'll activate our countermeasures."

"I am sure they are miracles of technology, but I hope that we will not need to use them," Dror said dryly. Amanda agreed completely. She had been fired at with surface-to-air missiles before and she wasn't eager to repeat the experience.

"The strike force is taking off now," Dror continued. There will be two squadrons of jet fighters, search-and-rescue helicopters and jamming aircraft. We will give the Syrian radar operators quite a show. Three terrorist camps in southern Lebanon will be hit as we go in. It will look like a reprisal for the attack on our border patrol. With luck, the Syrians will never see us."

Amanda hoped the Israeli colonel was right, but she wasn't going to bet her life on it. She concentrated on her flying. She would stay low and monitor her displays, ready to take instant action if the attack alarm sounded. She kept her eyes on the MFD, which converted the signals from the infrared sensors into a picture of the ground ahead, allowing her to fly low and fast in total darkness. Her aviator's night-vision goggles let her look to the left or right out the cockpit windows. It was an excellent system, but everything depended on Amanda's staying alert. When you were flying at one hundred fifty miles per hour and less than a hundred feet, there is no margin for error.

The minutes crawled by. The scene in the MFD showed only barren ground and an occasional dirt road. The control panel continued to indicate steady radar activity, but the attack-warning alarm remained silent. Amanda checked her moving map display. They must be getting close. Yes, at the upper edge of the MFD's picture, she could see a dark line snaking its way from east to west. That must be the Litani River. Beaufort would be five miles to the east. It was time to go up. The castle was twenty-two hundred feet above sea level. She would fly along the river as she climbed, keeping the mass of the mountain between the Blackhawk and the Syrian air-defense radars in the Bekaa Valley.

The whine of the turbines deepened as Amanda went to full power and began to climb. She looked out of the cockpit. To the north and west, she could see what looked like lightning flickering along the horizon. The Israeli jets were bombing and strafing the terrorist camps. The men in them probably had nothing to do with Colonel Sadiq, but the Israeli pilots didn't care. To them, the only good terrorist was a dead terrorist.

Colonel Dror touched her shoulder and pointed at the MFD. Amanda saw a small mountain ahead, topped by a flat plateau. On the top she saw what looked like a giant mass of jumbled stone. "Beaufort Castle! Excellent flying, Captain."

They were flying toward the plateau at more than two miles per minute. As they got closer, Amanda could see the individual towers and walls of the castle. Amanda was fascinated. She had never seen a castle before and had never imagined she would ever fly a mission to capture one. Parts of it seemed to be nearly intact. Others were in ruins.

Dror pointed to the display. "There is the upper castle. That is the citadel tower. Land on the tower or next to it in the courtyard. You are the pilot. The choice is yours."

The romantic thoughts were instantly forgotten. Amanda concentrated all her attention on flying. Either way, it was going to be a hairy landing. Here and there, from the walls and buildings, Amanda saw flickering lights and glowing dots streaking through the night. She had seen them before when she had flown assault troops into Iraq. People were shooting. Omega Force had captured the upper castle, but the defenders were still holding the lower section. She would land in the courtyard, where there would be more cover. She turned to the left to approach from the north, over the sheer cliff behind the upper castle. No use going in over the firefight and tempting people to shoot at her.

The north wall of the citadel loomed larger and larger in her MFD. Carefully Amanda brought the Blackhawk into the hover mode and started down. The helicopter shuddered and bounced as the down wash from the main rotors was reflected back from the walls of the citadel tower. She struggled with her controls. If the Blackhawk drifted sideways and her main rotor blades struck the tower wall, she was going to crash a very expensive helicopter. It took all her skill to bring the Blackhawk down, thirty feet, twenty, ten. Its wheels touched down with a jolt. She felt a surge of relief as she cut the power. It wasn't the prettiest landing in the world, but she was down and safe. Above her the second Blackhawk was heading down while a third circled, waiting its turn. She had done her job. Omega Force was landing in Beaufort Castle.

14

As Amanda unsnapped her flight harness, Colonel Dror was already moving to the door, an Israeli Galil assault rifle in his hands. Amanda could hear the crackle of rifle and machine-gun fire. Some of the castle's defenders were still putting up a fight. She took her M-16A2 rifle from its rack and chambered a round, then followed Dror. It wouldn't do to be in the middle of a firefight without being ready to fire. The large, rearward sliding doors on each side of the main cabin were open. The cabin itself was empty. General Sykes and the rest of her passengers were already outside.

Dror pointed to the citadel and ran toward the large door that led inside. Amanda quickly followed him, being careful to stay five steps behind. If there were any hostile snipers in the area, she wanted to be as difficult a target as possible. They dashed through the door and found themselves inside the huge, high-ceilinged main hall. General Sykes was standing near the door, talking to Dave Tower.

"We hold the tower, General, from the roof to ground level," Tower was saying. "But be careful. We haven't had time to search it completely, and there are stairs at the far side that lead down below ground. We haven't had the manpower to check them out yet. Major Cray is on the south wall with most of the assault party. As far as we know, the enemy has retreated to the lower castle, but we can't be sure that some of them aren't down below. My orders were to search the lower levels as soon as the main body arrived. Unless you want to do it differently, I'm ready to move out."

"All right, but wait a minute or two before you go. Dr. Hill was on the fourth Blackhawk. She should be here shortly. You may need her and her equipment before you're through."

Tower didn't like taking a civilian on a search-and-destroy mission, but Sykes was right. Cora Hill's specialized knowledge might be critical here. Besides, Tower had served with the general for several years. He knew very well that his chances of winning an argument with him were extremely small.

Sykes turned to Dror. "I'm going down to the south wall to check out the situation, Colonel. Do you want to go with me, or would you prefer to give Captain Tower a hand? You know the layout of this place better than we do."

Dror smiled. It was obvious that Sykes was being polite. He wouldn't give Dror a direct order, but like most generals Dror knew, Sykes expected his suggestions to be obeyed.

"I will be glad to go with Captain Tower. There are a number of chambers below the hall. They were used as dungeons and storage chambers in the old days. They may still be," Dror responded. Turning, he said, "I'm ready when you are, Captain. Give the word."

It was Tower's turn to smile. Now Dror was being polite. It was an Omega Force operation, and he was acknowledging that Tower was in command.

Cora Hill entered the hall. Tower signaled to Blake. He and six other men gave their equipment one last check and moved quietly toward the doors on the far side of the hall. The general hadn't told Amanda what she was supposed to do. Should she go with him or with Tower? She certainly didn't want to stay where she was. Even with her M-16 loaded with thirty rounds, she didn't like the idea of being alone in the gloom of the hall. She looked inquiringly at the general.

"Stick with Captain Tower, Stuart," Sykes said. "Look out for Dr. Hill. She's not used to this kind of thing."

Neither am I, Amanda thought. She was a helicopter pilot, not a Green Beret or a Ranger. Although competent with a rifle or pistol, she felt far safer with Tower and Blake than alone. She motioned to Dr. Hill and led her across the hall to where Tower and his group stood by an open door. Beyond it a flight of stone steps led down to the lower levels of the tower. Blake was checking the area around the door carefully. Logically the enemy hadn't had time to rig any elaborate booby traps, but Blake didn't consider any place safe until he checked it out.

At last satisfied, he led the way down the stone steps. One by one the party moved down the steps, nerves taut and weapons ready. Amanda brought up the rear with Cora Hill. At the bottom of the stairs, a wide corridor led off into the darkness. Amanda couldn't see well. There was little light for her night-vision goggles to amplify here, underground. She didn't like it. She could almost feel the crushing weight of the giant stone tower above her. The walls and the darkness seemed to be closing in.

Blake risked turning on a flashlight. Quickly he swept the hall ahead. There were several doors leading off to either side. "Storage chambers," Dror announced. Blake moved forward carefully, his submachine gun ready. One by one they checked the rooms, finding only stacks of wooden crates, some of them open. Blake looked at the nearest one. "Russian 122 mm artillery rockets," he said, disappointed. Blake liked modern high-tech weapons. Amanda gathered that 122 mm Russian artillery rockets weren't in that class.

Dror, looking down the corridor, suddenly stiffened and snapped his Galil to his shoulder. Amanda saw a flash of light as a door was flung open and two men leaped into the corridor, weapons in their hands. Instantly Dror fired. The roar of his rifle was almost deafening as the muzzle-blast echoed from the stone walls. Both men staggered under the hail of .223 bullets and went down. Tower reached for a grenade, then hesitated. Through the open door he could see tables and what appeared to be scientific equipment. If any of the chemical agent was inside the room, to throw a grenade could be suicidal.

He shouted something in Arabic. No reply. He shouted again.

"Do not shoot! For god's sake, do not shoot! I don't understand your language. I am a civilian. I am unarmed. I surrender. Do not shoot. You are in terrible danger if you shoot." It was a man's voice, speaking English with an accent Amanda could not place. She was sure of one thing— there was genuine terror in his voice.

Tower and Blake moved carefully forward. From either side of the door, they swept the room beyond with the muzzles of their weapons. Tower signaled the rest of the party forward. Amanda followed the others through the door. The lights were blinding. Amanda switched her night-vision goggles off and looked around. A generator was humming in one corner, several heavy wooden tables were covered with equipment that Amanda could not identify. On one table there were several rockets or missiles, each about five inches in diameter and ten feet long.

A tall man with graying blond hair was standing against the back wall, peering at them through thick glasses. Blake was covering him with his Heckler & Koch. The man showed no signs of resistance. That was wise. Blake had his usual pleasant grin on his face, but the casual yet competent way he held his submachine gun showed that he was ready to shoot to kill.

"I am a civilian. I am a citizen of the Russian republic. I am a scientist. I am not involved in this fight. Do not shoot."

"I won't, if you don't move," Blake said.

Somebody gasped.

"Kamov!" Cora Hill exclaimed. "Yuri Leontyevich Kamov!"

"Do you know this man, Doctor?" Tower asked.

"Not personally, but I know who he is. I've read some of his papers and heard him lecture once in London. Professor Kamov is one of the world's leading authorities in biochemistry and genetic engineering. I'm surprised to see him here."

Tower wasn't surprised. He had never heard of Professor Kamov, but his presence in Beaufort Castle answered a lot of questions. "Take a look at this equipment, Dr. Hill. Can you tell what they were doing here?"

Cora Hill appeared startled by the question. To her the answer was obvious. "They were transferring the agent from storage cylinders to the warheads on those rockets. Many chemical-warfare agents are too dangerous to be left loaded in warheads for long periods of time. It's common practice to load them into warheads shortly before you intend to use them."

She stepped closer to one of the tables and pointed. "See, here is one of the storage cylinders. It's identical to the ones we've seen before. It's connected to the transfer machine here, and this hose leads to the rocket warhead. If I were to push this button—"

"No! Don't touch anything!" Kamov shouted. "You don't understand. If you make a mistake, if the agent is released, we will all be killed!"

Cora Hill looked at Kamov icily. "Calm yourself, Professor. I am not stupid enough to try to operate biological-warfare equipment I don't understand."

Kamov didn't appear to be calm. "This operation should never have been carried out here. The safety facilities are totally inadequate. These men are crazy. They said that they would kill me if I didn't do what they said."

He glanced around the room. "Who is in command here? You must leave this place immediately. You must take me with you. I demand to see the Russian consul."

"I am Captain David Tower, United States Army. I am in command," Tower said coldly. "You aren't in a position to demand anything, Kamov. The evidence is clear. You are here working for a group of international terrorists. You've sold your scientific technology to them. You are helping them to use biological-warfare agents against civilian targets. That violates international law. The penalties for that are severe. Unless you tell us everything you know, you'll get what you deserve. You won't get out of here alive."

Kamov took a deep breath and glared at Tower. "I am not stupid, Captain. If I give you information, you will say I am confessing to what you call crimes. I will tell you nothing."

"That's your choice, Professor," Tower said, and pointed his submachine gun at Kamov's chest. "Do you want a few seconds to say your prayers?"

Kamov turned pale. He was looking straight down the muzzle of the Heckler & Koch's silencer, and Tower's finger was on the trigger.

He smiled faintly and shook his head. "No, you will not shoot me. You would kill me in battle easily enough, but you will not execute an unarmed civilian in cold blood. You are bluffing."

Tower sighed and lowered his submachine gun. Kamov was right. He wouldn't shoot an unarmed prisoner in cold blood. It was against all U.S. Army standing orders and regulations, and perhaps even more important, it was something that Tower was simply unwilling to do.

"See, I knew you wouldn't do it," Kamov said with a superior smile.

He was pushing his luck. Tower had taken an instant dislike to Kamov. It was true that he wouldn't shoot him, but the thought of bending Army regulations and breaking Kamov's jaw was extremely tempting.

"He will not kill you, but I will," someone said quietly. Colonel Dror stepped forward. He had slung his rifle over his shoulder. He held a big Beretta 9 mm automatic pistol in the steady, two-handed hold of an experienced combat shot.

"They will not kill you, because they are Americans. It is a game to them, a hard game perhaps, but a game with rules. I am not an American. I am Colonel Eli Dror of the Israeli defense forces. All my life, I have fought people who want to destroy Israel and wipe its people off the face of the earth. It is not a game to me. I don't arrest terrorists and take them to see their lawyers—I kill them. You are a terrorist, and I will kill you."

There was a moment's silence, broken only by a metallic click as Dror cocked his pistol.

"No! No!" Kamov said frantically. "I am a scientist, not a terrorist. For the love of God, someone stop him!"

"You are worse than a terrorist," Dror said coldly. "I understand the Arabs. They are fighting for a cause. It is a bad cause, but they believe in it. They fight and die for what they believe in." Dror spit on the floor. "You are a brilliant scientist, but you believe in nothing. You sold your knowledge to terrorists to kill thousands of innocent people who aren't your enemies. You are like the Nazi scientists in Germany who gassed the Jews. You deserve to die."

Dror aimed the big Beretta directly at Kamov's head. His finger began to tighten on the trigger.

"Stop him!" Kamov shrieked at Tower. "I will tell you everything you want to know. Everything!"

"Don't shoot, Colonel," Tower said quickly. "He deserves to die, but if you kill him, we'll never get his information. We've got to find out what he knows. It may save thousands of lives, Israelis and Americans."

"Very well, Captain. He deserves to die, but you are right and you are in command." Dror uncocked his pistol and holstered it.

"I need to find General Sykes and tell him what we found," Tower said. "Blake, take command. Dr. Hill, question Kamov, find out everything he knows. Colonel Dror, Captain Stuart, you'd better come with me."

Cora Hill began to talk to Professor Kamov. His attitude appeared to have changed completely. He seemed eager to tell everything he knew as long as he didn't have to go anywhere with Colonel Dror.

Tower was smiling as he moved through the corridor for the stairs. "Remind me never to play poker with you, Colonel. You run a wicked bluff. Kamov was scared to death," he said.

Dror stopped and stared at Tower. "You are mistaken, Captain," he said quietly. "I never bluff."

JAMAL TAWFIQ STEPPED through the door of the underground bunker. Colonel Sadiq sat at a battered wooden desk. Concentrating deeply on the map in front of him, he didn't seem to hear Tawfiq enter. Tawfiq worried about his leader. Sadiq was showing the effects of constant strain and fatigue. That was bad. Tawfiq was a competent combat officer. He could lead a mission, and the men would follow, but he knew he could be replaced. Sadiq was the heart and soul of the movement. If anything happened to him, the movement would be finished.

Sadiq looked up and smiled. "What news, Jamal?" he asked.

Tawfiq didn't like what he was about to say, but the colonel needed men who told him the truth, not what they thought he wanted to hear. "I have checked, Colonel. The air raids were unimportant, but I am afraid they were a diversion. The Americans have attacked Beaufort Castle. Somehow the sons of Satan took our men by surprise. Ten minutes ago we received a message that many helicopters were landing. Since then, nothing. I am afraid the castle is lost, along with the Russian and his equipment. Shall I assemble our men and try to retake it?''

Sadiq swore bitterly. It made him feel better, but it didn't solve the problem. Tawfiq's suggestion was tempting. It would be glorious to put his faith in God and retake Beaufort Castle, to lead his men in victory or to die a holy martyr. No, that was foolish! He was willing to die for his cause if it came to that, but he wouldn't throw away his life or the lives of his men as long as there was the slightest chance his plan could still succeed.

"No," he said. "We have lost too many men already. Besides, it doesn't matter. One attack or two, it makes no difference as long as we hit the damned Israelis so hard that they must strike back. Give the orders. I want every weapon and launcher we have here ready to move south as soon as possible. I will go and coordinate the attack with our Syrian allies."

Tawfiq smiled. This was the leader he was used to. Sadiq's fatigue seemed to be gone. He radiated total determination. "At once, Colonel," he said. "Go with God!"

15

Amanda Stuart stood in the castle courtyard and watched the Israeli CH-53D helicopter touch down. She admired the Israeli pilot's skill. It was a big machine, much larger than Omega Force's Blackhawks. It wasn't easy to land in the confined space inside the upper-castle wall, but it could lift ten tons of payload. It would take Kamov's equipment back to Israel for detailed analysis. The CH-53D's six-bladed rotor whined to a stop. The side door opened, and two Israeli crewmen jumped out, assault rifles ready. They scanned the courtyard and walls with a practiced air. They had been told that Beaufort Castle was secure, but they weren't going to take any chances. To Amanda, some of the Israelis she had met seemed abrupt and condescending, but she had to admire their professional skill.

Apparently they were satisfied. A dozen Israeli soldiers and technicians moved rapidly toward the citadel door where Sergeant Blake was waiting to lead them down to Cora Hill. Amanda waited by the door. Her orders were to coordinate helicopter operations, but since the Israeli CH-53D had landed, there was nothing more for her to do at the moment. She started for the CH-53D's side door. She would check with the Israeli pilot to be sure he had no problems and was ready for the return flight. Besides, she had never seen the interior of an Israeli assault transport helicopter. It would be interesting to see how the Israelis did things.

She was almost to the door when Dr. Kaye stepped out. He was a startling sight. Someone had given him an Israeli AC-T Kevlar armored vest and a steel helmet. He was carrying a pistol in a holster on his belt. They contrasted strangely with his rumpled gray suit and expensive civilian shoes. He looked apprehensively around the courtyard, which still wore the signs of battle. Fired cartridge cases littered the stones, and here and there bodies lay where they had been dragged out of the way. It was not a pretty sight, but Omega Force had other things to do besides police up the area. Amanda didn't think Kaye was happy to be back in Lebanon.

"Captain Stuart," Kaye said sharply, "I must see General Sykes and Major Cray at once. Take me to them immediately."

Amanda snarled under her breath. Kaye was his usual charming self. If prizes for tact and good manners were going to be handed out, he wouldn't get one.

"They are inside the citadel, Doctor," she said icily. "If you will please follow me?"

Kaye wasn't lovable, but neither was he stupid. He noticed the tone in Amanda's voice. "I'm sorry if I sounded abrupt, Captain. The flight here was unbelievable. That Israeli helicopter pilot seemed to be trying to commit suicide. I don't believe we flew above fifty feet during the entire trip."

Amanda smiled. It was a smile of satisfaction, not sympathy. She didn't think Kaye understood assault-helicopter tactics, but this wasn't the time or the place to enlighten him. She led the way into the main hall, where Sykes and Cray were sitting at a table, talking to Colonel Dror. They looked up as Amanda and Dr. Kaye approached.

"Gentlemen, allow me to congratulate you," Kaye said cheerfully. "Omega Force has done it again. It was a brilliant operation. I have been talking to Washington and Tel Aviv. They are extremely pleased."

Cray and Sykes smiled. It was nice to be appreciated, but both of them would have bet a month's pay that Kaye hadn't flown to Beaufort Castle on an assault helicopter to tell them how wonderful they were. They waited for Kaye to go on.

"I am here because the director wishes me to make an on-site inspection to verify that the operation has been successfully completed before he makes his report to the National Security Council and the President." Kaye pronounced the words reverently. It was obvious that to him the director of the CIA ranked just below God.

"No one is doubting you, gentlemen," Kaye continued smoothly. "After all, you have taken Beaufort Castle and you have captured Kamov and his weapons. The operation certainly seems to be over. But remember, it is a CIA operation. We discovered Colonel Sadiq's plot. The director merely wishes one of his own senior officers to confirm that the threat has been eliminated."

Cray didn't remember seeing any CIA agents during the assault on Beaufort Castle. If Kaye was the first wave, he was a little late. Still, there was nothing to be gained by trading insults with him.

"How are you going to report to Washington, Doctor?" he asked quietly.

"Via satellite. I understand you have a SATCOM radio here. Is there some problem, Major?"

"Not with the radio, Doctor. You can use it whenever you wish, but I would wait a minute if I were you. We aren't absolutely certain of the situation. Dr. Hill and Sergeant Blake are down in Professor Kamov's lab, checking things out. They should be here in a few minutes. Better wait and hear what they have to say. You wouldn't want to confuse our friends in Washington with a false report."

Kaye shuddered. If he gave the director a false report that was relayed to the President, it would be the end of his promising career. "How long will we have to wait?"

Cray smiled. He noticed that it was suddenly "we" again. Kaye wasn't always eager to share the credit, but he had no problem sharing the blame. "Not long. Here's Blake now."

Blake entered and walked quickly to the table. He was carrying what looked like a child's toy truck. Two soldiers followed him, pushing a dolly that held a slim, finned object. Blake set the model on the table and smiled with the air of magician introducing a new trick.

"This is a model of a Russian BM-21 Grad multiple-rocket launcher system. 'Grad' means 'hailstorm' in Russian. This is a standard Ural-375D 6 military truck. It has excellent cross-country mobility."

Kaye looked at the model doubtfully. It didn't look particularly impressive. He saw a six-wheeled truck, painted a dull green. On the bed of the truck, behind the cab, there were several rows of tubes that looked like pipes mounted on a rotating pedestal. Nothing he saw implied advanced technology.

Blake pointed at the tubes. "These are the weapons. The forty tubes are the individual rocket launchers. Each launcher holds a standard Russian 122 mm artillery rocket with a high-explosive or chemical warhead. The rockets are preloaded, ready to fire. No preparation or checkout is required before launching. All forty rockets can be fired in a single salvo in less than forty seconds. BM-21s are normally used in groups. They are designed to saturate a target area with large numbers of rockets striking in less than a minute. Reload rockets are normally carried on supporting trucks. Each BM-21 normally has a crew of six. They can reload the launchers and be ready to attack again in less than ten minutes. In an emergency it can be operated by two men, but then you cannot reload rapidly in the field."

Kaye was impressed with Blake's knowledge, but not with the BM-21. It seemed like a crude and obsolete weapon system, unlikely to be effective in modern combat.

"Are you sure this is the weapon that Sadiq intends to use?" he asked. "His movement seems to have plenty of money and excellent contacts. He seems able to get what he wants. Surely he would use something more advanced. Scud missiles, perhaps?"

"I don't think there can be any doubt. We found several hundred 122 mm chemical rockets here. Kamov was modifying their warheads and refilling them with his cobra venom agent. We have found no other rockets or missiles which can deliver chemical agents at Beaufort Castle. It has to be the 122 mm rockets."

Kaye stared at Blake. "I am not convinced, Sergeant. Surely Colonel Sadiq has more effective weapons available." The tone of Kaye's voice was almost a sneer, but Blake wasn't intimidated. Kaye might know more about some things than Blake, but foreign weapon systems wasn't one of them.

"You're making a common mistake, Doctor," Blake said firmly.

Kaye reacted as if he had been slapped. His stare changed to a glare. People didn't talk to him that way. "Would you care to explain that remark, Sergeant?" he said coldly.

"Certainly. You are confusing the weapon with the delivery system. Kamov's agent is the weapon. As long as it gets to the target area and is released, it doesn't matter whether it got there in rockets or was delivered by hand. Scuds are large, complicated missiles. They require special fuels and highly trained crews. Their transporter-launcher vehicles are large and specialized, easily recognized from the air. The Israelis have Patriot missiles. If a few Scuds were launched at them, they could be shot down."

Blake paused and smiled infuriatingly at Kaye. "Is that clear, Doctor?"

Kaye nodded. He was still furious, but he could think of nothing to say. It was hard to win an argument with Blake, particularly if the subject was weapons.

"On the other hand, the BM-21s and their rockets are extremely cheap and simple to operate. The rockets are fueled with a solid propellant at the factory. They have no guidance units or any other electronics. They don't need computers or radar. They don't radiate. There is no way to detect them except visually. And they're common all over the world. All you have to do is get within ten or twelve miles of the target, stop the trucks, aim the launchers and fire. Once the rockets are in the air, nothing will stop them. The Russians normally use them in groups of eighteen. Work it out. That means seven hundred twenty rockets coming at you in forty seconds. Nothing in the world can shoot them all down."

"Everything Sergeant Blake says is true," Cora Hill said quietly. She had entered the room unnoticed while everyone was listening to Blake. "Let me add just one thing. Kamov's selection of the BM-21 system is completely logical. Russian artillery rocket systems have always been designed for chemical warfare. The BM-21 is no exception. It was designed to deliver massive, surprise, saturation chemical attacks. It was originally designed to use hydrogen cyanide, blood gas. Kamov's agent makes it many times more lethal, and we have no defense against it. Believe me, if any military unit is hit like that, there will be no survivors."

No one doubted Dr. Hill. The cool, quiet tone in her voice was utterly convincing.

"Very well, Dr. Hill," Kaye said. "We must accept what you and Sergeant Blake say. After all, you are the experts." He looked at Blake. "How many of these BM-21 systems were here at Beaufort Castle, Sergeant? Can we destroy them before we leave? And can we be sure that

Colonel Sadiq doesn't have other BM-21s and rockets at other locations?''

Blake smiled. He didn't think anyone was going to like what he was about to say, but facts were facts. ''There are no BM-21s here. There is no evidence that there ever have been. Sadiq was preparing Beaufort Castle as a base to support attacks against the Israelis. He is keeping his BM-21 launching systems safe in a bunker complex in the northern Bekaa Valley. They will move south from there to launch the initial attack. Their plan is to bring the launch vehicles here and reload them for a second attack.''

Kaye turned pale. This news would not be popular in Washington. The director wouldn't be pleased. ''What is Sadiq's capability? Do you have any idea how many of these systems he has? Are they ready to be used?''

''Professor Kamov says there are approximately forty BM-21s in the Bekaa Valley. He hasn't personally seen all the vehicles, but he prepared rockets for that number. He supervised the loading of two BM-21s personally to be sure that there were no problems with the modified rockets. By now all the BM-21s are probably loaded and ready for action.''

Kaye frowned. ''A lot of this hangs on what Professor Kamov says. Can we trust him?'' His expression implied that only a fool would say yes. That was understandable. It was part of Kaye's job to trust no one.

Blake shrugged. Mind reading was not his specialty.

''I believe we can,'' Cora Hill said quietly. ''Kamov is afraid he will be killed unless we help him. He thinks Sadiq will kill him for giving us information or the Israelis will get him if Sadiq doesn't. We are his only chance. He desperately wants to get out of the Middle East and be given political asylum in the United States. He is trying to show us how valuable he can be so that we will put in a word for him.''

Kaye smiled bleakly. He could accept that. He was far more comfortable with people who were trying to get something they needed desperately than with idealists. He looked back at Blake. "Assuming everything you say is true, Sergeant, what can we do to stop the attack?"

Blake turned to face Kaye. Policy was decided above Blake's pay grade. Still, it was a reasonable question. "They can be ready to fire ten minutes after they reach the launching area. That's cutting it too fine. We have to attack and destroy the BM-21s before they get there, and the farther from the Israeli border, the better."

Kaye smiled faintly. It was time to put the ball in the Army's court. "Thank you, Sergeant, that was an excellent briefing. Let's assume that everything we've heard is true. General Sykes, this is obviously a military matter. Will you have Major Cray prepare a plan to destroy these rocket launchers? Perhaps Colonel Dror can assist him."

Cray frowned. It was always a bad sign when Dr. Kaye began to say "you" instead of "we." But Kaye was right. It was a military responsibility to destroy enemy forces. If Americans had to do it, there was no one else but Omega Force. Cray couldn't pass the buck. He glanced at Sykes. The general nodded. Cray sighed. No rest for the wicked. "Blake, get Captain Tower. Captain Stuart, get me a complete helicopter status and report back as soon as possible. We have planning to do."

16

Amanda Stuart gave her MH-60K Blackhawk one more check. It was fueled, armed and ready to go. The Hellfire missiles and 2.75-inch rocket pods beneath the short stubby wings of the ESSS gave it a lethal look that contrasted strangely with the utilitarian appearance of the standard transport versions nearby. She had faith in the armed Blackhawks, but she wished that Omega Force had more than four. She smiled wryly. While she was wishing, she might as well wish for an air combat brigade with three battalions of Apaches. Four armed Blackhawks were what they had, and they would have to get the job done.

Waiting was not something Amanda did well. She knew she was getting premission nerves, but there was nothing to do but wait and worry until someone located the targets. She bent down and checked the rocket-pod firing cables one more time. Hearing footsteps, she stood up quickly. Tower and Colonel Dror were rapidly approaching her Blackhawk. Amanda felt a cold knot in her stomach. She could tell by the way they moved that it was time for action.

She climbed into the cockpit and strapped herself into the pilot's seat. Dave Tower slipped into the copilot's seat to her right. Colonel Dror got in and leaned over her shoulder. She brought up the moving map display and looked at them expectantly.

Dror pointed at the map. "They are coming down the Bekaa Valley. One of our remotely piloted vehicles picked them up. Its sensor indicated approximately fifty vehicles.

Most of them appeared to be trucks. The rest looked like tracked vehicles.''

Amanda noticed that Dror was using the past tense.

''Are your people still getting data from the RPV?'' she asked.

Dror shook his head. ''Its controller sent it in for a closer look. It stopped transmitting suddenly. They seem to have shot it down. Another one is being sent up, but it will take time to reach the area. We cannot wait. Let's go.''

Amanda started her engines. The Blackhawk vibrated as its twin turbines whined into life. She checked her instrument display. All set. The whine of its twin turbine engines rose to a shriek as Amanda went to full power, and the Blackhawk lifted into the air. As soon as she was clear of the castle walls, Amanda turned to the south and started down. She would keep the mass of the mountain between her and any radars to the north until she had descended to the valley floor. She watched the radar altimeter and took quick glances out her cockpit window. The closer she stayed to the side of the mountain, the less likely it was that any radar to the north could detect her. But if she made a mistake and flew into the mountain, it would kill her just as dead as a surface-to-air missile.

The reading on the radar altimeter was dropping rapidly. Amanda leveled off smoothly at one hundred feet above the valley floor and turned to the right. She followed the base of the mountain around to the north. She could see the Litani River below her, beginning to curve toward the north. This was it! The mass of the mountain no longer shielded the Blackhawk from radars to the north. She would have to depend on low flying, hugging the contours of the ground to protect her.

She checked her displays. Her engines were running smoothly, and the radar altimeter still indicated one hundred feet. A number of lights were blinking on the display and control panel. Amanda glanced at the display. It indi-

cated heavy radar activity to the south, in Israel, and to the
north, in the Bekaa Valley. The Syrian air-defense surveillance radars were alert and maintaining a steady search of
the area. There were no indications that a fire-control radar was tracking her. That was good, but the situation
could change rapidly. She stayed low and watched her displays, ready to take instant action if the attack alarm suddenly sounded.

She glanced at the moving map display. The glowing
green dot was moving slowly toward the Bekaa Valley.
Tower was sitting quietly in the copilot's seat, and Dror was
still looking over her shoulder. Neither of them had said
anything since they took off. They knew better than to distract their pilot when she was flying fast and low in the
dark.

She could relax for a moment as long as she didn't take
her eyes off her display. There was one thing she had to
know. "How's the international politics going? Are the Israelis going to support the attack?"

"Not at the moment," Dror snapped. Amanda could tell
from the tone in his voice that he was angry. "Your government is still demanding that we take no action in Lebanon. We have forces standing by, but Tel Aviv and
Washington are still arguing. It is ridiculous. There are at
least fifty vehicles to destroy. Your people are good, but
four helicopters are simply not enough to get the job done."

Amanda agreed with him, but it wasn't her decision.
There was nothing more to say. They flew on through the
dark. The glowing green dot seemed to crawl across the
moving map display, but that was deceptive. Every minute
brought them two miles closer to the target area. They
would find out the hard way if four Blackhawks could do
the job.

"TARGET AREA in one minute," Amanda announced.

Tower armed the Blackhawk's weapons system. A row of

green lights on the weapon-control console came on. The 2.75-inch rockets and Hellfire missiles were checked out and ready to fire. Amanda checked the .50-caliber machine gun she controlled. It was loaded and ready to fire. They were as ready as they would ever be. She stared at the display on the MFD. Now the Blackhawk was flying along a dirt road at one hundred twenty miles per hour.

Amanda continued staring at her MFD, which showed the road and the low-lying hills to the side. She glanced at the moving map display. It insisted they were in the right place. All right, she should see the target now. She went to maximum magnification and looked again. There, at the upper edge of the display, a series of dots were moving down the road, headed south toward the border of Israel. She turned the Blackhawk away from the road and began to fly along the tops of the hills. Colonel Sadiq's force might have air-defense capability. In that case, a hill, even a small one, would be a mighty comforting thing to duck behind.

The picture in the MFD seemed to grow larger and fill the screen as Amanda flew closer and closer. She looked at Tower. She didn't think that there could be two large truck convoys coming south out of the Bekaa Valley on the same road. Still, Tower was the strike force commander. It was up to him to call the shot.

"Multiple-vehicle convoy approximately eight thousand yards ahead. I estimate fifty or more. That should be the target. Shall I go closer and make an identification pass, or shall we attack now?"

Tower thought quickly. They would have to get considerably closer to see more details or markings on the trucks. There was no sign the men in the vehicles ahead had detected the Blackhawks yet. But helicopters are inherently noisy. They could hardly be expected to ignore a Blackhawk making a low pass. He wanted desperately to take the enemy by surprise.

"What do you think, Colonel?" he asked. Tower wasn't trying to pass the buck. He was in command, and the decision was his responsibility, but Dror was a highly experienced combat officer and he knew Lebanon better than Tower. His opinion was worth hearing.

"One moment," Dror said. He spoke rapidly into his radio in Hebrew, stopped, listened and spoke again. "We have an RPV about fifteen miles to the north. It confirms that there is no other large group of vehicles moving in this end of the Bekaa. It must be them. It is your decision, but I say attack now. Take them by surprise if you can. There are a great many vehicles for four helicopters to destroy."

Tower agreed. "Let's go, Captain Stuart. Tell your people we are attacking now, Colonel."

Amanda spoke quickly into her microphone. "Omega Flight, this is Omega Leader. Prepare to attack at thirty second intervals. Break left after you make your first run, and make a second attack. I am attacking now."

She went to full power as the acknowledgments crackled in her head set.

"Rocket run first pass," she said, and turned the Blackhawk until she was flying straight up the road at one hundred twenty miles per hour. The images of the vehicles in the MFD grew larger. Amanda could see a long column of six-wheeled trucks moving along the road, broken here and there by a full-tracked vehicle. Tower pushed a switch, and the Blackhawk's stub wings were suddenly wreathed in orange fire as 2.75-inch rockets shot from the launchers. Amanda could see each rocket as a brightly glowing dot as it streaked at the enemy. She pulled the trigger, and the Blackhawk shuddered as her .50-caliber Browning machine gun raked the oncoming trucks with bursts of armor-piercing incendiary bullets.

Amanda saw a series of bright flashes along the road as the rockets struck and their five-pound high-explosive warheads detonated. The leading trucks were caught in a lethal pattern of explosions as the shower of rockets struck like a giant shotgun blast. The BM-21 trucks had no armor to protect them, so one hit was more than enough. Three were already burning. One exploded in a ball of fire. Amanda was fascinated, but she knew she must avoid target fixation. Flying into the ground at one hundred twenty miles per hour could kill you just as dead as an enemy weapon.

She pulled the Blackhawk into a hard left turn and glanced out the cockpit window. She saw another series of explosions flashing along the road as Omega Two started its attack. Suddenly she heard a sound that froze her blood. The attack alarm was beeping insistently. An antiaircraft fire-control radar was operating nearby, trying to lock on. She shot a glance at the display even as she twisted and dived toward the cover of the closest hill.

"Zoos!" she shouted into her microphone. "Omega Flight, break! Break! Zoos in the area. Zoos!"

Tower and Dror didn't understand. They weren't Army aviators. If they had been, they would have known that "Zoo" is the warning word for a Russian ZSU, a self-propelled armored vehicle with multiple automatic cannon and built-in radar fire control. Nothing was more dangerous to a helicopter at low altitude.

The cockpit seemed to rock and tilt crazily as Amanda took violent evasive action. Streams of glowing, bright green tracers tore through the air where the Blackhawk had been seconds before. She shot over the crest of the hill. The down wash from her main rotor blades threw up clouds of sand behind her helicopter as she cleared the top of the hill by less than twenty feet. She slowed and brought the Blackhawk into the hover mode. The ZSU was a direct fire weapon. It couldn't hit her unless it could see her. As long as she was behind the hill, she was safe. But that cut both ways. None of the Blackhawk's weapons could hit a target she couldn't see. To continue the attack, she would have to go up again and take her chances.

She checked her survivability-systems display and control panel. The threat-warning display indicated "multiple Soviet ZSU-23-4s with Gun Dish radars." That was bad news. The ZSU-23-4 was armed with four 23 mm automatic cannon. It could fire a 30-round burst of high-explosive incendiary shells in less than a second. The Blackhawk had no armor. A burst from a ZSU-23-4 could tear it to pieces. Amanda thought hard, trying to remember everything she had ever heard about the ZSU-23-4. The damned thing must have some weakness!

Think, Stuart! Think! Its range was short, less than three thousand yards, but that didn't help. There was no way she could stand back and attack it at long range, Suddenly something came to her. She could almost hear the voice of the bored warrant officer as she remembered that the Gun Dish radar was an excellent design, but had clutter-rejection problems when trying to lock on and track targets below two hundred feet. A low-altitude engagement could take twenty to thirty seconds from the time the radar detected the target until the guns opened fire. She hoped the warrant officer was right. She was about to bet her life on it.

Ten seconds had flashed by. Dror was speaking rapidly into his radio, doubtless giving his friends in Israel a play-by-play account. That didn't matter, since there was no time for a council of war. They had only one weapon system that could take out a ZSU, the Hellfire missiles. Amanda spoke quickly to Tower.

"Stand by, we're going up. Use the missiles. The targets are ZSU-23-4s. They will look like tanks. They have large, boxy turrets with a radar dish on top. Take the nearest one out. Do it fast, before they can lock on us."

Tower nodded and checked his controls. There were other things he would have rather done than play tag with a ZSU-23-4, but the Army paid him to take chances.

"Missiles armed. Any time you're ready."

The Blackhawk's twin turbines shrieked as Amanda went to war emergency power and took her up. She watched the picture on her MFD as the Blackhawk rose from behind the hill like a dull black ghost. The MFD suddenly showed the road, illuminated here and there by shattered burning trucks. Something erupted in a flickering fountain of flashing, flickering lights. Amanda's heart almost stopped as she saw a ZSU-23-4 firing burst after burst down the road.

Someone was making a rocket run. It was brave but risky. More green tracers shot skyward as a second ZSU opened fire. Tower didn't hesitate. He triggered the laser designator and fired. An AGM-114 Hellfire missile hissed from its launcher and flashed toward the ZSU. The Hellfire struck, and its warhead detonated. Its effect on the ZSU was spectacular. A white-hot jet of gas and molten metal lanced through its armor and struck one of the cannon magazines. Dozens of 23 mm rounds exploded like a string of giant firecrackers. The ZSU began to burn and explode spectacularly.

One down! Amanda looked up. She saw a series of rapid yellow flashes as a burst of 23 mm shells ripped into the Blackhawk flying up the road. It nosed up and began to burn, trailing a tongue of orange flame. The pilot fought the controls for a few seconds, then the main rotor failed, and the Blackhawk struck the ground and vanished in a huge ball of fire.

The second ZSU's turret was traversing rapidly. Amanda could see the round disk of its Gun Dish radar swinging toward her like an accusing eye. In a few seconds she would be looking straight down the muzzles of four automatic cannons. To stay up and try to fire another Hellfire was suicide. She started down, dropping toward the cover of the hill. The ZSU gunner knew his business. His radar wasn't locked on, but he must have caught the Blackhawk's mo-

tion in his optical night sight. Instantly he took a chanc
and fired by eye. A swarm of 23 mm cannon shells flashe
at Amanda at three thousand feet per second. A spot on th
hill twenty yards to the Blackhawk's left suddenly ex
ploded in flashes of fire and fountains of dirt and sand a
thirty shells tore into the hill.

The gunner corrected and fired again. Too late! His shel
shrieked through empty air. Amanda was safe for the mc
ment behind the hill. Forcing herself to stop shaking, sh
spoke urgently into her microphone.

"Omega Flight, this is Omega Leader. Report."

"Leader, Omega Two. I am behind cover about tw
hundred yards to your north. They got Omega Three. F
blew up. I'm ready to attack again, if you give the order."

Omega Two's pilot didn't sound enthusiastic. Amanc
didn't blame him. The ZSU-23s were murderous. Nov
where the hell was number four?

"Leader, Omega Four. We've got trouble. We took
couple of hits. One of my engines is out, and my copilot
wounded. We've lost weapons control. I'm headed for t
border."

Amanda couldn't argue with that. "Good luck, Four,
she said, and looked at Tower. He had heard the message
It wasn't going to work. There were only two Blackhaw
left. They might get another ZSU and a few more trucks
they attacked again, but they weren't going to win. It w
Tower's decision, as he was in command. Amanda wou
attack again if he gave the order, but she knew th
wouldn't survive.

"All right," Tower said reluctantly, "let's go. Atta
in—"

"Stop, hold your position!" Colonel Dror's voi
crackled with authority. He was not in command, but
had been giving orders in combat for twenty years. I
stinctively Amanda turned toward him. Dror smiled wic
edly. "Stand by, Captain Stuart. I think you are about
receive a message."

As if on cue, Amanda heard an unknown voice in her headset, speaking in precise, slightly accented English. "Omega Leader, this is Omega Star Leader. Stay clear of the road. I am attacking in thirty seconds."

Omega Star? The message was on the correct frequency and the basic call sign was correct, but there was no Omega Star. What the hell was going on? She glanced at Tower. He seemed equally surprised. Only Colonel Dror seemed to understand.

Amanda heard Omega Star's voice again in her headset, speaking a language she didn't understand. Colonel Dror's smile grew broader. "Take us up for a look, Captain Stuart," he said. "I think our Arab friends are going to be too busy to shoot at us."

Amanda increased her power and took the Blackhawk up. She hovered a few feet above the crest of the hill, ready to drop back instantly if a ZSU fired. She respected Colonel Dror's opinion, but she wasn't willing to bet her life on it. She stared at her MFD. Something was going on. She could see a ZSU a few hundred yards ahead. It was paying no attention to her. Its turret was turning rapidly, pointing its guns and radar south along the road.

Amanda looked to the south. For a moment she saw nothing. Then a flash of motion caught her eye. Four dim shapes were flying up the road at high speed, less than fifty feet above the ground. They suddenly seemed to explode into balls of fire and streaks of flame. Amanda's night-vision goggles were almost overloaded. She knew what she was seeing, attack helicopters, blasting Colonel Sadiq's force with rockets, guns and missiles.

The nearby ZSU was bathed in yellow fire as a dozen cannon shells struck and tore through its thin armor. There was a tremendous explosion. The ZSU's turret was blown off the hull and hurled through the air by the force of the blast. The road and the valley around it were filled with burning and exploding vehicles. The four attackers were turning left, flashing over Amanda's hill, but the attack didn't stop. Another flight of helicopters was coming up the road, firing continuously. The surviving ZSUs fired back. Red and green tracers crisscrossed as they fired frantically, and the attackers returned devastating bursts of heavy automatic-cannon fire that seemed to never miss.

Amanda watched tensely, ready to take evasive action as the first four attackers shot by the Blackhawk. One was less than a hundred feet away. Her night-vision goggles showed it clearly, a lethal angular shape that looked like a giant enraged dragonfly. It was the ugliest and the deadliest attack helicopter in the world, an American AH-64A Apache. Amanda shrieked with glee. She hoped she hadn't deafened Tower, but she knew what Apaches could do. If Colonel Sadiq's men didn't know, they were finding out the hard way.

But where had the Apaches come from? There were no U.S. Army Apaches closer than Germany. Had General Sykes worked a minor miracle? A second group of Apaches flashed by. Amanda saw the six-pointed star painted on their sides. Then she knew. The U.S. Army wasn't the only military force in the world that operated Apaches. That was fine with Amanda. She loved Apaches with a burning passion as long as they were on her side, and these were.

She had to be sure Tower understood. "Israeli Apaches! A squadron of Israeli Apaches!" she said gleefully.

"Disregard that last remark, Tower!" Dror's tone was stern though he was almost laughing. "Captain Stuart is obviously suffering from combat fatigue. She is imagining things. There is only one squadron of Apaches in the Israeli Defense Forces, and they are conducting night firing exercises twenty miles south of the border. It is impossible for them to be here in Lebanon."

Tower smiled. "If you say so, we believe you, Colonel. You are the expert. If you don't see any Israeli helicopters, they're not there."

He glanced at the picture on his MFD. A third and fourth group of Apaches were attacking. All the ZSUs had been knocked out. The Apaches' computer-aimed 30 mm cannon fired where their gunners looked, and the heavy explosive-incendiary shells were devastatingly effective against the unarmored BM-21 launchers. Truck after truck was hit. It was a slaughter now, and the Israeli Apache crews were pitiless. They knew what the trucks carried, and they were grimly determined that none of them would survive. In three or four minutes it was over. Nothing was left along the road but the shattered hulks of burning and exploding vehicles.

Cray, General Sykes and even Dr. Kaye would be happy when they got the report. Tower started to key his microphone. He could see a small problem. Just what was he going to report? He smiled at Dror. "It looks like we are going to have to be a little creative in our reports, Colonel. We'd better get our act together. What do you want to say?"

Dror looked pained. "I hope you are not implying that I would distort my report for political purposes. I will tell the exact truth. The enemy force was located and completely destroyed." He smiled. "I will also add that American helicopters are amazingly effective in combat."

17

The whine of the Blackhawk's engines died away as Amanda Stuart cut the power. Dave Tower sat in the copilot's seat and looked out the cabin window. The flight line of the Israeli air base was crowded with Omega Force Blackhawks. The evacuation of Beaufort Castle must have gone without incident. That was fine with Tower. All he wanted out of life at the moment was a hot meal and twelve hours of sleep.

He followed Colonel Dror and Amanda out the cabin door. A flash of headlights caught Tower's eye. Two jeeps were moving rapidly down the flight line. They pulled to a stop by the Blackhawk, and an Israeli soldier climbed quickly out of the lead vehicle. He was heavily armed and looked ready for combat. That wasn't unusual, but the man's steel helmet was. It was painted a glossy white with two large red characters in Hebrew. Tower looked inquiringly at Dror.

"Shoter Tzavi," Dror said. He smiled. "Excuse me, Israeli defense forces military police." Tower winced. Something was up. He couldn't remember having committed any crimes in Israel, but the two MP jeeps weren't there as welcoming committee. The MP saluted and began to speak rapidly in Hebrew. Dror nodded and turned to Tower. "There are new developments. We are wanted immediately. Also Captain Stuart."

They climbed into the jeeps and were driven rapidly to the headquarters building. They followed the Israeli M into the briefing room. Cray and Dr. Kaye were already there. Kaye looked up and smiled. "Gentlemen, Captain Stuart, allow me to congratulate you. From all reports, your mission was a complete success. The Israeli commanders say the performance of our helicopters was amazing. Omega Force is a credit to the United States Armed Forces."

Tower smiled and studied the wall map. The Israelis had obviously not told Kaye what had really happened. It would be interesting to see how he felt if he ever found out.

"That is not why I asked you here, however. The Israeli high command is pushing the United States to agree to a military operation to destroy the terrorist base in the northern Bekaa Valley. General Sykes is talking to Washington now. If there is to be an attack, Omega Force may well be involved. We should know shortly."

Tower sighed. He had seen enough of the Bekaa Valley to last him a lifetime. He doubted that his feelings mattered much to Washington.

The smile vanished from Kaye's face and was replaced by his usual look of cold superiority. "In the meantime, there is the question of security. You will recall that Captain Tower suggested that our plans have been repeatedly compromised during this operation. I believe I have evidence indicating who is responsible." He reached into his briefcase and took out a tape recorder.

"After Captain Stuart and Miss Almori were rescued in Beirut, I took the liberty of recording Captain Stuart's report. Let me play it." He pushed a button, and Amanda heard herself describing what had happened when she and Saada Almori had been kidnapped. She shuddered. The fear and humiliation she had suffered was one of the worst experiences of her life. The tape stopped. Kaye looked at Amanda.

"Is there anything you wish to add, Captain Stuart?"

Amanda was puzzled. She shook her head. "No, that's

exactly what happened. I'm sure. I saw or heard everything."

"Yes, Captain, and you understood everything you heard. I wasn't aware that you understood Arabic."

Amanda looked startled. "I don't speak Arabic, but I didn't need to. Everything they said was in English."

"Precisely, and it was in English so that you would understand it and believe what you thought was happening."

"Just a minute, Doctor," Tower broke in. "If you're suggesting what happened to Saada Almori was faked, I can tell you you're wrong. I led the rescue party. Saada Almori was naked when we got there. There were marks all over her body. She was really hurting. They beat the hell out of her."

Kaye smiled coldly. "You are not showing your usual intelligence, Captain Tower. Concentrate on the main point. Saada Almori's native language is Arabic. The men who kidnapped her were Arabs. Stop and think. If you were going to torture a woman, would you talk to her in a foreign language?"

Tower could see the logic in what Kaye said. Still, he wasn't completely convinced. "But they did beat her," he persisted. "I saw the marks. That wasn't faked."

"True, but I spoke to the Israeli doctor who examined her. Her injuries are spectacular but superficial. It was undoubtedly painful, but if Miss Almori is what I think she is, a fanatic and a terrorist, what better way to convince us that what she says is true? If I'm right, and I believe I am, she'd certainly be willing to suffer for her cause, to appear to be tortured for helping us."

"I don't know," Tower protested. "I understand what you're saying, but she has given us information and most of it has checked out. Would she have done that if she is a terrorist?"

Kaye smiled coldly. "Yes, she has given us information, and every time we have acted on it, we have encountered some kind of trap. You are lucky you are still alive. On Cyprus and in Lebanon, every time Saada Almori has been involved, it's been the same. Now, think again. Since we moved to Israel, we haven't told her what we intend to do and she has been unable to communicate with anyone. At Beaufort Castle and in the Bekaa Valley, we achieved total surprise. As you said yourself, Tower, 'The first time is happenstance, the second time coincidence, but the third time is enemy action.' In Miss Almori's case, we are long past coincidence. It is clearly enemy action."

"All right, Doctor, you make a strong case," Tower said reluctantly. "I'm not sure she's guilty, but we can't take a chance. What do we do with her, turn her over to the Israelis?"

Kaye smiled coldly. "Certainly not. At least, not yet. Miss Almori is our friend. We have been neglecting her. Now we will do everything we can to show her that we love her. We will gain her confidence and give her false information to feed to Colonel Sadiq. We have already started. Preston has had her personal possessions flown in from Beirut. He will give them to her and keep a friendly eye on her."

PRESTON WAS indeed keeping a very attentive eye on Saada Almori. He could count on the fingers of one hand assignments as pleasant as this during his career with the CIA! Whatever else Saada was, she was an exceptionally attractive woman. It would have been difficult not to notice that.

Saada had just stepped out of the shower. She was wearing a loose Israeli army bathrobe that kept falling open as she moved around the drab room. The Israeli army didn't believe in giving its women officers fancy quarters. There was nothing for Preston to look at but Saada. Since she was wearing only a semitransparent bra and panties under the robe, Preston found the view entrancing.

She smiled winningly at Preston. "I cannot thank you enough for getting my clothes and other things from Beirut. It means a great deal to me to have clean clothes and my cosmetics. You cannot know how much."

She moved closer to Preston and continued in a low husky voice. "You are my only friend here. You care for me as a person. The Israelis hate me, and your leader thinks of me as a thing to squeeze information from and then throw away. But you are different, you care." She let the robe fall open again as she turned to her cosmetics case.

Preston smiled. The view was certainly entertaining, but Saada was putting on a show for some reason. It was sad but true; all women didn't find him irresistible. She wanted something. Most Arab women were modest, particularly with strangers. She was acting this way for a reason. He didn't feel that he was in danger. He had a Smith & Wesson 9 mm automatic in a shoulder holster under his coat, and it was obvious that Saada was unarmed. There was no place for her to get a weapon. The Israelis had x-rayed and searched her suitcases carefully. There was nothing in them but clothes and cosmetics.

Saada reached in her cosmetics case and took out a can of hair spray. She looked in the mirror. She didn't think that Preston was a fool. If the Americans didn't suspect her, he wouldn't be here. He was watching her, of course, but he didn't seem particularly alert. He was relaxed and enjoying the show she was putting on. With her back to Preston, she examined the can of hair spray. It showed no signs of tampering. She turned a ring on the bottom of the can and put her hand on the nozzle. She made sure that the arrow was pointing away from her. Ready. She took a deep breath, held it, turned toward Preston and sprayed him in the face.

For a second nothing seemed to happen. Preston's face showed a look of sheer surprise. Saada's action was totally incomprehensible. Then he reacted, but it was too late. He eyes and lungs were burning. The room seemed to blur around him. He tried to reach for his pistol, but his hand and fingers didn't respond. He fell heavily to the floor and lay still. Saada snatched his pistol from his holster and moved quickly to the far corner of the room. Her lungs were burning as she tried to keep holding her breath. Her instructors had warned her to do that as long as possible whenever using the spray. It didn't contain Kamov's agent, but the chemical it sprayed was bad enough.

She could stand it no longer. She took a deep, gasping breath. Nothing happened. God is great! She looked closely at Preston. He was dead or unconscious; it didn't matter which. She felt no remorse. She considered herself a soldier, and Preston was the enemy. Time to go. She opened the door and darted into the deserted hall. She slipped inside the room two doors down. An Israeli army captain lived there, but he was not there.

Saada moved to the closet. The Israeli captain was about her size and build. She took a uniform from the closet and slipped into it. It was a little tight in places, but it would have to do. She set the officer's cap on her head at the same jaunty angle Israeli woman soldiers favored. She looked in the mirror. She would pass if no one looked too closely.

The front door was at the end of the hall. Saada walked confidently to the door and stepped outside. It wouldn't do to look as if she had anything to hide. There were two jeeps parked near the door. She slipped into the closest one, turned the ignition switch, let the engine warm up for a few seconds and drove away toward the main gate some six or seven hundred yards away. Her nerves screamed as she fought the urge to drive as fast as she could. It seemed to take forever, but she reached the gate and stopped.

The sentry in the gate house was bored. His attention was concentrated on keeping unauthorized people out, not keeping people in. He glanced at the vehicle's markings and looked casually at Saada and smiled. If only all army captains looked like that. He gave her a casual salute and waved her through. Saada smiled and drove out onto the road. Dawn wasn't far away, but she was only six miles from the nearest town. She knew how to contact members of the Palestine underground there. Once she disappeared into the Arab population, not even Mossad could find her. She looked into the rearview mirror. There was no sign of pursuit. She drove on into the night.

CRAY SAT in the briefing room and tried to stay awake. He was tired of endless briefings. Perhaps he was being punished for his sins. Hell might merely be an endless series of briefings he must attend. At least Colonel Dror had brought some hot coffee. He poured himself another steaming cup and tried to concentrate on what Dr. Hill was saying.

"I think the evidence is clear, gentlemen. Professor Kamov was very forthcoming. He is desperate and will do anything to get political asylum in the United States. The Israeli experts concur in my evaluation. The main terrorist base is a large bunker in the northern Bekaa Valley, close to the Syrian border. Kamov was installing equipment and training people to produce his cobra venom agent there. It was nearly complete when he was sent to support the attack on Israel. Within a few days it will be capable of producing the agent in significant quantities."

Kaye leaned forward. "Can this facility operate without Professor Kamov's personal supervision?"

"Yes. Kamov had trained a number of people in the techniques required. It was part of his contract with Colonel Sadiq. It would be safer, and things might go faster if he were there, but the people he trained will be able to operate the facility."

Kaye frowned. "Are you absolutely certain, Dr. Hill? Can Sadiq's people or the Syrians operate the equipment by themselves? Think carefully. This is an extremely critical point. Everything depends on it.''

It was Cora Hill's turn to frown. She wasn't used to having her professional judgment questioned, even by the CIA. ''It is my professional opinion that they can,'' she said firmly. ''It is not wise to underestimate the capabilities of Arab scientists, Dr. Kaye. Many of them are brilliant men. Believe me, they can.''

Colonel Dror had been sitting silently, listening to Cora Hill's words. He rose to his feet and spoke before Kaye could reply. ''Gentlemen, Dr. Hill, Captain Stuart,'' he said formally. ''Let me say that our experts have examined the evidence carefully. They agree completely with Dr. Hill. They have briefed the cabinet and the general staff.''

He looked around the room. ''You are not going to like this, but that cannot be helped. Israeli security cannot be risked. You have all done the best you could, but it hasn't been enough. My government has reached a decision. It was unanimous. That facility must be totally destroyed. Preparations for the attack have been authorized. Our air force has been alerted. They will use low-yield tactical nuclear weapons. The attack will be conducted during the next twenty-four hours.''

Kaye looked stunned. ''Surely you can't be serious, Colonel! That is what we have all been working so hard to prevent. I will agree that Kamov's facility must be destroyed, but there is no need to consider an Israeli attack. We will send in Omega Force. They will destroy the facility. There is no need for an Israeli attack, certainly not one using nuclear weapons. You must contact your government at once and tell them to cancel their plans.''

Dror shook his head. ''With all due respect, Dr. Kaye, you are a brilliant man, but you don't understand military matters.'' He pushed a switch and flashed a slide on the screen. ''Look at this. The map shows the situation in the Bekaa Valley. The red symbols show the location of Syrian

military units in the area. You will notice that there are a
great many, well over a hundred, and they are concentrated in the northern end of the valley near the Syrian
border. I will not bore you with the details, but the Syrian
forces include a full armored division, two commando brigades and more than thirty surface-to-air missile batteries.
A mechanized infantry division is in the process of cross-
ing into Lebanon to reinforce them. We are speaking of
over forty thousand soldiers, well-trained and fully
equipped with modern weapons."

Dror picked up a pointer and indicated a spot on the
map. "We were able to determine from the information Dr.
Hill obtained that Kamov's bunker is located approximately here. You will notice that it is surrounded by Syrian military units. Omega Force cannot get there, and it is
extremely unlikely that they could destroy the bunker if
they could. Our information indicates the facility is de-
fended by a Syrian commando battalion, eight hundred
officers and men. Syrian commandos are elite troops. I
have fought them more than once. Believe me, they are
good, and they are well dug in behind minefields and
barbed wire. There are thousands of other Syrian soldiers
who could reach the site in ten or fifteen minutes. It is impossible. It would be a suicide mission, and your men
would die for nothing. They would fail."

Kaye wasn't convinced. "There must be another way,"
he insisted, "one that doesn't involve nuclear weapons.
Suppose your air force supports Omega Force and you
could reinforce them with a battalion or two of your para-
troops. We could attack the same way we did at Beaufort
Castle. Wouldn't that work?"

Dror sighed. Working with civilians, no matter how
brilliant, wasn't easy. He flashed a second slide on the
screen. The mass of red symbols vanished, replaced by a
network of interlocking red circles. "No, and here is the
reason. These circles show the areas covered by the Syrian

air-defense missiles. Any planes or helicopters that attempt to carry troops into the Bekaa Valley will be detected and attacked repeatedly. These are not obsolete missiles. Just before the breakup of the Soviet empire, the Russians sold the Syrians their latest models, SA-8s and SA-10s. It would require two dozen planes at a minimum to carry in a battalion of paratroopers. It would be a slaughter. I doubt that a single aircraft would reach the target.''

He paused and smiled bleakly at Dr. Kaye. ''Believe me, Doctor, we Israelis are not always lovable, but we do understand war. We are not eager to use nuclear weapons, but we have considered every alternative. We see none that will work. A large air attack with conventional weapons? We could lose a hundred planes and still not be certain of success. A large-scale ground attack? We could take the Bekaa Valley if we had to, but it would require several divisions and take five or six days of hard fighting, at best. A nuclear strike with a few planes may achieve surprise. It has the best chance of success. I know that this is not what you want to hear, but those are the facts. If you do not believe me, ask your own experts.''

General Sykes didn't wait to be asked. ''Colonel Dror is right,'' he said quietly. ''I don't like the answer any better than you do, but I don't see any workable alternative.''

''I can't accept that answer,'' Kaye said. ''You are the military experts, but I don't think you realize what will really happen if Israel uses nuclear weapons against an Arab state. You'll see the damnedest war the Middle East has ever seen. That has to be prevented at all costs. General Sykes, please come with me. We will contact Washington immediately. Colonel Dror, contact your government at once. Tell them the United States will destroy Kamov's facility completely in the next twenty-four hours. They must delay action until then. Major Cray, in the meantime, study the situation again. See if you can come up with a workable plan. This meeting is adjourned.''

Kaye rose and stalked out the door. Cray stared at the red circles on the screen. He had been shot at with guided missiles. He knew what they could do. Kaye's words seemed to hang in the air, "at all costs." Cray had a dismal feeling he knew who would have to pay those costs. Well, the Army didn't pay him to make national policy. Combat operations was what he did. He turned the problem over in his mind again and again, but he could see no solution. It reminded him of another famous situation in military history, the charge of the Light Brigade. He didn't like that comparison.

For the next hour they went at it. Amanda Stuart pored over the map, trying to find a route that might let their helicopters slip through the Syrian defenses. Cray and Tower discussed attack options once they got there. It was an exercise in futility. The building that housed Kamov's equipment was a large, concrete structure, with heavily reinforced roof and walls. It would take heavy weapons or large quantities of explosives to destroy it. Even if they had the weapons, the problem of the Syrian commando battalion remained. Omega Force was good, but so were the Syrians. Man for man, Omega Force was better, but not enough to overcome odds of six to one.

They were still spinning their wheels when General Sykes and Colonel Dror entered the briefing room. Sykes didn't waste time on formalities. "Washington says we will destroy the facility. The Israelis have agreed to wait twenty-four hours while we try. The Air Force will send in a special attack unit to do the job."

Cray almost breathed a sigh of relief, but something in Sykes's expression told him that they hadn't dodged the bullet yet.

"That's the good news. There is still one problem. The Air Force commander says they will have to use laser-guided weapons and that the target must be pinpointed.

Somebody has to go in and laser designate the target from the ground."

Cray didn't have to ask. He knew who that somebody was.

Sykes turned to Amanda Stuart. "Captain, is there any way you can see that we can get one helicopter into the target area?"

Amanda thought hard. She was the best MH-60K Blackhawk pilot available. If it could be done, it was up to her. She didn't like the odds, but she had volunteered to be a special-operations helicopter pilot. It was time to pay her dues. "I think I can, General," she said quietly. "It will be a hell of a flight, though. I'll have to fly so low I'll be scraping the ground most of the way. I can't promise anything, but I'll do the best I can."

Sykes smiled. It was the kind of answer he liked. "All right, I'll inform the Air Force it's a go. Cray, pick your party. Be ready to go as soon as it gets dark."

18

Amanda Stuart was flying with every ounce of skill an concentration she could summon. She hadn't been exag gerating when she told General Sykes it would be a hell c a flight, but she hadn't realized just how bad it would be Fortunately the extra eight men in the passenger compar ment made no difference to the helicopter's handling.

She had crossed the Israeli border fifteen minutes ea lier. Now she was working her way north and east, thread ing her way through the hills that formed the western edg of the Bekaa Valley. The survivability-systems control pan was a mass of glowing, blinking lights as the radar senso detected dozens of Syrian radars. Amanda glanced quick at the display. It showed intense radar activity from do ens of points in the Bekaa Valley.

She was flying lower and faster in the dark than she ha ever flown before. The terrain-avoidance radars were gi ing continuous warnings. If this had been a peacetime e ercise, she would have been court-martialed for breakir every safety regulation in the book. She had no choice. H only chance was to stay so low and so close to the sides the hills that radar beams bouncing off the Blackhaw would be lost in the stronger return signals from th ground.

A quick glance at her displays told her that her speed w sixty miles per hour and that both engines were runni smoothly. The radar altimeter indicated thirty feet, but s couldn't count on it. This close to the ground she could something before it could warn her. She stared at the i frared picture of the ground ahead in her MFD and concentrated on her flying.

Tower was sitting at her side in the copilot's seat, checking the moving map display. It was up to him to tell Amanda if she strayed off the planned route. If she took thirty seconds to look at the map display, it could be fatal.

She pulled the nose up to avoid an outcrop of jagged rocks. They were coming to the end of the hill. A small valley lay ahead. There was a gap ahead of a mile or two before she reached the cover of the next large hill. It would take perhaps sixty seconds to cross. Now she was out, over the valley floor. The attack-warning alarm suddenly emitted a series of bloodcurdling beeps. Fire-control radar! Instantly Amanda went down, pulling the nose up at the last desperate second, and shot across the valley floor a few feet above the ground. She kept her eyes glued to the MFD. The infrared picture showed the barren ground flashing by with blurring speed.

The attack-warning alarm continued to sound. The missile fire-control radar was pointing in her direction. The missile battery would fire as soon as it could lock on. Amanda would have prayed or sworn, but she didn't have time for either. The whine of the turbines rose to a scream as she went to full emergency power and streaked toward the hill ahead. The Blackhawk's cockpit tilted suddenly to the left as Amanda swerved to keep the tips of the rotor blades from striking the side of the hill.

Amanda held her breath, waiting for a missile to flash out of the dark, but the attack alarm went silent. Radar beams worked only in straight lines and couldn't penetrate solid earth. For the moment she was safe. She glanced at Tower. He was all right. His flight harness had kept him safely in his seat, but he didn't look as if he was enjoying the ride. At least he could see what was happening. It must be worse for Cray and the rest of the men in back.

She checked her clock. Another five minutes passed. She wasn't worried about fuel. The MH-60K's extended fuel system gave it an endurance of seven and a half hours, but time was critical. She must get to the target area in time to let Cray and his team get in position.

She concentrated on her flying, staying low, ready to take instant action if the attack alarm sounded again. The minutes crawled by, five, ten, fifteen. The scene in the MFD showed only rocky hills and an occasional narrow dirt road as Amanda threaded her way through the hills. The survivability-systems display and control panel continued to show steady radar activity, but the attack-warning alarm didn't sound again. Amanda checked the moving map display. The navigation system was receiving inputs from the global positioning satellites in space and computing the Blackhawk's position. The display said she was almost there. It was supposed to be accurate to fifty yards. She stared at the MFD picture. Yes, the landing zone should be just over the next ridge.

She skimmed over the ridge line, hovered, reduced power and went down. The Blackhawk's wheels crunched down in the sandy soil. Amanda cut her engines, and the whine of the twin turbines faded away. They were there! Now it was up to Omega Force.

MAJOR CRAY LAY PRONE on the sandy soil and tried to wait patiently. It wasn't something he did well. The march from the helicopter landing zone had been gruelling and nerve-racking. It had taken far longer than planned. Every man in the team had carried sixty pounds or more of weapons and equipment, and even with night-vision equipment, the darkness and the need to move quietly had slowed things down. Now they were in position. Their equipment was set up, but there was no time to spare. The Air Force had given them a half-hour time slot for the attack. Cray's watch showed the attack window opening in sixteen minutes. They had to be ready then.

Cray scanned the target again. At least, he hoped it was the target. Israeli Intelligence had been right. There were many bunkers in the area, and they were all alike, large concrete structures with heavily reinforced roof and walls. They had been built to protect and store valuable weapons to support the Syrian forces in Lebanon. Most of them probably still fulfilled that purpose. One of them must be Kamov's facility, but from twelve hundred yards away and looking through night-vision devices, it was hard to tell which was it. They had detected movement in and around the nearest bunker, vehicles leaving and arriving, and small groups of men moving in what looked like security patrols around the perimeter. In a way the activity was reassuring. It showed that the bunker was occupied and contained something important. The knowledge that they were probably less than a mile away from an elite Syrian commando battalion was far less comforting.

Cray had sent Tower and Blake to take a closer look. There was nothing to do but wait until they got back. In the meantime, he took another look around. The laser designators were set up. The SATCOM and tactical radios were checked out and ready. Ten yards away Sergeant Sam Hall lay behind his big .50-caliber sniper's rifle, patiently scanning the landscape for targets. The other team members were carefully positioned, their rifles and machine guns ready. Everything was in place. There was nothing left for him to do but worry.

"Major," Hall said softly, "Captain Tower and Blake are coming in."

Cray watched tensely as Tower slipped quietly into the team's position and moved quickly to where he lay waiting. "That's it, Major," Tower said. "We've found it. The closest bunker is the target."

Cray felt a surge of relief. He didn't know what he would have done if Tower had reported that he couldn't find the target. "You're sure?" he asked. It wasn't that he doubted Tower, but Cray was in command. It was his responsibility; he had to be certain.

"It has to be. The bunker matches Kamov's description. It's in the right general area, and we got close enough to see the guards. They're wearing lizard-pattern camouflage uniforms. Only Syrian elite troops wear those, and they're only around this one building, none of the others. One other thing. Blake spotted three BM-21 rocket launchers parked near the entrance. They are unloading 122 mm rockets from the launchers and moving them inside the bunker. Everything checks."

Jackpot! All they needed now was the Air Force. "Good work," Cray said. He looked at his watch. Two minutes to go until the attack window opened. "You and Blake man the laser designators. Fill Colonel Dror in and stand by. The Air Force squadron has our call sign and our radio frequencies. They'll break radio silence and contact us as they enter the area. As soon as the attack is over, we get the hell out of here and get back to the helicopter."

It sounded simple, but Cray was nervous. He might have been more confident if he knew the details of the attack plan, but Sykes hadn't told them. All Cray knew was that an Air Force squadron was on the way and would attack within the half-hour interval. It wasn't that the General didn't trust him; he was merely being grimly logical. If something went wrong and some of them were captured, neither drugs nor torture could make them tell something they didn't know.

Dror wasn't happy. He thought that sending a single American squadron to do the job was insane. But Cray had faith in Sykes. The General was not the kind of man who would risk their lives on a fool's errand.

He looked at his watch. There was twenty-six minutes left in the half-hour attack window. Now, all he could do was—

"Major," Hall said suddenly, "better look at this. We've got trouble. It looks like a patrol coming in our direction."

Cray moved quickly to Hall's side, staying close to the ground in case the Syrians had night-vision equipment. He looked down the gentle slope that led from Omega Force's position to the bunker on the valley floor. The ground was open, broken here and there by clumps of bushes and stunted trees. He looked in the direction that Hall was pointing.

At first he saw nothing. That wasn't surprising, since Hall's sight gave a magnified view but Cray's night-vision goggles didn't. Cray kept looking. Hall wasn't a man who was frightened by shadows. Then he caught a flicker of motion, then another. Hall was right. Men were moving slowly and carefully up the slope. They weren't walking casually or marching in formation. They were advancing individually, moving from cover to cover, keeping ten or twelve feet apart in the classic manner of infantrymen moving toward contact with the enemy.

"What do they look like?" Cray asked softly.

Hall turned the magnification knob on his rifle's telescopic sight to maximum. Cray waited tensely. It was no use asking Hall to hurry. The big sergeant was a professional's professional. He would report as soon as he was sure of what he saw. Hall stared intently through his scope for sixty seconds.

"It's a patrol, all right. I estimate a reinforced platoon, forty or fifty men. They're wearing Soviet-style steel helmets with camouflaged cloth covers, and lizard-stripe camouflage uniforms. Their weapons look like AK-47s and RPK light machine guns. From the way they're moving, I think they have some kind of night-vision equipment. I don't think they know where we are, but they're alert. They look like they expect trouble."

Cray didn't like the sound of that. A platoon of Syrian commandos wasn't a routine security patrol. "What's the range?" he asked.

Hall didn't want to turn on his laser sight until he was about to shoot. Enemy night-vision equipment might be able to pick it up. He looked carefully through his scope again. "I make it eight hundred yards, just outside their wire. Wait a minute, they've stopped. It looks like they're waiting for something."

Cray stared down the slope. He saw a sudden glare of light. The Syrians were looking at the ground, using a flashlight. Cray's night-vision goggles amplified the dim light until it looked like a searchlight. He had a dismal feeling he knew what they were looking at. The soil was sandy. Anyone moving across it would leave tracks, and Tower and Blake hadn't had time to try to wipe out their trail. The footprints left by American military boots were different than those made by Syrian boots. The Syrians would know that someone had been close to the facility they were guarding. They wouldn't like that, and they would follow the tracks. They couldn't do it rapidly, perhaps, but they could do it, and the tracks would lead them straight to the American position.

Cray thought furiously, but he could think of nothing to do but stand his ground. If they retreated, they wouldn't be able to laser designate the target. Without the laser designation, the mission would be a failure. Perhaps the Air Force would get there before they were discovered, but he had better not count on that. He had no alternative but to stay and fight.

"Keep your eyes on them," he said. "When they get close, pick out the patrol leader. Get your sights on him and get him first. Don't shoot unless I give the order or you're sure we've been detected. Let me know if the situation changes."

"Right, Major," Hall said quietly.

Cray thought for a second. Perhaps he should try to say something inspiring, something that would keep up Hall's morale, but he could think of nothing grand to say. He and Hall had served together for years. Hall understood the situation as well as he did.

"Good luck, Sam," was all he said.

Cray moved carefully to each man, explaining the situation, telling them to pick their targets carefully, to hold their fire and not shoot until Hall fired, to fire semiautomatically, one shot for each pull of the trigger to conserve ammunition, and not to use grenades until the enemy got close. His men already knew this, but Cray was a worrier before combat. It made him feel better to tell them one more time, and the familiar routine made his men feel better.

He moved carefully back to Hall's position. Hall knew what Cray needed to know. He didn't wait to be asked. "They're coming on, Major," he said softly. "Range is five hundred yards and closing. I think I've spotted the patrol leader."

Cray looked at his watch. Twenty-two minutes left. If the Air Force didn't come and he waited too long, none of them would get out alive. The minutes crawled by while Hall called out the range to the Syrian patrol.

"Four hundred yards."

"Three hundred."

Cray stared at his watch. The time seemed to be passing incredibly slowly while the Syrians advanced with impossible speed.

"Two hundred yards. They've stopped. I think they see something."

"Have you got the patrol leader spotted?"

"I think so, Major. He's not wearing any insignia that I can see, but the radioman is moving with him. The two of them are together by that white rock."

Cray made up his mind. To wait any longer risked disaster. He must achieve surprise. He put his own sights on the two men Hall had indicated. "Get the radio man, Sam," he said quietly, "and then get the radio if you can."

"The radioman," Hall acknowledged, and slowly, carefully, began to squeeze the trigger of his big .50-caliber rifle. Cray put his finger on the trigger of his M-16A2 and took up the first bit of slack. Careful! He would feel like an utter fool if he broke his own order and fired before Hall's shot. He concentrated on the rifleman's mantra, Squeeze The Trigger, Don't Jerk, Squeeze The—

Hall's big rifle boomed. The huge .50-caliber bullet tore through the Syrian radioman's chest. Killed instantly, he fell to the ground like a puppet whose strings had been cut. Hall sent a second round tearing through the radio on his back. Cray squeezed his trigger and sent a 3-round burst at the patrol leader. He staggered and fell. Cray heard the snarling crackle of M-16s and SAWs as his men opened fire. The rest of the Syrian patrol seemed to vanish as men were hit and fell or dived for cover.

Muzzle-flashes flickered as the Syrian commandos opened fire. Green tracers streaked through the dark toward the American position. Cray thought he had hit the patrol leader. That should slow them down a bit, but the Syrians were elite troops. If the patrol leader was dead, one of his sergeants would take over. Cray ducked as a burst of .30-caliber bullets tore into the ground two feet away. He could hear the boom of Hall's big rifle as he fired again and again.

Cray risked a quick look. He could see five or six bodies sprawled on the ground, but the Syrians were coming on. Some of them were firing while others dashed forward a few yards, took cover and opened fire. It was classic infantry tactics, fire and maneuver, exactly what he would have done if he were the Syrian leader. Cray fired two quick shots and snatched a look at his watch. Thirteen minutes left. He glanced up. The Syrians were getting closer. They could delay them, but they weren't going to stop them. Where in hell was the damned Air Force?

MAJOR PAUL RIGGS FLEW steadily on through the night toward the coast of Lebanon. He was alone in the cockpit of his F-117 stealth fighter. The only light came from the softly glowing multifunctional displays in front of him. He scanned the displays one more time. Both of his F404-GE 100D engines were running smoothly. His computer was in the navigation mode. The data appearing on one of his MFDs showed he was on course and maintaining correct speed and altitude. He should be approaching the coast of Lebanon now. He looked at the picture on another MFD. His plane's infrared sensors were detecting the heat radiating from the surface of the earth and converting it to a black-and-white picture of the scene ahead.

At first the MFD showed only the calm waters of the Mediterranean twelve thousand feet below. Then he saw the blurred line of the coast in the distance ahead. Riggs flicked another switch and looked at the data his electronic warning system was gathering. He whistled softly under his breath. Dozens of radars were active ahead. Russian-built surveillance radars and missile target-acquisition radars were clustered thickly in the Bekaa Valley. The Syrian air-defense system was on a high state of alert. He hadn't seen that many air-defense radars operating at once since he had been in the first strike against Baghdad in 1991. There was no way to avoid them. His target was in the middle of that lethal cluster. He had to go in. It looked as if he was going to earn his pay tonight.

He was approaching southern Lebanon at five hundred miles per hour. It was time for the fence check, the last detailed check of his plane and its systems before he crossed into enemy territory. All warning and caution lights were off. Check. All external running lights were off. Check. Fuel status. Check. Weapons ready, master arm switch safe. Check. All right, fence check satisfactory. Go!

Things happened rapidly at five hundred miles per hour. The coastline was looming up ahead. He could see the mouth of a river flowing from east to west. That must be the Litani, good, that confirmed what his navigation system was telling him. Riggs watched the display intently as the seconds ticked by. He had a lot of faith in computers, but there is no real substitute for the human eye and brain. Now the river below him was turning to the north. He was entering the south end of the Bekaa Valley.

He checked his threat-warning display again. Radars were everywhere! He didn't think the Syrians could know that the 416th Fighter Squadron was coming. They were simply on war alert, waiting for an Israeli attack. That made no difference. He didn't have the Syrian identification codes. If he were detected, the Syrians would fire. He hoped the miracle of modern technology he was flying would get him in and out again. In the meantime, he would do everything he could to make it work. He began to "jink," making small, repeated changes in heading around his basic course. That would change the reflection from any particular radar frequency. If any radar down there was getting a small return signal from his plane, the sudden changes in target aspect would make it extremely difficult for it to establish and maintain target track.

He was nearing the target area now. The infrared sensors showed bunkers, weapon emplacements and unpaved roads. There were a great many bunkers. Which one was the target? He pushed the target-position button and watched as the navigation system positioned the aiming cross hairs over the computed target position. The cross hairs began to track one group of bunkers. Riggs flicked the master arm switch to On. Power flowed to the guidance systems of the two 2,000-pound laser-guided bombs in the weapons bays.

Now if this mysterious bunch of Army supersoldiers was ready to do their thing! Riggs pushed the button on his low-probability-of-intercept radio and spoke into his microphone.

"Omega Force, this is Ghostrider. Laser designate. I am ready to attack."

DAVE TOWER KEPT his eye glued to the laser designator's telescopic sight. The crackle of small-arms fire was growing steadily louder as the Syrian commandos closed in on the American position. The high-pitched snarl of M-16s and AK-47s was punctuated by the flat booming roar of

Sergeant Hall's big .50-caliber rifle. They were making the Syrians pay for every foot of ground, but they weren't stopping them. He fought the temptation to pick up his rifle and start shooting. One more rifle wasn't going to make any difference one way or the other. Colonel Dror was speaking rapidly into his radio. Tower couldn't understand what Dror was saying, but he could tell from the tone of his voice that the Israeli colonel wasn't happy. He said something in Hebrew that threatened to sizzle the paint on his radio.

Dror switched to English. "Nothing! Nothing at all!" he exclaimed. "We have a Grumman E-2C Hawkeye early-warning plane at thirty thousand feet. It can detect planes at over two hundred fifty miles. There are no aircraft flying over Lebanon except Syrian MiG patrols. Nothing else can be detected. Something has gone wrong. This American supersquadron is lost or they are not coming."

Tower glanced at his watch. "Nine more minutes, Colonel," he said quietly.

"Don't be a fool, Tower. If your planes were nine minutes away, the Hawkeye would see them. Perhaps your famous State Department has decided to sacrifice us in the interests of peace! I wouldn't put it past them," Dror said bitterly.

Tower shrugged. He wouldn't put it past them, either, but international politics wasn't his responsibility. He was a soldier. His orders were to stand by to laser designate the target. That's what he would do.

"We are accomplishing nothing here. We must get out now, while we still have a chance! Tel Aviv will honor our commitment. They will wait until the time is up. But nine minutes from now, our planes will be taking off, and some of them will be carrying nuclear weapons. They will wipe this place off the face of the earth, and us with it if we are still here. We will all die for nothing!"

Tower could see the logic in what Dror said. There was no such thing as a friendly nuclear weapon when you were a thousand yards from the target. No one survived that kind of friendly fire, but it wasn't his decision. "Major Cray is in command, Colonel. Talk to him if you want to, but I don't think he'll change his mind."

"Very well, I will—"

Dror stopped in midsentence as the radio at Tower's side came to life.

"Omega Force, this is Ghostrider. Laser designate. I am ready to attack."

For a moment Dror thought Tower had gone mad! The tall blond Green Beret beamed with joy, and he shouted "Ghostrider!" at the top of his lungs as if it were some kind of magic spell. Perhaps it was! Tower knew that call sign. He had heard it a dozen times behind enemy lines in Iraq. He knew who the Ghostriders were and had seen what they could do. Instantly he pressed the trigger on the laser designator. A beam of light, invisible to the human eye, shot from the designator at the speed of light. A spot of light, pulsing rapidly in an intricate coded pattern, appeared on the side of one of the enemy bunkers.

Tower pushed the button on his radio. "Ghostrider, this is Omega Force. Target designated. You are clear to attack."

"Roger, Omega Force. Ghostrider Leader attacking now."

MAJOR PAUL RIGGS PRESSED and released the target designator button and slewed the cross hairs until they were precisely on the center of the bunker roof. He pushed and released the button again. The computer now knew the DMPI, the designated mean point of impact, the precise point where the bombs should strike. Instantly the plane's own laser designator sent a continuous, invisible beam of light to the DMPI and began to keep the laser spot locked on the aim point as Riggs's black jet moved rapidly toward the target.

He checked his MFDs. He was in range now. The computer was in the weapons-delivery mode. The weapons' ready lights glowed green as power flowed to the laser sensors in the noses of the two laser-guided, improved-penetration GBU-27 bombs in the weapons bay. Time to put them in the basket! He pushed the red weapons-release button on the top of the control stick. His weapons bay doors snapped open. There was a dull thud. The F-117 shuddered as the first huge two-thousand-pound guided bomb dropped from the rack inside the weapons bay and hurtled down toward the target. Riggs waited ten seconds and pushed the red button again. The second GBU-27 dropped away and down through the darkness. The weapons bay doors slammed shut.

The two huge guided bombs fell through the darkness, silent and invisible as they arced toward their target. The laser sensors mounted on each bomb's nose detected the laser energy reflected from the target and sent signals to the guidance units. Their aim was excellent, but not perfect. Signals flowed to the control fins on each bomb's tail assembly, and the trajectory of each changed slightly until it was falling straight at the laser spot that marked the aim point.

Riggs stared at the infrared display in his MFD intently. Twenty seconds to go, ten, five—at the last second, he saw the first bomb appear at the edge of the display and streak toward the target. There was a small flash and a puff of dust as the bomb struck the aiming point. The bunker was strongly built, constructed from concrete reinforced with steel, but the GBU-27 was designed to penetrate the hardest targets. It crashed through the bunker's roof, and its delay-action fuze fired. As the bomb detonated, the tremendous explosion blew the bunker's doors off, and Riggs saw a huge flash of light as the blast tore through the roof and hurled blocks of concrete into the night sky. Ten seconds later the second GBU-27 struck, and another giant explosion rocked the target.

Riggs turned and dived. The Syrians hadn't known that they were under attack. That was about to change. The dull black stealth fighter shot toward its exit route. Behind it the sky exploded in streaks and flashes of light as dozens of antiaircraft guns opened fire and missiles shot upward. Riggs looked at his warning display. There was no sign anyone was tracking him. The Syrian gunners were firing blind, blasting intense barrages into the night sky.

One by one, invisible and undetected, the Ghostriders attacked. Explosion after explosion tore the big bunker to pieces and made the rubble bounce. Huge columns of smoke and dust drifted into the sky as the black jets of the 416th left the Bekaa Valley and turned toward home.

Cray watched as Kamov's facility burned and exploded. He didn't feel triumph, just an overwhelming sense of relief. The mission was accomplished. Omega Force had done the job. He hoped it was worth what it had cost. The Syrian commandos were confused, dazed by the overwhelming attack from the dark that had blasted to pieces the bunker they had been guarding. Time to go before they recovered.

"Break contact. Withdraw to the landing zone," he ordered.

Quickly, silently, the Omega Force team vanished into the dark.

19

Major Cray sat by himself in the Israeli briefing room waiting for General Sykes. For once he didn't mind waiting. Ten hours of sleep had improved his view of things remarkably. There was nothing Cray had to do at the moment. Dave Tower was supervising the loading of men and equipment on the huge C-5B. In a few hours Omega Force would be flying back home. He looked up as the general entered the room. Sykes was smiling. That was a good sign.

"I just finished talking to Washington," Sykes said. "Everybody there loves us, even the CIA. The Israelis are happy. They're going to write you a letter of commendation. It will have to be highly classified, of course, because none of this ever happened. You spent the last few days participating in highly successful maneuvers. A few fanatics tried to sabotage the peace process. The Syrian government swears it will hunt them down and punish them. Syria and Israel are back at the conference table. The State Department says the prospects for peace are excellent. Mission accomplished. Omega Force did a damned good job."

Cray smiled. He was glad everybody was happy. At least it was over, and he could relax. Until the next time!

COLONEL SADIQ SAT in the webbed seat in the passenger compartment of the C-130 and sipped a mug of hot, sweet tea. The plane was crowded with his officers and men. Most of them were asleep, worn out by the constant strain of days and nights of fighting and rapid movement. They had been

lucky to get out of Lebanon alive. The Syrians who ha
supported him had turned against him when his plan ha
failed. He smiled bitterly. Men were fickle. He would hav
been a great hero to most Arabs if he had won, but he ha
lost. Now he was called an international terrorist, to be a
rested or shot on sight.

Someone was coming down the aisle. It was Jamal Taw
fiq. The burly major had a thermos in one hand and
clipboard in the other. There was a look of concern o
Tawfiq's face as he looked at his colonel. Sadiq was th
heart and soul of the movement. If he lost faith in the
cause, it was over. As long as he still believed, the move
ment was alive.

Tawfiq smiled and lifted the thermos. "More tea, Colc
nel?"

Sadiq shook his head. It would take a great deal of tea
wash the bitter taste of defeat from his mouth.

"There are two messages, Colonel. One is from Captai
Kawash. The other planes took off all right. They are o
the way to the rendezvous."

Sadiq nodded. That was good news. He had lost to
many good men in Lebanon.

"The other message is from Ahmed Heikal. He say
'The sun has risen in the south. Its light is very bright.'"

Tawfiq didn't understand what the message meant, b
he could see that Colonel Sadiq was happy to hear it.

"God is great! I could not have better news. Tell the p
lot to change course. We are going south. Soon we will
ready to strike again, and this time we will hit the Amer
cans themselves. We will shed their blood! This time we w
not fail! As God is my witness, we will not fail.

WELCOME TO

JAMES AXLER

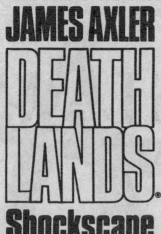

DEATHLANDS®

Shockscape

**A shockscape with a view—
and the danger is free.**

Ryan and his band of warrior survivalists chart a perilous journey
across the desolate Rocky Mountains. Their mission: Deliver the hired
killers of a small boy to his avenging father.

In the Deathlands, survival is a gamble. Death is the only sure bet.

America's toughest agents target a Golden Triangle drug
pipeline in the second installment of

SLAM

by DAN MATTHEWS

The scene has switched to the jungles of Southeast Asia as the
SLAM team continues its never-ending battle against drugs in
Book 2: **WHITE POWDER, BLACK DEATH.** SLAM takes fire
in a deadly game of hide-and-seek and must play as hard and
dirty as the enemy to destroy a well-crafted offensive from a drug
lord playing for keeps.

Take
4 explosive books
plus a
mystery bonus
FREE

Communism's death throes bring the
world to the edge of doom in

DON PENDLETON'S

THE EXECUTIONER®

FEATURING

MACK BOLAN®

BATTLE
FORCE

The dynamic conclusion to the FREEDOM TRILOGY finds Mack
Bolan, Able Team and Phoenix Force battling to avert World
War III. From the war-torn states of Eastern Europe to the urban
hellgrounds of Los Angeles, Bolan's army fights to head off a
nightmare of chemical warfare.

THE FREEDOM TRILOGY

JOIN MACK BOLAN'S FIGHT FOR FREEDOM IN THE FREEDOM TRILOGY...

Beginning in June 1993, Gold Eagle presents a special three-book in-line continuity featuring Mack Bolan, the Executioner, along with ABLE TEAM and PHOENIX FORCE, as they face off against a communist dictator. A dictator with far-reaching plans to gain control of the troubled Baltic state area and whose ultimate goal is world supremacy. The fight for freedom starts in June with THE EXECUTIONER #174: BATTLE PLAN, continues in THE EXECUTIONER #175: BATTLE GROUND, and concludes in August with the longer 352-page Mack Bolan novel BATTLE FORCE.

Available at your favorite retail outlets in June through to August.

Book 1: BATTLE PLAN $3.50   ☐
   (THE EXECUTIONER #174)

Book 2: BATTLE GROUND $3.50   ☐
   (THE EXECUTIONER #175)

Book 3: BATTLE FORCE $4.99   ☐
   (352-page MACK BOLAN)

Total Amount	$_____	
Plus 75¢ Postage ($1.00 in Canada)	_____	
Canadian residents please add applicable federal and provincial taxes.	_____	
Total Payable	$_____	

To order, please send your name, address, zip or postal code, along with a check or money order for the total above, payable to Gold Eagle Books, to:

In the U.S.
Gold Eagle Books
3010 Walden Avenue
P.O. Box 1325
Buffalo, NY 14269-1325

In Canada
Gold Eagle Books
P.O. Box 609
Fort Erie, Ontario
L2A 5X3

GOLD EAGLE ®

FT93-2